Waiting for the Sun

The harrowing story of a peasant boy
in occupied Tibet

Mary Craig

Hodder & Stoughton
LONDON SYDNEY AUCKLAND

British Library Cataloguing in Publication Data
A record for this book is available from the British Library

ISBN 0 340 72199 5

Typeset by Avon Dataset Ltd, Bidford-on-Avon, Warks

Printed and bound in Great Britain by
Clays Ltd, St Ives plc

Hodder & Stoughton Ltd
A Division of Hodder Headline PLC
338 Euston Road
London NW1 3BH

For
Emme-la and his family

This centre of heaven
This core of the earth
This heart of the world
Fenced around by snow mountains
The headland of all rivers
Where the peaks are high and the land is pure
A country so good
Where men are born as sages and heroes
And act according to good laws

From an early ninth-century document about Tibet

Contents

Acknowledgments

I had hoped to say a profound thank you to Tsewang Topgyal, my indispensable and efficient interpreter during Emme-la's visit to England in November 1997. He encouraged me to write this story, insisting that the personal testimony of someone who had survived the appalling Cultural Revolution in Tibet was rare and worth recording for posterity. It was with shock and sadness that I heard, a few months later, that Tsewang had died. So my thanks – and condolences – go to his wife, Kunsang, instead.

Thanks are due also to Emme-la's friend, TCV Accountant Jamphel Dorjee, who wrote letters on his behalf in admirable English; and to my old friend, Tashi Tsering of the Amnye Machin Institute in Dharamsala who offered advice and e-mail facilities. Caroline Symes took a further set of questions for me to Emme-la in Dharamsala. Robbie Barnett and Riki Hyde-Chambers checked the manuscript in its final stages. To all the above and in particular to Anne Jennings Brown, who not only suggested the book and provided the illustrations but gave me steadfast support throughout, my heartfelt thanks.

Introduction

Shortly after I began work on this, my third book on Tibet, a friend sent me a Canadian review of my second one, *Kundun: A Biography of the Dalai Lama and His Family.*[1] The reviewer regretted that I had given no account of the sufferings of the *ordinary* people of Tibet, the peasants. It was fair comment, though it must be said that in that particular book the peasants were not part of my brief. In my earlier work, *Tears of Blood*, however, I had written about the sufferings inflicted on every section of Tibetan society by the occupying Chinese, including the peasants who made up the bulk of the population.

While doing the research for *Kundun*, I returned many times to Dharamsala in North India where several thousand Tibetan refugees have lived since the military crackdown on their country in 1959. On one of these visits in 1995, my travelling companion, Anne Jennings Brown, introduced me to Jinpa Ngodup (aka Emme-la), a young man of peasant stock whom she had sponsored ever since he had arrived in Dharamsala as a refugee from Tibet in 1982. She remarked that his story was a moving one, and that one day I ought to go and talk to him. In 1982 Emme-la had been among the first of a new wave of refugees who had lived through the ten terrible years of the Cultural Revolution and its aftermath.

In November 1997, Anne, who lives near me in Berkshire, invited Emme-la to stay at her house for a few weeks. One morning she rang me. 'Why don't you come and listen to Emme-la's story?' she asked. 'You might want to turn it into a book.' As I was then undecided about my next project, I agreed to think about it.

Alas, I neither speak nor understand Tibetan, and Emme-la has little English. Fortunately we were able to find an interpreter, Tsewang Topgyal, who had lived in England for many years. Convalescing after a car accident, Tsewang was available to spend much of the next few weeks in the Berkshire countryside. Emme-la had already written up his experiences in Tibetan in a slim manuscript which he brought with him from India, and his notes provided me with some of the basic information from which to start my questions.

I did indeed find his story moving, but I knew that it would have to be put into a wider context for Western readers who knew little or nothing about what had happened to Tibet. So I began at the beginning, trying to piece together the landmarks of Emme-la's life and slot them into what I already knew of recent Tibetan history. Emme-la, like most people, seemed ignorant of the wider historical framework within which his life had unfolded. His own part in the story was as much as he could cope with. Reflecting on its larger context was a luxury he had never been able to afford.

When I began to write, I immediately came up against a specific difficulty: Emme-la was not born until six years after the 1950 Chinese takeover of Tibet, and his own personal saga did not begin until he started school at the age of seven. Yet what happened in the intervening years following the Chinese invasion was crucial to his story and set the scene for everything that happened later. It could not be omitted. I had to give some sort of account of those years, even though Emme-la himself had no part in them. Born into a family of hard-working farmers, designated 'rich peasants' by the Chinese Communists, Emme-la's life was blighted from the moment of his birth in 1956.

In any case, I came to realise that Emme-la's story does not belong to him alone; it is, in a sense, everyone's story. No family in Tibet remained or remains untouched by the Chinese occupation of their country. Many have suffered incalculably more than Emme-la, many somewhat less. But by and large his experience was shared by everyone else. He was just one of the vast anonymous multitude of ordinary Tibetans of all ages who, after 1959, suffered the destruction of everything they had previously held dear and who were henceforth mere pawns to be pushed around or liquidated at the whim of their Chinese masters.

In the early days, over a hundred thousand Tibetans managed to escape. Of those who remained, huge numbers were starved to death, imprisoned, tortured, executed. Others kept their heads down, knowing that at any time, any one of these fates could befall them too. They had to come to terms as best they could with the insane regime that had taken over their lives. For them the name of the game was survival pure and simple. They did not retaliate – how does one retaliate against an all-powerful and ruthless machine? – they merely did what they were told, in order to go on living. When despair took over and they could endure no more, many resorted to suicide – an appalling solution for a Tibetan Buddhist with a belief in karma and in the sacredness of all life.

No one who has never experienced life under a totalitarian regime can really understand what it is like to live under a system where an ever-watchful Big Brother seeks to control not only the physical activities but also the mind and spirit of the human beings in his power. There can be no dissent. The great Polish philosopher and poet, Czeslaw Milosz, summed it up in the word *ketman*: the anguish of knowing that one's life depends on asserting beliefs in public which are diametrically opposed to what one knows in one's heart to be true. In that situation, a human being does violence to his or her inner integrity in order to survive. Such was the fate of the Tibetans particularly during the infamous Cultural Revolution of 1966–76.

In exile too the Tibetans get on with the business of surviving. When they talk about the past they offer little but the bare facts, for much of their experience is buried too deep for words. Often it takes a sympathetic outsider to present their story in its fullest dimension, and so speak for them to the world outside. But often even the sympathetic outsider has blind spots. For instance, I spent many hours listening to refugees when I was writing *Tears of Blood*, and while I wept at what they told me, there was one thing that I took at face value – their actual escape from Tibet. 'Then I escaped,' they would say. End of story. 'Then he escaped,' I would jot down in my notebook, as though the escape were a mere postscript to what had gone before. It wasn't until I read Joe Simpson's intensely moving account[2] of meeting a group of escaping Tibetans in the high Himalayas between Tibet and Nepal that I suddenly got a glimpse of the reality. Simpson brought home to me with a stab of understanding what the act of escaping must have involved – the terrifying cold of sub-zero temperatures, the snow-blindness, the loss of fingers and toes to frostbite, the inadequacy of flimsy clothing in the face of bone-chilling winds, the hunger, the natural perils of the high Himalaya themselves. The countless and unrecorded deaths. Emme-la's description of his own escape was as undramatic as all the others and, though I tried to push him on it, I have not attempted to embellish his account. But Joe Simpson's book made me realise at last the inner truth of such a traumatic experience, the anxiety, the terror, and finally 'the brief voluble excitement of crossing the pass and leaving Tibet erased all too quickly by the knowledge of what they have lost'.

Since 1981, when Emme-la fled Tibet, thousands more have followed suit, usually at the rate of about forty or fifty each month. Today, smarting under the knowledge that in spite of all their efforts to turn Tibet into an integral part of the People's Republic of China, most Tibetans still regard themselves as Tibetans, as Buddhists and as followers of the Dalai Lama, the Chinese are stepping up their onslaught on the culture and traditions of that unhappy land. As a result of this new repression, the number of refugees has risen tenfold in the last months. In October 1998, the reception centres in India and Nepal were flooded by over five hundred new arrivals. Every week men and women are desperate enough to brave the rigours and perils of the mountains, risking death, for the sake of the freedom that lies beyond. Like Emme-la, they have nothing to lose but their lives, and they consider the risks to be well worth taking.

Prologue 1981

The young Tibetan stood at the top of the mountain pass, almost waist-deep in snow. He looked around at a world of extraordinary contrasts: to the south, covered now in low cloud, lay Bhutan, lush, green, fertile, the ancient Kingdom of the Thunder Dragon, gateway to a long dreamed-of freedom, but alien, unfamiliar. Slowly, he returned his gaze to the land of his birth. Tibet, roof of the world, the jagged, icy peaks of its high Himalayan plateau clawing the sky, uncompromising, terrible, but beautiful beyond description. He had come to the moment he had longed for and dreaded: for what lay ahead was not just the next stage of a journey, but exile into the unknown. He was saying goodbye, perhaps for ever, to his country, his family, his friends, and the knowledge that this was so brought anguish. Briefly, and for the thousandth time, he reviewed in his mind the reasons which had driven him to this parting of the ways. They were always the same: the Chinese usurpers of his country had, since years before his birth, made life in Tibet a nightmare, and he could stand it no longer. None of his ancestors had done any harm to the Chinese, he reasoned, nor had he done anything against them. 'So again and again I had to ask myself why these people had been able to take over my life and make it unbearable for me to live in my own land. They had taken everything from me: my education, my religion, my human freedom, my health, my pride in being Tibetan, everything.'

The decision had in fact been made long since, and it was too late to turn back now. Bowing his head for a moment in silent prayer to the gods, the young man removed the Chinese People's Liberation Army cap from his head and flung it defiantly into the void, laughing aloud as he did so. Then with a firm step he began his descent towards freedom.

CHAPTER 1

Honey on the Knife

Their smooth talk, their presents and their silver dollars blinded us while they drew their noose around our necks. It was too late when we remembered the old adage: 'Beware of the sweet honey offered on the blade of a knife.'

Jamyang Norbu, *Warriors of Tibet*

His name was Jinpa Ngodup, though most people called him Emme-la, a nickname meaning Little Grandfather. He was small and slight, broad-chested like all mountain people, with a flat Mongolian face, relieved by the fine bone structure and high chiselled cheekbones typical of those who live in the central Tibetan provinces of Ü and Tsang. A shock of blue-black hair, dull and lacklustre now from years of neglect, hung in a heavy fringe over almond-shaped black eyes flecked with amber. He looked, in short, like most of

3

his countrymen, the olive hue of his face tinged, like theirs, with the pallor caused by fear, malnutrition and chronic exhaustion. Aged twenty-four, he had never known a time when the Chinese had not ruled his homeland, for when he was born, in 1956, the occupation had already been in force for six years.

His family had lived for generations in Gyantse, a small town in south-western Tibet, considered to be the third largest in the country, after Lhasa, the regional capital of the province of Ü (and indeed of all Tibet), and Shigatse, capital of Tsang (only Lhasa had any political importance). Twelve thousand feet above sea level, perched on a crescent of mountains soaring out of a wide, level plain, it was dominated by a massive medieval fort (built in 1268) on top of a near-vertical 500-ft hill known as Gyantse, or Royal Peak, which gave the town its name. At its foot three major caravan tracks converged: one leading towards Lhasa (264 kms to the north-west) and thence to eastern Tibet and China; a second to India and Sikkim (a Tibetan kingdom which had become a protectorate of British India); and the third, via Shigatse, to Nepal and points West.

From time immemorial, this small market town, with its densely packed white-washed houses and narrow, winding, dusty streets had been the main centre for Tibet's important wool trade with India, Nepal, Sikkim and Bhutan. The Tibetans were passionate traders and Gyantse's busy thoroughfares used to teem with little shops, where merchants from many countries haggled and chaffered over their wares. The town's woollen cloth was inferior to none, and its carpets were famous all over the Indian subcontinent.

Emme-la's parents were farmers in Chagri-gyab, one of five little hamlets which surrounded the Fort. Indeed, most Gyantse people were either farmers or semi-nomadic herdsmen. Tibetan society was semi-feudal, in that all land was owned by the government and was leased directly to the monasteries and aristocrats who in turn rented it out to the peasants. The rent was paid in grain and in a certain amount of compulsory labour for the landlord (known as *ulag*), in exchange for which they received adequate food and clothing. By modern standards it was not ideal as a social system but for centuries it had worked, producing little serious discontent. With inevitable exceptions, the landowners for the most part were not oppressive and did not interfere in their tenants' private lives, and although it is true that most of the latter were poor and tied to the land, they were not downtrodden and had all they needed in the way of food, clothing, festivals to celebrate and the popular barley beer (*chang*) to drink. They were free to visit friends and relatives in other areas, go on pilgrimage to far-off regions, and, if they wanted to get on in the world,[1] join a monastery.

In the early part of the century, Emme-la's great-grandfather had prospered sufficiently to build a house of his own on the site of an old stable belonging to a local estate-owner. Renting one piece of land from this man and another from the local monastery, Pelkhor Choede, he agreed to pay the annual rent in harvested grain, knowing, as did everyone else, that if emergencies such as hailstorms, floods or unexpected drought came along, there would always be enough surpluses stored in monasteries and government granaries to cope. Then, since no Tibetan would dream of undertaking any important project without first checking the auguries, his next step was to consult the lamas. Only when the latter had decided on a propitious date, did he go ahead and build the house, calling it Tara Sampa or Stable of Dreams.

It was a typical two-storeyed flat-roofed Gyantse farmhouse, with white-washed stone foundations topped by mud-brick walls, which kept the place warm in winter and cool in summer. And from every corner of the flat, slate-edged roof flew blue, green, white, yellow and red prayer flags. All Tibetans, being deeply religious, believed that there was more to life than mere outward appearances, and prayer played a large part in their lives. *Om Mani Padme Hum* – Hail to the Jewel in the Lotus – the Buddha prayer that was inscribed on the flags or packed into the prayer wheels that people spun as they walked, the rosary beads they told, or the papery 'wind-horses' (*lungta*) that they launched into the air for the winds to carry to the high heavens and the ends of the earth. The compassionate prayer that all sentient beings might one day become enlightened.

Though most of Gyantse's inhabitants had no land of their own and had to perform casual labour for others in order to survive, there were about fifty families like Emme-la's in its villages, industrious peasants scratching a fair living out of subsistence farming, eating the produce of their own fields, spinning and weaving their own clothes, making their own Tibetan boots – and bartering for whatever else they needed. And though there were twenty or so much richer, land-owning families in Gyantse's fertile plain (an unusually large number for Tibet), no one was actually rich in the way Westerners understand the term. Some had more horses, more cattle, more grain or more land, but the way of life was much the same for everybody and the gulf between rich and poor had never been the huge problem it was in countries like China. On the whole, Buddhist belief gave rise to at least a smidgin of generosity from the rich and an absence of envy on the part of the poor. The Tibetans' firm belief in karma (the

Buddhist law of cause and effect) meant that they accepted their status in life as the result of good or bad behaviour in a previous existence, their well-being in a future life depending on how they behaved in this one.

For everyone, it was a tough, spartan existence, with little in the way of material comforts: no electricity, no wireless, no newspapers, no clocks, watches or sewing machines – no roads, no wheeled transport of any kind, not even animal carts. From time to time, Gyantse had come within a whisker of being dragged into the modern age, but its powerful and deeply conservative senior monks were frightened of change and had always managed to keep it at bay.[2]

At the turn of the century, in the wider world outside Tibet's borders, a power struggle was being waged between British India and Tsarist Russia, for the mastery of Central Asia. It became known as The Great Game. In 1904, during the reign of the Thirteenth Dalai Lama, the British grew alarmed that the Russians might be getting a foothold in Tibet, the isolated Land of Snows beyond the Himalayas. So in April of that year (the Tibetan Year of the Wood-Dragon[3]) a British Military Mission under the command of Colonel Francis Younghusband was despatched to save the situation. Younghusband stormed his way to Gyantse in order to draw up a trade treaty with the Tibetans, by force if necessary. This modern expeditionary force inflicted a terrible carnage on Tibetan troops equipped with little more than matchlocks and prayer wheels, and then dumbfounded the survivors by binding up their wounds rather than, as they had expected, despatching them forthwith. On arrival in Gyantse, Younghusband and a small force of men captured the Fort, raised the Union Jack there, then proceeded to set up their HQ on more congenial ground at Changlo, a mile to the south. Here they lingered for some months while awaiting permission from the government in London to proceed to Lhasa.

Perceval Landon, a *Times* special correspondent with the expedition, has left us a beguiling portrait of Gyantse and its inhabitants.[4] He writes of 'a land dotted with willow-thorn and ... carpeted from end to end with iris', of a patchwork of small cultivated fields without trees or hedges. Circling overhead are the ever-present lammergeiers, as well as golden wagtails, rosefinches, redstarts, hoopoes, ruddy sheldrake, green-black magpies and bar-headed geese. The skies are of that startlingly clear, deep indigo blue seen only in high altitude lands, the 'hard and vivid' sun 'beats off the coarse and strong-grained whitewash' of the houses, and the flat plain 'shivers a little in the heat, confusing the lines of leafless willows beside a whitewashed mill'. As for the sunsets, they are 'perhaps Tibet's most exquisite and peculiar gift; the double glory of the east and west alike, and the rainbow confusion among the wide waste of white mountain ranges'.

Although it was Spring, the season at which 'the daily, driving dust-storm wrapped ... all the valley in a tawny fog', Landon notes how the stars invisibly assert themselves day and night, making the Himalayan peaks stand out, as though against moonlight. 'The colour of Tibet', he concludes wonderingly, 'has no parallel in the world. Nowhere, neither in Egypt, nor in South Africa, nor ... Sydney, nor Calcutta nor Athens, is there such a constancy of beauty, night and morning alike, as there is in these fertile plains inset in the mountain backbone of the world.'

The Gyantse people he pronounced 'friendly and hospitable', not at all shy, and, considering the circumstances, incurious to the point of seeming indifferent. They were matter-of-fact: 'The spring work has to be done, there is no-one but themselves to do it . . . and there is much to do.' Their courtesy was unfailing. 'The small boy jumps off the harrow upon which he has been having a ride, and, stopping his song, bows with his joined hands in front of his face, elbows up and right knee bent. A householder smiles and exhibits two inches of tongue, and gives a Napoleonic salute as we pass by, pulling his cap down over his face to his chest.'

Courteous they may have been, but the Gyantse people were not as indifferent as Landon believed. To them, the invading British were Pi-lings, foreigners from the West, 'the demon-masked ones from England' who quite probably intended to destroy their beloved Buddhism;[5] 'an enemy people scarcely recognisable as human, since they were different in appearance from themselves and carried strange and deadly weaponry. Although throughout the expedition, the soldiers had been ordered to refrain from raping and looting, many of them had disobeyed, as a local street-song[6] lamented:

> Gyantse, the turquoise valley,
> Is filled with marauding outsiders.
> Oh! When I see such things happen,
> I wonder what the use is of gathering riches.

Before the British left, there were many skirmishes both within and without Gyantse, in the course of which it was estimated that about 2,000 Tibetans were killed. The townsfolk were traumatised by these terrible events. Yet in July, when the bloodbath was over, a Treaty was signed in Lhasa and good relations and mutual respect were somehow established between the

Tibetans and the British. The latter withdrew from Tibet, having obtained, among other benefits, the right to establish a trading post in the town of Gyantse.[7]

Over the next ten years, Tibet underwent many changes. Angered and humiliated by the success of the British Younghusband Expedition in 1904, in the following year the Chinese, who since the early eighteenth century had held a loose and shifting kind of suzerainty over the country,[8] invaded and captured the eastern borderlands of Tibet, with the intention of reasserting an authority which had dwindled to the point of extinction. Leaving a trail of slaughtered monks and lay Tibetans behind them, the Imperial Chinese forces swept through Tibet and by 1910 had reached and occupied Lhasa, which they proceeded to loot and pillage. Pursued by Chinese soldiers and with a price on his head, the Thirteenth Dalai Lama fled to the protection of British India, where he was given asylum and a warm welcome in Darjeeling. In the two years he spent there, he formed a close friendship with the British Political Officer, Sir Charles Bell, and established a good working relationship with the British.

Only the Chinese Revolution of 1911 and the overthrow of the Manchu Dynasty by Dr Sun Yat-sen saved the Tibetans then. The Imperial army was demoralised and the Tibetans were able to throw the occupying forces out of Lhasa and recapture many (though not all) of their eastern territories. Returning to Lhasa in 1913, the Dalai Lama broke off all ties with China and declared Tibet to be well and truly independent. For the next several years, China would be far too busy wrestling with the chaotic situation inside its borders to focus on problems outside.

But the Thirteenth Dalai Lama knew that the threat

from China was dormant rather than dead and that Tibet must quickly build up its defences. Accordingly, among many other reforms, he decided to create an army, and (after due consideration of the Russian and Japanese varieties) to do so on the English model. A garrison was established in Gyantse, British instructors were brought in, and the sounds of 'Att-E-e-en-shun', 'Pre-sE-ent arms', 'Yes – SAH' and 'Lef-righ, lef-righ', together with marching feet, gunfire and the somewhat garbled strains of God Save the King, Auld Lang Syne and It's a Long Way to Tipperary were frequently wafted over the Gyantse plain.

Unfortunately the Tibetan bureaucracy was run by dyed-in-the-wool lay and monk officials, and though the Dalai Lama had vision, the reactionary nobles and monks did not. They could not believe that the Chinese would ever pose a threat to Buddhism and that was the only thing that mattered. They had – with the greatest reluctance – to accept the army and certain other reforms, but on some things they refused to give way. In 1923 an Englishman, Frank Ludlow, tried to open a boys' school in Gyantse. But the monastic hierarchs saw it as threatening to the Buddhist religion and put such pressure on the Dalai Lama that in 1926 the school was closed. They were resistant to other plans of His Holiness also. In 1924 the latter put forward a plan for a proper road to be built from Lhasa to British India, leading through Gyantse. But the local landowners and abbots whose lands lay along the proposed route soon saw off that idea, complaining to the government in Lhasa that if roads and motor cars were allowed to replace dusty old caravan routes with their yaks, donkeys and mules, the people would be unable to fulfil their tax obligations – the *ulag* services – to their masters.[9] Despite the Dalai Lama, Tibet was reasserting its old isolationism, regarding all foreigners as a threat to their sacred religion. 'If only,' sighed a government official in present-day India, 'the religious establishment had had less power and influence, we might indeed have seen some progress.'[10] The Tibetans would pay dearly for the abbots' refusal to enter the twentieth century.

In October 1949, after years of bloody civil war between China's ruling Nationalist Kuo-mintang Party and Mao Tse-tung's Communists (interrupted for the period of the Sino-Japanese War when both sides fought the Japanese invaders), the Reds came to power in mainland China and founded the first peasant dynasty in that country for six hundred years. Scarcely had the new People's Republic been proclaimed than Peking Radio began promising the imminent 'liberation' of Tibet – from American and British imperialism. (There were no Americans and no more than five foreign nationals – three British, two Austrian – in the whole of Tibet.[11] One of the Britons, the radio operator Robert Ford, was the first to hear the Chinese announcement, and realised with a shock that 'I was not down on the list for liberation; the Tibetans were to be liberated from me.'[12]) The threat was no idle one, for almost exactly a year later, Chinese Communist troops – having already grabbed the disputed borderland territories with their overwhelmingly Tibetan populations and culture – now swarmed into those areas of Tibet which had for centuries been ruled by the Dalai Lamas.

Driven by a nationalism every bit as powerful as that of their Nationalist enemies; and presumably not unaware of the strategic advantage of controlling the Roof of the World, the Chinese Communists marched into Tibet. In vain did the Tibetans protest their independence, their protests were simply ignored. In May 1951, a Tibetan delegation was forced to sign a Seventeen-Point Agreement in Peking proclaiming their country to be an integral part of the Chinese Motherland.[13] The alternative, with the well-equipped and hardened battle-troops of the People's Liberation Army already occupying part of Tibet and poised to take the rest of it, could only have been a massacre.

In July 1951, an advance party of Chinese generals and senior officials passed through Gyantse, on their way to Lhasa, and Emme-la's parents were among those who gathered to watch them in mingled curiosity and fear, clapping their hands to ward off evil spirits, murmuring *Gyami, Gyami* (*Chinese, Chinese*) in awestruck whispers, never having seen a Chinese person before. Three months later, in October, the 52nd Division of the People's Liberation Army, under its Commander Yin Fa-tang, arrived in Gyantse to start building a military base.

At this early stage of the occupation, it was possible to believe that Tibetan Buddhism and Chinese Communism might be able to co-exist. The Han Chinese[14] in Tibet had been instructed to treat the local inhabitants with deference and respect, to 'make friends and do good deeds'. They quietly camped in tents throughout the area, didn't rape, didn't pillage, were polite, well behaved and self-disciplined.

'My parents,' says Emme-la, 'told me that a few weeks after they arrived, Yin Fa-tang and his men went out and about to meet the local people personally. After that, they abandoned their tents and went to live with families in the villages and monastic estates round about. They were all put up by local Tibetan families; Yin Fa-tang himself stayed with a family called Kyolo who lived right opposite the District Magistrate's house. We had one Chinese soldier and an interpreter in our house, and they were model guests. They paid for everything, their own food, fodder for their animals, services rendered and all sorts of little things. Whenever they slept under someone's roof, they paid handsomely in Chinese silver dollars (Da Yuan[15]), insisting on paying, even when their hosts tried to refuse the money. And they made sure everything was in order before they left. My parents said they were very friendly and helpful, their body-language was really warm.'

The Tibetans made the best of their new situation, hoping that this invasion, like earlier ones, would not last long and the Chinese would soon go away and leave them in peace. Meanwhile, they were not averse to the silver dollars. 'From the revolutionary East, showers of silver dollars rain upon the land of snows,' went a song. 'The mountains of silver dollars are higher than the snow-capped peaks of our own country.' The Chinese were sweeping the dusty thoroughfares, planting vegetables, helping with the harvest, and carrying water when water was scarce. And they insisted that as soon as they had 'liberated' the ordinary people from the 'feudal lords and imperialists' they would go home again. There may have been an element of wishful thinking on the soldiers' part here, since there is no doubt that Tibet, with its rarefied air, dizziness-inducing altitude, sub-zero cold, monotonous food, lack of roads and of even the most basic modern facilities, was regarded by most as a hardship posting. Privately, the Chinese despised Buddhism and considered the Tibetans to be dirty barbarians and 'green brains'. But for the time being they were under orders to keep such opinions to themselves.

The dread word 'communisation' was also banned.

In fact, the Chinese fell over backwards to avoid giving offence and, as there were no home-grown revolutionaries to assist them, they wooed the local officials and aristocrats (the 'patriotic Upper Strata'), many of whom welcomed the prospect of the progress the Chinese might bring to Tibet. They used mass meetings, films, dramas and a ubiquitous tannoy system to get their main message across – the promise to take the land away from wealthy landlords and redistribute it among the peasants.

In reality the Fourteenth Dalai Lama had tried to do this some years earlier. After the Chinese invaded in 1950, the Tibetans had rushed to invest the 16-year-old youth with the full powers of secular and spiritual leadership, and he had immediately put forward his own proposals for social equality.[16] But although the 1951 Agreement allowed for the political system to remain unchanged, and in the short term the Chinese were paying lip-service to the Dalai Lama's sovereignty over Tibet, they intended to use him as a mere rubber stamp for their own purposes. They blocked his plans for land reform, partly because they did not fit with the Communist aims of destroying the religious and national identity of Tibet, and partly because they were determined that no one but themselves should be given credit for sweeping social change. Later on, the Dalai Lama could conveniently be blamed for all the social ills in the land. (It must be admitted that in the matter of land reform the ultra-conservative abbots and property-owners were every bit as opposed to the Dalai Lama's radical ideas as the Chinese were.) Nevertheless the young leader managed to slip some reforms through, cancelling agricultural debts and bringing an end to the *ulag* (corvée labour), that forced provision of unpaid services which was such a burden on the poor.[17]

So the Chinese put their own best efforts into more high-profile signs of progress, opening schools and clinics, introducing Western medicines and medical training, bringing in modern agricultural implements and suggesting new methods of farming, never doubting in their revolutionary fervour that the Tibetans would be humbly grateful. It didn't seem to occur to them that to the Tibetans they were not long-awaited saviours but uninvited foreign intruders – they simply couldn't understand why they were resented.

There were some 20,000 PLA troops scattered over central Tibet, and their mere presence made food shortages inevitable. The troops paid for the food they ate, but as there was simply not enough to go round, the price of food soared. Inflation rocketed and the cost of all basic commodities shot through the roof.

Then there was the road-building programme. Only when there were motorable roads and bridges to link the vast, inaccessible Tibetan plateau to China would the Chinese invaders be able to bring in the tanks and military equipment needed to make their power a permanent reality. As yet they had no supply bases, no infrastructure, and all communications were of the most primitive kind. It was because there were no roads that so far they had only been able to bring in the infantry.

When the Chinese began recruiting large numbers of Tibetans to build the new roads (plus an airport far away to the north of Lhasa), the people of Gyantse faced a difficult problem. No matter how well the Chinese were prepared to pay for their road-building services, most of them were farmers, and at harvest-time they needed all the help they could get in the fields. They turned the Chinese proposal down flat. The latter, not yet in a position to enforce their wishes directly, leaned on the local Tibetan officials and made them *order* a labour force to go off and build the roads – whether they would or no. Whatever the cost to others, the Chinese were determined to have their roads.

Until 1954, the Tibetans went on hoping and praying that the Chinese would soon go away and leave them in peace. But in April of that year came the news that India, Tibet's neighbour and long-time friend, had signed an agreement with China which recognised Tibet as a part of China.[18] This shattering betrayal was followed by a natural catastrophe which to the superstitious Tibetans seemed like the most horrible of black omens. In Gyantse's upper valleys were a 'white', a 'yellow' and a 'black' lake. On the fifteenth day of the fifth month of Wood Horse Year – June 1954 – the huge Black Lake burst through a natural dam which had confined it for thousands of years and flooded the surrounding river-valley.

A number of Tibetan government officials had been wont to go on pilgrimage every year to the Black Lake to appease the spirits by casting precious stones and religious artefacts into its waters. Alas, that summer, almost everyone who was anyone in the government had gone off with the Dalai Lama on a much-hyped official visit to China – which itself had the people worried to death that their beloved leader was being abducted and they would never see him again. In the general excitement and confusion, the officials had neglected to pay their annual respects to the sacred lake. And now it had burst its banks and the people knew whose fault it was.

The flood caused havoc throughout the Gyantse area, 170 small villages and over 3,000 houses were washed away, agricultural lands were completely submerged, thousands of people and animals drowned. A large part of Gyantse itself was washed out, and the muddy torrent rushed on as far as the regional capital, Shigatse. A small Indian military base was washed away and 300 of its personnel were lost. 'Water covered the entire valley,' wrote an eye-witness, 'the dry mud houses absorbed the water and began to crumble away.'[19] Emme-la's parents' house was badly damaged, their cows, oxen, goats and yaks drowned, their crops ruined. The water soon subsided, but the flood had destroyed all hopes of a harvest that year. And the natural beauty of Gyantse's fertile valley had been wiped out. Acres of land had been turned overnight into a barren wilderness of stones and rocks.

When news of the catastrophe reached them, the Lhasa noblemen, lamas and traders sent money, grain, cloth and medicines for the survivors; and what remained of the Tibetan government in the city hastily appointed two officials to assess the damage. 'We left for Gyantse immediately,' reported one of the two, Tsipon Shuguba,[20] 'and we met the Chinese representative who helped with the distribution of blankets, coats, shoes and hats from the Chinese Army post.'[21] The two men recommended that every farmer in Gyantse should receive an emergency ration of 80,000 khels of barley-grain[22] from the government stores, to be used as food and for replanting. The Peking government capped this with a gift of 800,000 silver dollars for the flood victims.

According to Emme-la, the farmers of Gyantse saw nothing of this gift. They knew it had been promised, but not only did they receive no money from the local Chinese commander, Yin Fa-tang, they later discovered that he had siphoned off half the emergency grain supplies from the Tibetan government stores to feed the People's Liberation Army.

Worse was to follow, he says. The sympathetic Indian

government donated a large quantity of medicines, rice, wheat, margarine, sugar and bedding, and a group of émigré Tibetans living just across the Indian border in Kalimpong[23] collected 500 sacks of these commodities from the traders and merchants passing through. At the Tibetan border all these supplies fell into the hands of Yin Fa-tang who, instead of allowing the flood victims to receive this gift from their compatriots in India, cynically declared them to be a gift from the Chinese government in Peking and used them to pay off the destitute road-workers in lieu of salary.

Recovery from the flood damage was slow. 'Months and months went by without much sign of progress,' wrote the official, Shuguba. 'There was not time nor energy enough to give each person a proper funeral nor to hire the corpse-slayers necessary for all to be given the traditional Tibetan return. Many families had lost everything and were confused about how to make a new beginning.'

A new beginning was indeed just around the corner, but it was not one the Tibetans might have had in mind. At the end of this catastrophic year the roads leading from Xining and Chengdu to Lhasa were finished. The Chinese press claimed piously that the roads were a symbol of the 'great care and concern' the Chinese Communist Party and Chairman Mao had for the Tibetans. In a veritable lather of self-congratulation, they neglected to mention that the roads had been built at an appalling cost in terms of human life and were first, last and all the time intended for the build-up of the Chinese military machine. Without further ado, more troops, tanks and weapons were brought in from the mainland. The centuries of on-going Tibetan hostility to China, in which the two sides had competed on equal terms, were at an end. Moreover, from now on, the Chinese would monopolise the Tibetan economy, putting an end to Tibet's centuries-old trade with India and Nepal.

It is doubtful, however, whether peasant families, such as Emme-la's in Gyantse, realised the momentous difference the completion of the roads would make. How could they know that a line had been irrevocably drawn under their old lives, and a new one was about to begin? There would soon be no further need to placate the peasants with silver dollars since their subjugation was already safely assured.

CHAPTER 2

A Deadly Mockery

For us Tibetans the phrase, 'the liberation of Tibet', in its moral and spiritual applications is based upon a deadly mockery. The country of a free people was invaded and occupied under the pretext of liberation – liberation from whom and from what? Ours was a happy country with a solvent Government and a contented people until the Chinese invasion in 1950.

> Manifesto by Tibetan leaders in
> 'The Question of Tibet and the Rule of Law'[1]

Tibetan women took an active part in social life and business affairs, and were considered as equal partners by their husbands. On the farms, both partners cut firewood, gathered fuel, and saw to the sowing, reaping and threshing in the fields. Farmers' wives did the chores, cooked, swept, carried water and milked the cows, but much of the household sewing – especially when leather was involved – was considered to be man's work. Wives were in general strong and competent managers in the home, ran their homes efficiently when their husbands were away, and usually controlled the money. Yet there is no doubt that the husband was head of the household. Though love matches were not unknown, the woman usually had to have her marriage arranged for her, the idea being that 'it would not be right to talk to her of it for it would distress her, the thought of leaving home, her father and mother, she would refuse to go'.[2]

Most marriages in old Tibet were arranged. After careful consideration, the parents or older relatives of both partners would decide on a suitable match, and the local Oracle would be called on to perform a number of divinations to assess its prospects. 'Both my parents came from the Gyantse district,' says Emme-la, 'and my father's uncle arranged their marriage. He was a captain at the Tibetan Army garrison in Gyantse before the Chinese came – the one that was set up by the British. The family consulted the Oracle for the final verdict, and he had to choose a date which would be auspicious for both bride and groom. When my mother moved in with my father's family, seven horsemen accompanied her and there were seven days of merry-making, drinking chang, singing and dancing, and lots of food for everyone present.'

In 1954, the year of the great flood, Emme-la's mother, who already had two little girls, Dawa Phentok, aged four, and Pasang Dolma, two, found herself pregnant for a third time. It used to be whispered in old Tibet that sometimes, when the first thunder struck in summer, a child might disappear from its mother's womb, taken, it was said, 'by the Dragon'. Early that summer, thunder struck Gyantse and, whatever the cause, Emme-la's mother miscarried. The baby she was carrying, she told Emme-la later, simply abandoned her womb. The distressed parents consulted the Oracle who reassured them that within two years they would have a male child, and that they must name him as 'a gift of the gods'.

Thus did Emme-la, born two years later, in the Year of the Fire Monkey (1956), receive the names Jinpa Ngodup, 'precious gift of the gods'. (The nickname Emme-la was given to him later at school.) The astrologer, however, like the Bad Fairy in a Western folk tale, had added a more ominous prediction: the family were to have a statue of a certain divinity made and placed in their altar room.[3] Failure to do so would ensure that precisely twelve years after the child's birth a terrible disaster would befall them. Joy at the arrival of Precious Gift was, therefore, mixed with despondency and foreboding, for even in these early stages of the Chinese occupation such a thing would have been impossible.

In those days, Tibetans had a relaxed approach to names, frequently changing them according to circumstances, after marriage or sickness, a long journey – or a meeting with some important lama. Most people did not know the actual given names of their parents, or indeed if they had any at all. A newly married man was referred to as Cho-la, Elder Brother, but when the children began to arrive he was usually called Pa-la, (Father). Emme-la's family went a step further, calling their father Pa-drung – a localised term which was a sign of very special respect. If Pa-drung had a given name of his own, none of the family knew it – to them he was always Pa-drung. His mother's personal name was Migmar Sithar, but after her marriage she was known only as Achi Pomo or 'new wife'. Surnames were unknown, except among big landowners who often took the name of their properties.

Though girls were not officially considered as inferior, the birth of a son after two daughters was an occasion for general rejoicing; and the chances were he would be seriously spoiled by the females of the family. The child came into the world, as was the custom in the Gyantse area, in the downstairs storeroom along with the animal fodder. (In other rural areas of Tibet, for example in Amdo where the present Dalai Lama was born, babies were traditionally born in the cow byre among the cows.) His mother had, in accordance with custom, woven a piece of woollen cloth into a sleeveless garment for the baby, with a gap in the front to leave access for nappies. Behind the neck of the jacket was a pouch into which she now placed the severed umbilical cord sewn into a small bag. That done, she wrapped her son into the two fine-wool shawls she had made, an inner small one and a much larger outer one. A striped woven blanket was ready and waiting to cover him at night.

In the villages around Gyantse, everyone knew everyone else, rich or poor, and their lives were interwoven on many levels. Although the man of the house usually made the felt uppers of the Tibetan boots his family wore, the cobbler often had to be called in to fashion and fit the sturdy leather soles. Then there were the weaver, the tailor, the tinker, the carpenter, the potter, the glue-seller. Tibetan houses at times could resemble busy market places. So it was no surprise that shortly after the birth neighbours, crowds of relatives and friends arrived bearing gifts. The custom, known as the 'bangse' – the 'getting-rid-of-bad-luck' ceremony – dates back, like so many Tibetan rituals, to the pre-Buddhist era.[4] When the new baby was a boy, this purification rite took place on the day after the birth. If it was a girl, the event was postponed until the third day.

The first visitor to arrive would start a small heap of *mani* (prayer-inscribed) stones by the door, burn pine and juniper twigs in a broken earthenware teapot beside the pile,[5] and sprinkle grains of roasted barley over the stones. The next arrivals would follow suit. Only after this ritual had been performed did they enter and present their traditional offering of a long white spun-silk scarf – known as a *khatag*[6] – to mother and baby. The visitors brought barley-beer (*chang*), and buttered tea which they poured out for the mother, and with which they wetted the baby's head while pronouncing a few words of blessing. There were other presents too: sheepskin bags full of tsampa, (the roasted barley-flour which is to the Tibetans what rice is to the Chinese) and butter, to symbolise the hope that the baby would grow up healthy. Occasionally, for good measure, someone would mix a pinch of butter into a few grains of tsampa and put it in the infant's mouth for luck. The visitors brought cubes of cheese, strips of dried mutton or yak meat to build up the mother's strength after the birth, cotton nappies for the baby, and sometimes (from better-off callers) warm scarves or even blankets.

A month later, and for this too a propitious day had to be chosen, the baby was taken out of doors for the first time, both mother and baby having new clothes for the occasion. The mother would first of all take a dab of soot from the bottom of a cooking pan and smear it on the tip of the baby's nose to protect it from evil spirits. Then, after visiting the temple to pray for long life for her child, she would call on any relatives and friends who were fortunate enough to have three generations living under one roof. The idea was that some of their good fortune might rub off on the new baby and that he too might be similarly gifted with offspring.

Religion pervaded every aspect of life. As Landon

commented somewhat scornfully (he was disgusted by what he saw as the Tibetans' superstition and the lamas' exploitation of it):

> At the summit of every pass, at the entrance to a village, at a cleft in the rock-side, at the crossing of a stream by bridge or ford, one is accustomed to find the flicker of a rain-washed string of flags, a fluttering prayer-pole, or a gaily-decked brush of ten-foot willow sprigs; evil spirits must be exorcised at every turn of the road. Wells, lakes and running streams also are full of demons who visit with floods and hailstorms the slightest infraction of the lamas' rule.[7]

Although there were six other monasteries in Gyantse,[8] the focal point for the whole town was without a doubt the great walled monastery of Pelkhor Choede, on a hill facing the great fortress about three-quarters of a mile away. (Unusually for Tibet, Pelkhor Choede housed representatives of all the Buddhist sects, not just those of the dominant Gelugpa tradition to which it officially belonged.[9]) All the most important local events took place there. The high point of the year and source of the most intense excitement was the two-week Getsa Dhamak Festival in June commemorating the anniversary of the monastery's founder. It was special to the Gyantse area. Part religious, part secular, it involved not just the prayer that the deceased founder had been reborn in a better form of life, but fun and games for everyone. Ten days of piety to start with (from the eighth until the eighteenth day of the fourth Tibetan month), followed by five days of fun. Emme-la has fond recollections of these innocent, long-ago festivities. 'All the Tibetans from the surrounding villages would gather in the main chapel of the monastery, dressed in our best clothes, everyone wearing at least one new item for the occasion. We would be shown all the freshly made mandalas, and new scrolls and thangkas (sacred scroll paintings) specially painted for the coming year. Over the next few days, various monastic colleges would perform their special dances for the public, and then towards the end there were offerings of *torma*, the ceremonial cakes made out of tsampa with various delicacies mixed in. We absolutely loved those. Last of all, and this marked the end of the religious side of things, a huge thangka of the Buddha Sakyamuni[10] would be displayed for us all to see. It was the grand climax. After that (from the nineteenth to the twenty-third day) we could simply enjoy the festivities. There were song and dance competitions for everyone – fathers, mothers, brothers and sisters, landowners and peasants, everyone joined in – except the monks. And lots of picnics, while the men took part in horse-racing, archery, tug-o'-war, weightlifting and all sorts of competitions.' With plenty of chang to get drunk on, the unsophisticated villagers were content. They looked forward to Getsa Dhamak the whole year round.

Agriculture in Gyantse, as everywhere in Tibet, was geared to basic survival. Better-off farmers like Emmela's parents who owned a few chickens, dogs and cats, a few cattle and a couple of free-roaming yaks, were its bedrock. Tibetans, most of whom lived at 12,000 ft and higher could not conceive of life without the yak – the hardy bison-like animal which supplied almost all their needs.[11] The yak indeed cannot survive below 10,000 ft. Shaggy-haired and short-limbed, it is a creature of the high altitudes, impervious to heat or cold or lack of oxygen. It forages for itself and requires no grooming, stabling or any other kind of attention. 'We used our yaks for ploughing. At night we used to tie them up by fixing one end of a thin yak-hair cord to their horns and the other to a pegged-out rope,' Emme-la explains. 'No animal could harm a yak, not even bears. When we needed them during the day for ploughing, we just went out and called them or put food out for them. When they came near, we lassooed them with a long rope fastened round a tree.' Robert Ford wrote:

> In a land without machinery [the yak] was vital for transport and on the farms. Its hair was used for tents, blankets, and very strong ropes. Its hide was used not only for boots and saddle-bags, but also for coracles, Tibet's only boats. Its horns were used as snuff-boxes, and its tail for making fly-whisks and Santa Claus beards (for export only). Its dung was used occasionally as manure, but almost universally as fuel, for no coal was mined and much of the country lies above the tree-line. And the yak was the Tibetans' staple diet in the form of milk, butter and meat. The butter was also used for lighting, making images and polishing floors.[12]

Together with the snow lion which adorned the national flag, the yak was a true symbol of Tibet. The very name, *yak*, is Tibetan, perhaps the only Tibetan word in use all over the world.

In addition to the pair of yaks, Emme-la's family had five dairy cows and several sheep and goats which were mainly looked after by semi-nomadic members of their extended family, who tended large flocks on the hillsides. The animals provided the family with meat, butter (for Tibetan tea[13] and for use in the butter-lamps which blazed in front of every altar), milk and cheese, and the wool and leather for use in clothing and handicrafts such as carpet-making. Then there were the

dogs, beloved of all Tibetans. 'Tibetan "mastiffs",' wrote
Landon wonderingly, 'bark from every roof until the
housewife quiets them with a stone. She throws better
than her European sister, in spite of a grimy coral and
turquoise halo round her head and a baby on her left
arm.'[14]

There were fields of the highland barley, known as
gingke (which provided not only chang but roasted
tsampa, the staple food of the Tibetan), wheat, buck-
wheat, mustard and peas. Because of the high altitude
and the thinness of the air, vegetables were scarce in
most of Tibet, but in Gyantse's fertile valley, watered by
the Nyangchu River and its streams, farmers grew
carrots, potatoes, radishes, cabbages, turnips, cauli-
flowers, onions and wild garlic. Before the flood there
had even been peaches, apples and pears. Wild flowers
flourished on the hillsides and the medicinal herbs and
roots which grew in profusion made Gyantse an important regional centre for Tibetan medicine.[15] Western
medicine too was available. With the British having had
a trading post in Gyantse since 1904, there was also a
hospital run by British and Irish doctors.

Thornwood and dried patties of yak dung were
stored on the roof, both of them indispensable for cooking in the bitterly cold sub-zero winter temperatures.
Sometimes grain was spread out there, ready to be
made into *chang*. On the ground floor were cattle pens,
and in the courtyard perhaps a horse or two. Above,
the dark living area, unlit apart from the light that came
in from doors and small square windows, consisted of
the kitchen – the hub of the family's activities – a few
smaller rooms and most important in any Tibetan dwelling, the altar-room. The family slept together on the
floor of the kitchen on mattresses stuffed with wild
antelope or goat hair – or even with discarded carpet

trimmings – over which they unrolled a thick length of woollen cloth. Those who could not afford even such a simple mattress built an outer frame of mud bricks and filled it with sheaves of wheat. Of furniture there was little or none. As Landon observed, 'Two or three brass or copper bowls, a big unglazed red porcelain tea-pot, a few lengths of thick red or gray cloth are (besides the implements of his trade) all you will ever find in a Tibetan house.'[16]

As the time round about dawn was considered the most auspicious for prayer, every day began in the altar-room with prayers, the offering of bowls of water, the lighting of butter-lamps and of an incense made from juniper twigs in a large earthen burner. Breakfast was Tibetan tea, made from brick-tea (imported from China, and preferred to Indian) churned together with yak milk, butter (often rancid) and salt and drunk from a wooden cup. Into the remains of the tea in the cup they would mix a little tsampa, the beloved roasted barley-flour. Most of them lived on little else. Sometimes a bit of dried cheese would be added to the tsampa, some-times even a little sugar. In a mountainous land so high that water boiled at a very low temperature, culinary skills were not advanced, and tastes in food were simple. In the middle of the day, they would have tsampa once again, this time with bread or possibly dried meat and a few vegetables. And in the evening, mutton broth, or tsampa with vegetables and meat.

Meat – dried – was an essential part of the diet, and, like every other vital foodstuff, had to be carefully prepared and stored at a time dictated by sun and stars. Tibet's farmers had long depended on a rule-of-thumb astronomy. Centuries earlier, in order to gain an under-standing of the climatic and seasonal changes which affected their ploughing, sowing and harvesting, they had worked out their own methods of recording the passage of time. 'There were four distinct seasons,' says Emme-la. 'The time for manuring the fields in the spring was shown by the four stars of Karma Jama; and when the six stars of Karma Mindrug set towards the west at dusk, it was time to sow the seed. The season for slaughtering the animals was in late autumn, when the nine-star constellation known as Karma Marwo began to set towards the east.' Professional animal slaughterers (usually Muslims originating from East Turkestan) were brought in during the winter, as no self-respecting Tibetan Buddhist would stoop to killing a sentient being of any kind, even for food. The meat – yak or mutton – would be left outside to dry which it did very quickly in the high altitude and thin, clear air. Or hung outside to freeze dry in the minus 25 to minus 30 degree arctic chill, after which the jerky was cut into strips to be used throughout the year. Cheese too was dried and cut into strips in the autumn. In fact, autumn was the time of maximum activity for all the farmers. It was then that the crops were harvested and the root vegetables buried in the ground, the other vegetables being dried and preserved along with the meat and cheese.

Until the age of seven or so, the younger village children led a carefree existence, loafing around and playing the games that Tibetan children had always played. Emme-la and his friends played hopscotch, paddled in the running streams, rolled down the hillsides, went birds'-nesting, ran all kinds of races and jumped off mounds of muddy earth, seeing who could jump highest and farthest. Another favourite game was played with the knuckle-bones of a sheep: instead of numbers, the surfaces had the names of animals such as horse, yak, goat and sheep. As with dice, 'You throw the bone and see which side it lands.'

The children made rough bows and arrows and practised target-shooting – with Tibetan boys, archery and horse-racing were a passion. They rode bareback, practising on anything that moved, horses, cattle, pigs and even sheep. The archery contests, the horse-races and the folk dances at the summer festival were the nearest approach they had to organised sports – but everything was on an amateur basis, there was no gambling.

They learned what was necessary from their parents and, as they grew older, were given odd jobs to do. 'I remember carrying messages to neighbours when I was quite small. I also had to light the butter lamps and incense sticks before morning prayer, and wash the sacred water-bowls in the evening, ready for the next day.'

It was a way of life that had existed for centuries, and there was no reason to suppose it would not go on for ever. People never even thought about change and few bothered their heads about learning to read or write. There were no newspapers or radios, no official schools; and most people were illiterate. But, in a timeless community where everyone had his or her appointed work and place, this was not a problem. What need was there for outside knowledge, what scope was there for ambition? (If you were ambitious for your children, you could always send them to a monastery.)

Nevertheless, there were four private schools in Gyantse, run by Buddhists who taught to gain merit through the teaching of religion. They were for children of eight and upwards, and entrance was open to all. There were no fees, but families who wished their offspring to attend were expected to make a substantial donation in the beginning, and to give a party for the whole school at which Tibetan butter-tea, sweetened rice, raisins and special biscuits would be served. All four schools concentrated mainly on the teaching of Buddhism, together with the Tibetan language and script, and basic mathematics. The clever ones might also learn astrology and the principles of Tibetan herbal medicine.

Scattered over various villages, the children would walk to the nearest school shortly after day break, seven days a week, with time off only on holy days and religious festivals. On arrival, they would recite in unison a prayer to Jampeyang, the Buddha of Wisdom, who was portrayed with a book balanced on his left shoulder and a sword in his right hand to scythe through the pupils' ignorance. This they were expected to learn by heart and recite every day. The main verse of this immensely long prayer was:

The impartiality of your love for all human beings,
Your voice like thunder waking up the sleep of the
   ignorant,
Your magic sword which cuts the root of all
   unhappiness;
From your loving knowledge, full of radiance,
Please light my dark ignorance with your
   sparkling light
To make me understand the teaching of Lord
   Buddha;
May you give me courage, and understanding
   of the great teaching.[17]

If events had followed their normal course, Emme-la would doubtless have attended one of these schools. But in 1956, the year of his birth, the tocsin was already sounding for this uniquely Tibetan way of life.

* * *

During a twelve-month visit to China in 1954–55, the Dalai Lama had been assured by Chairman Mao that he had abandoned his initial plan to rule Tibet directly from Peking in favour of a degree of self-government. Tibet, explained Mao (and in 'Tibet', he did not include the eastern borderlands with their massive Tibetan populations, but only the central provinces of Ü and Tsang which had been under the Dalai Lama's direct authority at the time of the 1950 invasion) needed careful grooming before it could fulfil its destiny as a constituent part of the People's Republic of China. To this end he proposed setting up a temporary governing committee made up mainly of Tibetans. The young Dalai Lama believed in the necessity for social change, and although during his visit to China he had realised the terrible toll in terms of human anguish and loss of individual identity which the 'grey fog' of Marxism had exacted, he was still convinced that Tibet could benefit from a degree of material progress without suffering the same fate. He rather admired Mao and believed he could trust him.

His optimism was somewhat dented, however, on the journey back to Lhasa in May 1955, as he passed through those regions of eastern Tibet which had been forcibly absorbed into the People's Republic of China (his own homeland of Amdo in north eastern Tibet was among them). In these Tibetan-populated areas, communism was being ruthlessly imposed, and what he saw filled him with foreboding. He could not fail to be aware of the 'boiling resentment', the mounting hatred, as a reign of terror was unleashed on an unwilling populace. He could do nothing to help them, but consoled himself with the thought that in his own central Tibet at least, out of fifty-six members of the new Preparatory Committee proposed by Mao, fifty-one were to be Tibetan. That surely was a hopeful sign.

In the provinces of Ü and Tsang, relief at the Dalai Lama's safe return from China was tinged with apprehension. With the roads now in place, the need for caution on the part of the Chinese had gone, the iron hand could be brought out of its velvet glove without further delay.

In August 1956, amid much fanfare, the Preparatory Committee for the Autonomous Region of Tibet was inaugurated, with the Dalai Lama as Chairman, the Panchen Lama (Tibet's second most prominent lama, whom the Chinese at that time appeared to have in their pocket) as Vice-Chairman, and Ngabo Ngawang Jigme (Tibet's foremost quisling, disliked by the Tibetans who called him 'the two-headed one') as General Secretary. It did not take the Dalai Lama long to realise that he had been conned: there were indeed fifty-one Tibetans on the Committee, but all but fifteen of them had been hand-picked by the Chinese for their willingness to play ball. Such power as these Tibetans had was in any case an illusion, since *all* real power lay with the five Chinese members, all of them members of the Committee of the Chinese Communist Party of Tibet, on which there was no place for Tibetans. At a stroke, the Dalai Lama's power had been wiped out. Though his Cabinet (*Kashag*) and the Tibetan National Assembly continued nominally to exist, from now on they could be out-voted by a two-thirds majority on any and every issue. The whole Tibetan government, and the Dalai Lama himself, had been effectively hamstrung. The pussy-footing was at an end – the Chinese were making it clear that they were the masters now.

A new, nightmarish factor was also entering the equation. Until now, Lhasa had only heard distant rumours about atrocities being perpetrated by the Chinese in eastern Tibet. But suddenly thousands of refugees from the eastern regions began to flood into the city, bringing with them reports of widespread tortures and massacres in the region of Kham, where a guerrilla movement was resisting the Chinese. Eyewitnesses described how:

> monks and laymen were tortured and many killed, often in barbarous ways; women raped and others publicly humiliated; venerated lamas subjected to brutal and disgusting degradations, other monks and lamas compelled to break their religious vows; men and boys deported or put to forced labour in harsh conditions; boys and girls taken from their homes, ostensibly for education in China; children incited to abuse and beat their parents; private property seized; and sacred images, books and relics carried off or publicly destroyed.[18]

The effect of these reports can be imagined. Popular disquiet spread alarmingly. As CHINESE GO HOME posters appeared on every Lhasa wall, the feeling gained ground among the Tibetans that violence might be the only course left to them. It could only be a matter of time before the popular fury and anguish boiled over.

At this point Mao appeared to back-pedal somewhat, promising to postpone the planned communisation of central Tibet for five years, or until the Tibetans were ready for it. But it was too late, the scene-shifting for the last act of the drama had already begun. In July 1957, as the Chinese began bringing more troop divisions, more truckloads of equipment, more tanks and heavy artillery into Lhasa, making it clear that they intended to enforce their political programmes through military control, the guerrilla groups of eastern Tibet resolved to sink their historic mutual rivalries and pool their resources in the defence of Buddhism. It was not so much then the independence of Tibet – they took for granted that Tibet had always been independent and would be so again – but the actual survival of Buddhism for which they were prepared to lay down their lives. Calling themselves first the Volunteer Force for the Protection of the Faith, they later adopted the name Chushi Gangdrug, which means Four Rivers, Six Ranges, an ancient name for the mountainous Kham and Amdo regions which formed the contentious border with China. By the early summer of 1958, the movement had established its headquarters in the Lhokha area of southern central Tibet, and as thousands poured out of Lhasa and the surrounding towns to join the guerrillas, the first united Tibetan fighting force was born. It was a nation-wide Resistance Movement.

Suddenly Gyantse, where the Chinese were stepping up their surveillance programme and becoming more repressive by the day, found most of its menfolk disappearing. Hundreds quietly left the area to join the national resistance force, others fled towards Nepal and India while the going was good; others again, realising that Lhasa was on the verge of an explosion, made their way to the city. There the Chinese were taking no chances: they were already digging trenches, putting sandbags in place, creating underground passages and surrounding their buildings with electrified barbed-wire fences.

In March 1959, Lhasa spontaneously combusted;[19] the Dalai Lama and his government fled into exile; the People's Liberation Army answered the Tibetan people's cry of despair by opening fire on the crowds and turning their heavy artillery on the city, reducing it to a smoking ruin. Almost 10,000 were killed in three days of fighting: corpses littered the streets, many lay wounded and dying; and Chinese soldiers rampaged through the sacred city, systematically destroying it. Thousands of Tibetans were marched off to prisons and far-away gulags in the Tibetan Siberia (the frozen wastes of the Chang Tang desert in the north), most of them never to be seen again. As the prayer-flags were torn down, the red flag of the People's Republic of China flew triumphantly over every town, village and mountain pass in the land.

CHAPTER 3
Socialist Paradise

In essence, what had occurred was not simply the conquest of one race by another, but the head-on collision of two opposing views of man's innermost nature: one spiritual, the other material. While the Chinese believed that Communism, as defined by Mao, was a panacea for all life's ills, the Tibetans felt that earthly existence could never be ultimately satisfactory. Liberation to them meant freedom from the inevitable suffering of birth, old age, disease and death, gained by enlightenment. Material well-being had never been an ideal in Tibetan culture.

John Avedon, *From Liberation to Liberalisation* (1982)

What price now the 'peaceful liberation' of Tibet? The Lhasa uprising was a genuinely popular revolt by ordinary Tibetans who longed to be rid of the 'Red Chinese Enemies of Religion', and were sick and tired of seeing their own traditional elites[1] collaborating with them. Yet this people's revolt had been crushed by the People's Liberation Army with unthinkable brutality.

To the victors, recent events merely confirmed what they had always believed: that the Tibetans were no better than savages. The revolt provided all the justification they needed for going back on their promises and imposing full-blooded socialism. They did not scruple to turn the facts on their head, declaring that the uprising had been a last-ditch attempt by 'upper-strata counter-revolutionaries and foreign imperialists' to regain control, that it was entirely unsupported by 'the masses', in coming to whose rescue they had regrettably been forced to use violence. Moreover, in spite of their best efforts to protect him, reactionary forces had kidnapped the Dalai Lama. (Whether or not they actually believed it, it was imperative for the Chinese to maintain this fiction for the time being, as they intended to attach His Holiness's name to the radical reforms they were about to impose.) But, they assured the stricken populace, everything had in fact turned out for the best, since now the Tibetan people could be incorporated into the sacred Motherland without further delay. First, of course, they must be purged of their bad old ways and learn how to behave in the socialist paradise.

Resistance in Lhasa continued to be viciously put down, 'peaceful liberation' went to the wall, and the Tibetan system of government was instantly replaced by a military dictatorship. In the absence of the Dalai Lama, the 22-year-old Panchen Lama was made Acting Chairman of the temporary government, backed up by the 'Patriotic Few', those upper-class Tibetans both clerical and lay who, for whatever reasons, had thrown in their lot with the Chinese.

The Chinese lost no time in eliminating the

opposition. On 8 April 1959, 20,000 soldiers of the People's Liberation Army (PLA) swept through the areas around Lhasa and south of the Yarlung Tsangpo river (known elsewhere as the Brahmaputra) which Chushi Gangdrug, the resistance movement, still controlled. The guerrillas continued to fight bravely, but they had few weapons and stood little chance against the full onslaught of the well-armed PLA. By the end of April, before the Chinese had contrived to seal off the borders, the guerrilla leaders had fled to India to continue the fight from there. By May, as resistance fighters swelled the growing numbers of escapees, the Chinese were able to claim that all opposition had finally been crushed.

Though Emme-la was only a small boy at the time when life as his ancestors had known it for centuries was turned upside down, he absorbed the atmosphere from his parents. 'Like everyone else, they had gone on believing that their beloved gods would protect them, and had confidently invoked their protection against the approaching evil. But the gods had unaccountably been deaf.'

The people of Gyantse were disorientated and confused. First of all, most of the men had left to join the Resistance or to take part in the protests in Lhasa. 'And now Chinese soldiers were suddenly milling about everywhere, no longer even pretending to be friendly, and accompanied by men in blue boiler suits – the political officers brought in to oversee social change. All those soldiers and officials had to be fed, housed and clothed, the prices of everything shot up and up and up, and the people began to feel that they were enveloped in total darkness. Most of those who lived near the borders were contemplating escape.'

41

The Chinese authorities acted swiftly to nip that particular problem in the bud, summoning the people to public meetings where a terrifying picture was painted of the fate awaiting those who might be thinking of escape to India. Certain misery and death by heat, poverty, starvation, disease and persecution would be the only result of such folly. The propaganda was laid on with a trowel, and it worked. For the time being at least, all thoughts of flight were abandoned.

The arrests started. In the short term, society was divided into those who had not supported the uprising and those who had – the *logchoepas* or 'counter-revolutionaries' – who had to be liquidated whatever class they came from. Anybody suspected of having belonged to Chushi Gangdrug, of sheltering or giving food or aid or anything at all to the Resistance fighters was automatically rounded up. Emme-la's great-uncle, the Tibetan captain who had brought his parents together, and who had later fought bravely with the Resistance, was taken away in this wave of arrests, as was his mother's youngest sister, a nun. 'My parents felt terribly sad and upset. But they were frightened too. They simply didn't dare talk about the arrests except quietly at home. There were spies and informers everywhere. If they'd protested, someone would have reported them and it would have been their turn next.'

PLA squads swooped on the houses of rebels who had been arrested in the immediate aftermath of the revolt; their families were evicted or, at best, allowed to move into the stables with the livestock. Then the soldiers returned and took away the livestock too, yaks, donkeys, sheep, cows, even the families' stocks of food and their agricultural tools. Any rebel estate-owners (their families and servants) who still remained, or anyone associated with the monasteries were rounded up and taken away, most of them never to be seen again.[2]

The local post office in Gyantse was converted into a make-shift prison and filled to overflowing with men aged from fifteen to fifty, all 'enemies of the people' for having fought in the Resistance or taken part in the Lhasa rebellion. On the pretext that the monasteries had supported the revolt, most of Gyantse's monasteries and temples were closed down and destroyed, the abbots and senior monks arrested, the novices evicted and sent home. Sacred images and books were smashed or burnt. The great monastery of Pelkhor Choede survived as a torture centre. Pasang Tsewang, a poor peasant forcibly undergoing re-education, was taken there with about 200 others.[3]

I saw more than two hundred people, monks and laymen, bound with thick ropes. They were brought there from the local post office where they had been imprisoned for some time. They were joined by about two hundred monks, chained and manacled, along with the Oracle of Cho[e]d[e] Monastery and its abbot, Lobsang. Both the abbot and the oracle were publicly assaulted and charged with terrible crimes. The abbot's ears were torn and his entire face was soaked in the blood pouring out of his mouth, nose and ears.

As for the Oracle, his captors dressed him in his ceremonial robes complete with its head-dress, which was so heavy that usually it could be borne only when the wearer went into a trance, then tortured him, forcing him to put himself into a trance, while they continued to beat him.

'Families were frantically searching for relatives,

many of whom had already been shot or had simply disappeared,' says a Gyantse woman. Later, Emme-la counted thirty-six families in his own village alone who had lost loved ones at this time. It would be many years before their fate would become known.

'One of the best-known families, for example, was that of Loden Katsanub. They had been successful traders before the Chinese came. Loden was arrested in 1959 and sent to four different prisons set up within Gyantse itself. First of all in Dzongdun, where most of the local prisoners were held, regardless of what they were supposed to have done. From there they were classified according to their "crimes" and sent on to a second prison. By the time he had been transferred yet again, it was obvious that the Chinese had found him guilty. The fourth prison was Kharmae where most of the serious Gyantse cases were locked up. Here he was made to work in the fields, before being sent away from the Gyantse area, to a prison in Tsetang, near the Samye Monastery. With him went about 120 others.

'It was the worst period of his imprisonment. The prisoners' daily diet consisted of half a pound of tsampa flour, with some thin soup in the evening. Occasionally there would be a cup of black tea to mix with the tsampa. That was all. On this diet they had to reclaim virgin land and convert it into arable land by digging with spades. This land had never been worked before, and it was as hard as granite. The prisoners' day began at dawn when they had a long walk to their place of work – and it ended at sundown. In between they worked non-stop, apart from a short midday break for tsampa. Each prisoner had his work quota for the day and any shortfall had to be added to the next day's quota.

'As time went on, the poor diet and the hard labour

took their toll, and the prisoners were less and less able to fulfil their daily quotas. They tried, as men were doing in prisons all over Tibet, to supplement their starvation diet by stripping the leather from their boots or from the prayer wheels around Samye – in order to cook and eat it. The leather from the prayer-wheels was apparently very unpleasant on account of the coloured dyes with which the thongs had been painted. But no matter. Every time they went into the monastery itself, they searched frantically for anything that might be made of leather, and which they could cook. Sometimes when they were working on the land, they would see a few mice running round. Whoever saw a mouse would lay claim to it, but was usually too weak to chase it and could do no more than weakly shout, "It's mine." Not one of them had the strength to catch it.

'Probably their best find was the carcass of a dead horse, belonging to one of the villagers who lived near the monastery. When they saw the carcass they fell on it like a pack of wild animals, hacking off huge chunks with their spades and eating them raw. It was, they said, the best food they had ever eaten, and for some reason it did not make them ill.

'But few of them could survive for long. On average about seven prisoners died each day, mostly during the night. They would lie down at night and simply not get up again.'

Those landowners, government officials or monks who had fled to India or Nepal were condemned in their absence as reactionary traitors who had fomented the rebellion and assisted the rebels. Their property and possessions were confiscated: estates, houses, ornaments, carpets, works of art, religious relics. In theory, these were to be handed over to the poor. Deeds to expropriated land were distributed with great fanfare to the poorer peasants and to beggars who knew nothing about farming and had no desire whatsoever to learn. (And who certainly did not suspect that the land would soon be taken away from them again.) The Chinese proclaimed that such generosity represented the sun of the Chinese Communist Party shining down at long last on the poor instead of on the rich, but it did not turn out quite like that. Items such as furniture and rugs were taken away by the Chinese military or civilians for their own private use, priceless artefacts were crated and sent to China for sale on the antiques markets of Hong Kong and Tokyo (or, in the case of gold objects, to be melted down into bullion). Only the rubbish – broken chairs and tables, empty boxes, old clothes and chipped crockery – was somewhat cynically distributed among the deserving poor. When the hopeful beneficiaries were summoned to the neighbourhood office to receive their share of the spoils, they were woefully disappointed.

Undeterred by the reality, the Chinese insisted that this new order of things symbolised the beating of Chinese and Tibetan hearts together in brotherly love. 'We have liberated you,' they boasted, though some of the Tibetans suspected that the only thing they were being liberated from was their freedom. Despite the continued dire warnings from the authorities, entire villages began abandoning their homes and making for India or Nepal. By the end of July 1960, more than 60,000 Tibetans had escaped from Tibet.

By that time the serious re-organisation of Tibetan society was well under way. After the revolt, Gyantse was divided into districts, each with its own zone, neighbourhood and block committee controlled by local collaborators – one for every ten inhabitants. Identity cards were introduced and had to be shown on demand. Nobody could now leave the towns or villages without official permission.

The next step was to set up a new class structure, and to this end the Tibetans were ordered to estimate the value of such property or land as they had. The upper class of landowners and officials and the lowest of have-nots were easy enough to identify, but the nomads and smallholding peasants in between could not by any stretch of the imagination be described as 'bourgeoisie'. In the end it was decided that if a family's income exceeded its expenditure, then the family were exploiters of the people, even if that family was actually quite poor. 'They divided us into classes on the basis of how much seed a family used for planting. Ours,' says Emme-la, 'used about 240 kg of seed a year, less well-off peasants used about 50–60, and the poorest, the seasonal hired workers, would use none.'

Five new classes were finally inaugurated: the owners of large estates; their agents and stewards; richer farmers or nomads; middle peasants and nomads; and the poorest peasants and nomads.

'The lowest categories were said to be pure and clean. They got no privileges as such, but they *were* given the opportunity to join the Communist Party and were eligible for promotion within the Communist hierarchy. It was unlikely they'd ever be victimised by the regime. And even the middle-ranking peasants were more or less safe. But the first two categories were doomed from the outset – they never stood a chance. Our family, because we had our own farmhouse, our cows, yaks and sheep, and because of the amount of seed we sowed each year, were classified as "rich peasants". And that meant that we were always in danger of being "struggled against" and imprisoned by the authorities.

If your class background was wrong, you could be arrested at any time for no reason at all, and your word would never be believed. Our lives became very restricted.'

Abandoning their 'United Front' policy of working with the traditional elites, the Chinese now turned to those in the two lowest categories whose existence they had so far ignored. The key to the planned re-organisation would be the mobilisation of the masses. Thousands of new cadres (officials) were recruited. 'When the Chinese first came to Tibet,' remarked a former activist,[4] 'they befriended the rich and the powerful to make them their agents. After 1959 they befriended the beggars, the criminals and the poor, the ones with personal resentment against the establishment, to make them their tools.' With the help of these disaffected elements of society and of the young Tibetan activists who had been sent to China for their political education during the 1950s, educating the masses in the rules of class hatred became a top priority.

Twice a day the people were summoned to political meetings and ordered to learn the new political theory by heart – and put it into practice. 'Our families were told,' says Emme-la, 'that there were three main evils against which they must "struggle" with all their might: those who'd taken part in the revolt; the former Tibetan government; and the landlords, including the monks. I don't think people were all that bothered about the landowners and the government officials, at least not in the beginning, but they were very upset about the monks.'

At the obligatory mass meetings aimed at whipping up class hatred to fever pitch, it was hammered home to the people that they had never known happiness before being 'liberated' by their Chinese brothers. They were ordered to say – and indeed to think – that thanks to Chairman Mao and the Chinese Communist Party they were now basking in limitless joy. It was now that the propaganda machine first began churning out atrocity stories about the old regime. (Though they had been in the country for a decade the Chinese had made no mention of these before.) On the basis of 'four legs good, two legs bad', the old society was held to be responsible for all Tibetan ills, no matter how trivial. In this version of events, people had lived like animals before the Chinese came, thousands had died of cold and starvation, or been tortured to death by evil monastic officials and landowners.[5]

However stunned they might be by such monstrous distortions of the facts, the Tibetans were not allowed to be a passive audience – they must dig into their own recollections of the past, unearth every possible grievance and grudge against the landowners, true or otherwise, naming names, while the activist in charge noted the charges in a big book. It was impossible to hide or to back away from the repellent task – active participation was insisted upon. Enemies of the People had to be exterminated – and be seen to be exterminated – by the People themselves.

Thus did the infamous struggle-session or *thamzing* arrive in Tibet, as karma, the Buddhist way of accepting one's life with its miseries as well as joys, was forcibly driven out. Hatred, in the Communist philosophy, was the true leveller, and *thamzing*, active class struggle, was the bloody crucible in which hatred could be fomented; it was the way in which the people would be forced – in pain and suffering – to become a hate-crazed mob in order to make the revolution for themselves. And if the 'green-brained' Tibetans were crass enough to feel no

hatred for their supposed former 'oppressors', the landlords, lamas, army officers and traders who were the
'Enemies of the People', well then, they must be made
to feel it. And because the Chinese in fact had a deep
contempt for the Tibetans, whose belief in karma and
'compassion for all sentient beings' made them unpro-
mising revolutionary material, *thamzing* in Tibet would
be even worse than it was in mainland China. It would
always be racist in character, with the Chinese insisting
that the horrors and humiliations, the tortures and the
ghastly murders which the Tibetans were driven to
carry out in the regular *thamzing* sessions were in their
own best interests. The very word *thamzing* would soon
strike terror and shame into all Tibetan hearts.

Before each *thamzing* session, the cadres would decide
who was to be struggled against that day, who would
lead the session, what the charges would be and how
the victims would eventually be punished. The next
stage was to give the Tibetan activists some key accusations to use. Only then was it time to order the general
public to present themselves at the village square or
monastery or wherever the *thamzing* was to be held.
Attendance was compulsory for everyone. But at this
stage they would not know who the victims were to be.

When the organisers, accusers and public were gathered together, the victim would be trucked in from
prison. 'The victim would be the last person to know,'
says Emme-la, 'and sometimes he or she would be
someone dragged out of the audience to face trial. The
person in charge of proceedings would then talk about
the Motherland and the joy of Socialism and how we
must all play our part in bringing it about.' The people
were skilfully worked on by their activist leaders, made
to sing rousing socialist choruses, to shout slogans and
shake their right arms and fists in the air, revolutionary-

style; briefed as to what accusations to make; rehearsed in the finer points of character-assassination; and skilfully whipped into a lather of frenzy. This piece of theatre was supposed to represent the serfs rising up as free individuals to claim their rights.

Then the real work of the day would start. As the prisoners were dragged centre stage in the temple, monastery courtyard or village hall, the howls of accusation began: 'You made us work like animals'; 'You kept us on starvation wages'; 'You exploited us for your own advantage'; or, in the case of revered and much-loved lamas, 'You cheated and lied to us'; 'You lived off the fat of the workers'; 'You taught us superstition.' And then, as the carefully stoked flames of mob hysteria ignited, came the beatings, the torture, the dragging by the hair, the ritual humiliations and – frequently – the murder. No one's hands could be clean; no one's hands were meant or permitted to be. That was the whole point. 'The cadres used to watch us carefully, taking note not only of what we said but of our facial expressions. If these were not satisfactory, it would be our turn next.'

'It was terrible,' Emme-la continues. 'If we had refused to turn up, we'd have had to face *thamzing* too. And we had to be seen to be taking an active part, screaming, shouting and beating whoever was the target for the day. If there were no crimes to accuse the victim of, we had to invent them. As time went on, the person being struggled against realised that what was happening bore no relation to reality, they knew that those of us who were doing the accusing had no choice in the matter.'

In practice, *thamzing* came to mean the setting of every Tibetan against every other: not only the poor against the rich, but the people against their former leaders; children against parents, relations and teachers; friends against friends. It meant that the Tibetans were coerced, threatened and bullied into becoming a race of spies and accusers and into holding kangaroo courts in which they were both judge and jury not only over their former 'oppressors', but even over their own families and friends. 'It was all a performance,' insists Emme-la, shame-faced. 'We didn't hate any of those people. They were Tibetans, and many of them had been our friends. We had to pretend to hate them, we had to say horrible things about them, we had to beat them and pull out their hair because the Chinese forced us to, but none of it bore any relation to what we really felt.'

The new State penetrated into every aspect of Tibetan life. The old economic set-up dependent on manorial estates was replaced by Mutual Aid groups and the paying of all taxes to the State. The peasants were divided up into small teams of about ten families, each of them under the leadership of the political progressives. They would not only farm but build dams and watermills, enlarge canals, undertake irrigation – in short, build the new Tibet with their bare hands. The aim was supposedly that the people themselves would transform a backward Tibet into a socialist paradise, but all that happened in practice was that Tibet's food and mineral resources were siphoned off and sent to China. In the early 1960s, the Tibetans went hungry. Many starved to death. 'We saw people with swollen bodies and greenish-coloured eyes,' recalls Emme-la. 'They went to the hospital where the Chinese gave them medicines that made them even worse and told them to go home and get some good food. Since there was no food at all, they went home and ate pig swill and grass. No one was allowed to beg. People were so hungry that they went to the mill where the Chinese soldiers ground the flour, and they scraped the remains of the flour off the millstones to eat there and then.'[6]

The thousands who continued to flee to safety over the mountains were indeed driven out partly by hunger, but the economic disaster was as nothing compared to the destruction of the monasteries and the desecration of the Buddhist faith. This was what drove the refugees in despair from their homeland. The Tibetan peasant's world had been axed at its roots. 'There is no hope either for our life in this world nor for our life in the next,' lamented one peasant woman as she prepared to leave her home in Phari and become a penniless exile in India.[7] Many in Gyantse must have reflected bitterly that the British invasion of 1904 had not, after all, represented the worst of all possible fates. There is a Tibetan proverb which says, 'When you have seen a scorpion, you look on the frog as divine.' Overwhelmed now by the all-conquering Chinese scorpion, the Tibetans may even have looked back on the old British frog with something approaching nostalgia.

CHAPTER 4

When the Wind of Destruction Blew

It mattered very little to the Chinese leaders what the Tibetans thought of their society or what type of reforms they wanted; the logic of Chinese politics dictated that Tibet should be subjected to class-struggle.

Tsering Shakya, *The Dragon in the Land of Snows*

One day early in 1963, Emme-la's father was allowed to make a pilgrimage to Lhasa.[1] He genuinely wanted to make the pilgrimage, though the secret reason for the journey was to visit the infamous Drapchi prison in Lhasa[2] where two of his relatives had been incarcerated since 1959. Both his wife's youngest sister, a nun, and his own uncle, the former Tibetan army captain, had been rounded up as class enemies after the Lhasa rebellion and imprisoned in Drapchi, where

54

torture was routine and starvation rife.

Seven-year-old Emme-la was taken along. Too young to comprehend the darker implications of this his first big excursion away from home, he was excited by the prospect of adventure. 'One freezing January morning, my mother woke me early, scrubbed me hard, festooned me with good luck charms, wrapped me in warm clothes and put a white khata around my neck. She rubbed black soot on my nose to protect me from evil spirits – this was the usual procedure when children were going on their first long journey. My father was dressed in his best *chuba* and fur hat, and my mother and younger sister came with us as far as the truck-stop. When the truck came, we seemed to travel for hours until we reached the Khamba-la Pass which marks the border with Ü province[3] and leads to Lhasa. I shall never forget arriving on top of the Pass and seeing the marvellous, sacred turquoise waters of Yamdrok Lake far below. It was a wonderful sight.'

The sight of Lhasa itself was more tragic for his father, for the city had changed out of all recognition. It had been mortally damaged by bombs and shells during the three-day orgy of destruction which was the Chinese response to the Tibetan uprising. The bodies of the dead had burned for three days, and after the carnage, the reprisals, arrests and executions had begun. The Tibetans' holy city had become an armed camp, divided, like everywhere else, into districts and zones and neighbourhood committees, all controlled by collaborators and ultimately by the Chinese. Everyone was hungry, no one dared speak out, for there were spies everywhere and everyone was under constant surveillance. The famous Tibetan medical college on the sacred Chakpori Hill had been destroyed along with so much else, the Hill itself renamed Victory Peak and boasting a brand-new ammunition dump. Streets now bore typical revolutionary names like Great Leap Forward Street, Liberation Street, Sunshine Street; and the Dalai Lama's Norbulingka Park had become the People's Park.

Pa-drung had many relatives living in Lhasa, but he dared not contact them for fear of endangering their lives. So he and Emme-la took a room in a small guesthouse. They went to the various pilgrimage sites, circumambulated the ruins of the Jokhang Temple, and visited the remains of the once great monasteries of Sera, Drepung[4] and Ganden, now mainly in ruins and with only a handful of aged caretaker monks remaining. The Dalai Lama's Potala and Norbulingka Palaces were strictly out of bounds.

Only when they had completed the pilgrimage circuit did they turn their attention to the Drapchi prison. In a small temple outside the prison precincts, they made offerings to the prison's protector deity, Drapchi Lhamo, before stationing themselves with their food bundles before the prison gates. They waited, and waited, but there was no one around to give them any information. 'If we saw an official,' says Emme-la, 'we asked if we could see our relations, but none of them would even speak to us, though one or two of them stared at us as though we'd come from another planet.

'They stayed put until dusk that first day, then returned, disappointed, to their guesthouse. Early on the morning of the next day, they resumed their vigil at the prison gates – together with several other families on the same hopeless errand. Many women were hawking food parcels around all of Lhasa's prisons in a desperate attempt at finding where their loved ones had been taken. And still no one would take any notice of them. Then, suddenly, hope surged, as two men were seen approaching the prison gates pushing two wheel barrows. At last! we thought. They're coming to collect the food parcels from us. Everyone got very excited. My father started mixing tsampa with some butter to send to his sister-in-law and his uncle. But it turned out we'd made a ghastly mistake. When the wheelbarrows came near, we could see that they were covered over. And then we learned that they contained dead prisoners who were being disposed of. We were sickened and horrified by this news. Later we learned that two or three cartloads of corpses were taken out every day from Drapchi and Taring prisons in Lhasa, for hasty burial or to be used as manure on the fields. And nobody was ever allowed to say those people had died of starvation. It was a capital crime to say so. Nobody could starve under socialism.'

Once again they took their food bundles back to the guesthouse. Again the next night, and the next one, and the one after that. Losar, the New Year festival which once had been the happiest of all the Tibetan festivals, came and went but there was no appetite for rejoicing. Hope took a long time to die, but in the end Emme-la and his father understood that their mission was hopeless. So, leaving all their food parcels behind, they reluctantly returned to Gyantse. Much later Emme-la would learn that his father's uncle had died in prison, while his mother's younger sister would remain a prisoner for sixteen more years before being released – with her eyesight totally destroyed.[5]

Among the village children, Emme-la gained considerable kudos from his journey to Lhasa. Had he not seen with his own eyes the famous statue of Buddha in the Jokhang Temple, the most precious statue in the whole of Tibet? The other children were green with envy, and Emme-la was thrilled with his new-found status.

As yet, the village children were scarcely aware of the momentous changes taking place in their country. Emme-la had continued to do the small jobs in the house and on the farm that Tibetan children had always done. He burned the incense sticks in the altar-room, ran messages for his family and for neighbours, fed and watered the animals when they were unable to be sent to the pastures for grazing.

It was nearly time for him to go to school. In old Tibet, education, outside the monasteries, was almost unheard-of,[6] neither of his parents could read or write and there had never been any question of his older sister Dawa Phentok attending school. She was good at sewing and handicrafts and was indispensable about the house, so she stayed at home – no one thought that strange.

But in 1959 when the Chinese built a primary school in Gyantse on the site of a former monastery, just half an hour's walk away from their home, the younger daughter, Pasang Dolma, was enrolled. And by May 1963 it was 7-year-old Emme-la's turn. 'Both of my sisters were excited when it was time for me to go to school,' says Emme-la. 'I suppose, being the youngest, I was the family pet. They both came with a good-luck scarf for me and lots of good advice.'

On the morning of the great day, Emme-la put on his best Tibetan *chuba*, with a bag of dried cheese and roasted barley stowed in its ample pouch for his midday meal. That first day his father was to accompany him. His mother solemnly placed a ceremonial scarf around his neck, then father and son set off, Emme-la clutching a new writing slate, his father carrying 'a smart bag containing books, ink and string for measuring straight lines on a slate'.

His father left Emme-la in the care of a teacher, Tashi

Kidzom, a Tibetan girl who had been educated in Chinese schools. She in turn handed him over to a prefect, who, after checking to see that his hands and face were clean, abandoned him on a bench in the most junior classroom. (The main hall of the former monastery housed three separate classes, each of them facing in a different direction.) With his father gone, Emme-la's excitement rapidly turned to panic. He knew only one other pupil, Tenzin Norbu, a boy from his own village who was in the top class. This turned out to be a lucky acquaintance, for Tenzin Norbu took him under his wing. 'As we all knew that there were spies everywhere, we had to be very careful what we said or did. Tenzin Norbu told me which pupils to avoid.' In spite of the age gap, they were to become good friends.

Alas, due to his family's new 'rich peasant' classification, Emme-la's school life was under a cloud from the outset. After the first day at school, he put away his *chuba*, both to prevent its getting dirty and because he had already discovered that Tibetan dress was frowned on by the school authorities. He was delighted when his father gave him a new corduroy jacket and a pair of woollen trousers to wear next day.

But these garments were to be his downfall. About a week after his arrival at the school, Emme-la's smart new clothes were singled out for condemnation at the political meeting held every morning to discuss the class structure of society (the main purpose of which was to humiliate and punish 'class enemies'). He was giving a bad example to the others, the terrified child was told, he should be wearing clothes which were more suitable for hard-working labourers. Seconds later, a group of prefects descended on Emme-la and hauled him to his feet. For the rest of the meeting – well over half an hour – the 7-year-old was forced to stand with his hands above his head, and three slates piled on each hand. 'It was horrible being punished like that before all those people I hardly knew. After only a few minutes, my hands began to shake and I felt I couldn't stand it any longer. I felt sick and dizzy and I began to cry. But it didn't do me any good, they made me stand there like that till the meeting finished.' When he went home, of course, he begged his parents for some old clothes to wear, but they had nothing else to give him. In fear and trembling, he returned to school next day, still wearing the hated new clothes. Thankfully, no more was said about them, either then or later.

No longer, of course, did the children study scripture nor recite prayers to the god of wisdom. The only thing they were taught about religion was that it was dangerous nonsense. In primary school, they were taught political theory, the rudiments of arithmetic, drawing, the Tibetan alphabet and basic Chinese. Chairman Mao had demanded that the culture of 'book-worship' should give way to one of 'work-worship', so when school finished in the afternoon, the children were given a variety of extra-curricular duties. They spent two days a week working on the roads, collecting up cowpats for manure-making, and, in the fields which belonged to the school, uprooting the weeds and thistles from among the crops. Even when they wore gloves, their hands were blistered and sore.

In October 1963, four or five months after Emme-la had begun school, his teacher Tashi Kidzom was sent away to China to study at one of the special colleges set up for the non-Chinese races within the People's Republic.[7] As no other teacher was available and harvest time was fast approaching, the school was closed down. In November, when the farmers had finished gathering in the harvest, the Chinese authorities put up a poster announcing the opening of a new district school in the same premises as before. Emme-la, studious by nature, was enthusiastic. 'My sister came with me to enrol. We went to the school office, and had to do certain tests: recognising colours, reciting the Tibetan alphabet, counting as far as we could, that sort of thing. They sent us home then, but two or three days later sent for us again and we had a medical check-up to see if we had any contagious diseases. After that we were enrolled.'

Now there were more subjects to learn. 'We still had all the political stuff, and we went on studying the Tibetan alphabet. But we also had two lessons of drawing, two of physical exercise and two of basic arithmetic. I enjoyed it all and got on well. When my class was asked to vote for the best student, they all voted for me. I was delighted, not only by the honour but because of the cash prize – a few coins – that was supposed to go with it.' But Emme-la's 'rich peasant' background dogged him: no matter how many times he topped the poll, the school authorities refused to let him receive his prize. 'I won lots of times, but they refused to give me the money. The first time it happened, I burst into tears and couldn't stop crying. It seemed so unfair, and I'd been looking forward to buying some sweets. But then, when they kept on refusing, I got used to it and stopped caring.'

Before long, the new school was divided up. The three senior forms were left where they were, while the six lower (primary and middle) ones were moved with their teachers to a new location. 'I thought it would be the same as before, but it wasn't, it was much worse. In the building we moved to, there were no desks and no chairs. We just had to sit on piles of bricks with a piece of matting over the top. Even the most basic equipment was lacking: there weren't even any dusters to clean up with. It made us realise how good our old place had been.'

The children were still kept busy with hard physical work. Like the Chinese soldiers, the teachers too kept pigs, as food for themselves and also to sell to supplement their meagre pay. The children had to look after the animals, as well as carry the manure to the fields which were about two hours' walk away from the school. Naturally, they were exhausted. 'We had to carry the dung in baskets on our backs,' says Emme-la. 'When we set off, the teachers made us start singing. But after a while we were so tired that we simply didn't have the energy. By the time we got home in the evening we were half-dead. And our feet were covered in blisters.'

One good thing about the new school was that Emme-la's new friend Tenzin Norbu was in the same class as himself. But Tenzin's political background – his father was a former landowner and Resistance fighter who had been arrested after the Lhasa insurrection – made him dangerous to know. He was in constant trouble. In fact, none of the children was really safe. One day, a boy of about twelve, Phurbu Tsering, criticised Chairman Mao while chatting with his friends. Someone reported him and the boy was summoned to attend a neighbourhood meeting where he was 'struggled against' in a public *thamzing*. Emme-la and all the other children were forced to attend. They were sick with fear, but there was no escape. 'Phurbu Tsering's hands were tied behind his back, he was beaten, they boxed his ears and forced shit into his mouth. Then they dragged him along by the hair. His head was streaming with blood as they took him off to prison. We couldn't bear to watch, so we all tried to turn our heads away. But they wouldn't let us, they made us look. It was horrible. There were two others being struggled against at the same session, a man called Lhakpa, and a woman, Zimzim Dolkar. They beat the woman up so badly that she died on the way home. I'd had to attend a lot of struggle sessions before, but none of them had been as violent as this one. We were all very scared and felt sick. It was so shocking to see this sort of thing happening in front of our eyes. We'd always known the Chinese were cruel, but this proof of their cruelty was more than we could bear.'

It was communist practice to admit the most industrious students into a special student group, with the aim of turning them into model socialist citizens steeped in Marxist-Leninist theory, dedicated to physical labour and to the Communist Party. 'We must love the Party more than our parents' was a core slogan. All the students dreamed of being admitted to this elite group but not all of them succeeded. Towards the end of his first year at primary school, Emme-la, despite his class background, was admitted to the group and allowed to wear its coveted red scarf, that 'unique badge of pride and honour which every child should strive to acquire'. 'Before we were presented with the scarf, we had to take an oath, promising to work hard, to show respect for our teachers, and most of all to obey every instruction from the Party.' The group had its own anthem which the children proudly sang while marching, especially on 1 June, National Youth Day. 'I became a leader and used to march at the head of my group,' remembers Emme-la proudly. 'Those of us who wore the red scarf were allowed to give the clenched fist salute as we passed the ceremonial dais, while the others had to just bow their heads in silence.' For a small boy it was a moment of sweet triumph.

* * *

At about this time, the Tibetans acquired an unexpected and tragic champion – the Panchen Lama. The Panchen, whom the Chinese had forced them to recognise as being the spiritual and temporal equal of the Dalai Lama,[8] had long been considered as a mere tool of the Chinese. As a boy in Amdo in 1949 he had 'invited' Mao to come and 'liberate' Tibet, and ten years later had sent Mao a telegram congratulating him on the suppression of the Lhasa insurrection and the intro-duction of the democratic reforms. No wonder the Tibetans despised him and called him 'Mao's Panchen'. But all was not as it seemed.

The Chinese made the 24-year-old Panchen Lama a Vice-Chairman of the Chinese National People's Congress in 1960, confident that he would underwrite whatever they chose to do in Tibet. But in the bloody aftermath of 1959, the scales had fallen from the lama's eyes. Travelling around, he saw to his horror the vast slave-labour camp that Tibet had become, a graveyard for countless thousands dying of famine.[9] In September 1961, as the Panchen left Lhasa to attend the celebrations in Peking for the twelfth anniversary of the Communist takeover of China, he was besieged by hungry and desperate men and women pleading with him to inter-cede for them with Chairman Mao. He investigated further, and by the time he arrived in Peking had drafted out a 123-page document for Mao,[10] detailing the sufferings he had himself witnessed: the desperate hunger; the deprivation; the imprisonment of a huge percentage of the population, many of whom had died of 'abnormal' causes; the destruction of Tibet's monast-eries along with their monks and nuns;[11] and the gener-ally brutish behaviour of the Chinese occupation forces. He wrote of 'the fierce, life-and-death class struggle' which had turned the Tibetan world upside-down, and accused the activists and cadres of over-kill in dealing with the rebels of 1959. Tibetans, he said, had suffered random and violent persecution, and many had resorted to suicide, 'throwing themselves into rivers or using weapons to kill themselves'.

In carrying out the political reforms, he accused, many activists had criminally exceeded their brief:

> They thought everything old was backward, filthy and useless; they made no distinction between what was in fact necessary and what was not, everything was mixed up and a wind of destruction blew. They neglected the Tibetan language, ridiculed Tibetan dress . . . showed dislike of women's head-dresses and men's ponytails, with the result that it has become impossible to wear a head-dress or keep a ponytail. They regarded white-washing the outer walls, gifts for marriages and funerals, going to the monasteries for worship, festivals and traditional sports as useless and superfluous, so that most of these practices were stopped.

But it was the wilful destruction of Buddhism which most distressed the Panchen Lama, and his report simply echoed the general despair: the smashing, burning, melting down, throwing into the river of the Buddhas. 'The Tibetans love Buddhism better than life itself,' he declared.

> They have had to take down the prayer-flags from their roofs . . . they have had to hide their statues of Buddha and their copies of the Buddhist scriptures; they do not dare chant scriptures or accumulate merit by praying in public; they do not dare to burn juniper incense, to make offerings for the holy places, to turn

their prayer-wheels, make offerings to the monks, or donate to the poor.

Worst of all perhaps, the ceremonies for the dead were no longer allowed, a tragic loss for the Tibetans. 'People are saying, "If we had only died a bit earlier, we could have had prayers said ... but now our deaths will be like that of a dog. As soon as we cease to breathe, we will be thrown out of the door." '

In short, at a time when even the faintest criticism of Chinese policy was a capital offence, the Panchen Lama courted disaster by this private plea to Mao for mercy for his countrymen, for food and medicines for them, for religious freedom, for an end to the destruction of sacred artefacts and to the terror of the mass arrests and tortures.

At the time of that twelfth Anniversary Congress, Mao, the most radical of revolutionaries, had temporarily lost ground to the more pragmatic members of the Chinese Communist Party. His crazy Great Leap Forward[12] had created such widespread famine that an attempt was being made to rein him in. When the Panchen Lama handed in his petition, it was not to Mao but to the Prime Minister, Zhou En-lai, and Zhou took the criticisms so much to heart that he promised to take steps immediately to improve the situation in Tibet. Much relieved, the Panchen Lama began his journey back to Tibet.

Alas, shortly after his return in 1962, the wind again changed in China as Chairman Mao regained the initiative. By September, all-out class struggle had been formally reinstated as the core of the Party's policy, and Mao scornfully dismissed the Panchen's petition as a despicable attempt by a class enemy to recover his lost authority, 'a poisoned arrow aimed at the party by reactionary feudal overlords'. Ominously, the Panchen was invited to 'consider his mistakes'.

His ultimate fate was not yet sealed, however. With Tibet on the verge of becoming an autonomous region within the Chinese Republic, and with the Dalai Lama now a refugee in India, it would be impolitic just then to remove him. He was therefore offered the chairmanship of the new Tibet, on condition that he should move into the Potala Palace in Lhasa and formally denounce the Dalai Lama. For the Panchen, this was a betrayal too far. He refused point blank, and used the opportunity to advise the Tibetans to do what they could to preserve their own culture from destruction. One memorable day in 1964, he publicly proclaimed that the Dalai Lama's continuing survival in India was a sign of hope for Tibet. 'I must proclaim my firm belief that Tibet will soon regain her independence and that His Holiness will return to the Golden Throne. Long live His Holiness the Dalai Lama.'

To make this public statement was an act of incredible courage. The Chinese revenge was as predictable as it was devastating. The Panchen Lama was branded a traitor and a counter-revolutionary, 'anti-Party, anti-Socialism, anti-People', a secret supporter of 'the Dalai bandit'. As Emme-la recalled, 'There was a campaign against him, in public meetings and at school. We were told that he was a traitor who'd opposed the Chinese liberation of Tibet. He was an enemy of Communism who wanted to bring back the old feudal system.' Blamed for all the failures of the past few years, accused of murder, mayhem and conspiracy, he was dragged before a kangaroo court and underwent a particularly brutal series of *thamzings* lasting seventeen days. In the course of this vicious public humiliation, he was physically abused, punched, beaten, kicked, spat upon and cursed. After the trial the Panchen, his parents, and a remnant of faithful supporters were chained, thrown into closed trucks and driven under heavy guard out of Tibet. The Lama would remain imprisoned in solitary confinement in Peking for thirteen years. It was, of course, decreed that this 'incorrigible running-dog of imperialist and foreign reactionaries' should be removed from office as Acting Chairman of the PCART. (The Dalai Lama was formally ejected at the same time.)

Thus in September 1965, as Tibet prepared for its new unwelcome incarnation as the Tibetan Autonomous Region within the People's Republic of China, its two most cherished leaders had been condemned as Enemies of the People. Though the people mourned, they had to put on a public show of joy. 'As the day for the establishment of the TAR drew near,' said Emme-la, who by then was nine years old, 'we were ordered to welcome the Central Government officials who were coming from Peking to celebrate with us. We children had to dress in our best clothes and line the streets on both sides waving paper flags. Then the celebrations started. We were all summoned to a mass meeting, where Chinese and Tibetan officials made a lot of very long speeches. They seemed to go on for ever, but eventually gave way to a song and dance entertainment – Chinese people performing in Chinese for the benefit of us Tibetans. I remember one of the songs they sang. It was about the Chinese army and the words went something like – "Mao's soldiers are the most obedient servants of the Communist Party and will go wherever they are sent." Then they performed a play about how the Chinese were helping the Vietnamese people in their struggle. We didn't have any idea what they were talking about and were very confused. But we had to look as though we were enjoying ourselves.'

Though the Tibetans had no option but to profess in public their deep love for the Chinese Communist Party in general and Chairman Mao in particular, without their own Dalai and Panchen Lamas they felt helpless and lost. That day of Tibet's 'emancipation' must have seemed like a waking nightmare. How could they have known that what was to follow would be unimaginably worse?

CHAPTER 5

The Graveyard

When some Western journalists were permitted to visit
Tibet in the late 1970s, they described it as 'the graveyard of a murdered civilization'. The tragedy is that
while the Tibetan race took nearly 1000 years to build a
rich, complex, Buddhist civilization and culture, it took
just three years to destroy it.

Dawa Norbu, *Tibet: The Road Ahead*[1]

Chairman Mao believed in permanent revolution, that
is to say periods of stability followed by rampant chaos
– out of which would come progress. His dream was to
turn the world upside-down at regular intervals and he
resented the moderates in the Party (now dubbed the
'capitalist-roaders' because they considered that improving the economy was more important than the sacred
class struggle) who had prevented him from imposing
undiluted Communism. For much of the early 1960s,

70

the moderates, led by China's President Liu Shao-qi, had prevailed, but by 1965 Mao had succeeded in purging his enemies from the Central Committee and putting the Left back on course. Class struggle was about to come into its own.

In August 1966 he announced a Great Proletarian Cultural Revolution whose avowed aim was to impose true Communism and bury the moderates once and for all. It was to be the Last Great Battle which would usher in the triumph of Utopia. Henceforth it would be the duty of the proletarian classes, particularly the young who had not been moulded into the values and culture of a bygone age, to smash all remnants of 'bourgeois' thinking wherever it was to be found, in art, in culture, in education, in the Communist Party or in the Government itself.

Supported by the Army under its commander, Defence Minister Lin Biao, new young Red Guard militias vowing death to Mao's enemies undertook to make war on everything bourgeois, to wrest power from their local Party organisations and to set up Revolutionary Committees as the new governing bodies of the People's Republic. Their sworn task was to root out 'the Four Olds', old beliefs, old culture, old habits, old customs, replacing them by their opposites, 'the Four News': the Thoughts of Chairman Mao, proletarian culture, and the habits and practices of radical Chinese Communism.

Thus was Mao, idolised by the Red Guards as 'the reddest red sun in our hearts', brought nearer to the total control he craved. As a carte blanche invitation to China's disaffected youth to let off steam, settle old scores, kick against authority and give vent to their general frustration, the Cultural Revolution was a stroke of political genius. A revolution against the Revolution.

A 'crazy kitchen' policy of smash-and-destroy-to-the-heart's-content. For China, it would prove to be a tragedy of enormous proportions. For Tibet, it would be a holocaust.

Stuck in its medieval time warp, Tibet represented everything the Maoists hated. The way of life to which it continued to cling was a deplorable obstacle to the country's absorption into China.

Red Guards poured into Tibet and began recruiting young Tibetans to their ranks. Only members of the Communist Party were eligible, so Emme-la with his 'unclean' class background would not have been allowed to join even if he had wanted to. 'But many young Tibetans from the two "clean" classes did join them. Mainly because, being "clean", they had to. Chinese and Tibetan officials came to their homes, appointed them as Red Guards, and told them where to go and what to do. Very few of them dared refuse.'

It was a bizarre situation for the authorities, having to authorise a revolution whose central aim was to destroy them. At first they confined themselves to rhetoric. The official Tibetan language newspapers began proclaiming the new Party line, declaring that all those in the two lowest social classes were duty bound to carry out the aims of the new Cultural Revolution with 'all determination and speed'. Then they published a 16-point instruction manual which everyone had to learn by heart. 'The gist of it was,' says Emme-la, 'that we were ordered to smash the Four Olds and replace them by the Four News. We had to "show our contempt" for the old society.' Most of the Tibetans had no idea what that meant.

They would soon find out. A start was made in Lhasa, as Red Guards invaded and vandalised the Jokhang

Cathedral, smashing its famous statues and images, burning its sacred texts and – when they had finally turned it into a rooming house for themselves – underscoring their contempt by keeping pigs in its courtyards. The Norbulingka Palace was next in line for destruction, and there followed an orgy of blind destruction throughout the city.

The Revolutionaries knew that Mao wanted to be rid of the existing Communist Party structures and officials, and once they had attracted enough new recruits they felt strong enough to move onto the attack. In December, when fifty Red Guard groups joined forces in an attempt to seize power, calling themselves the Revolutionary Rebels (Gyenlog), the situation turned nasty. The authorities declared the Red Guards to be 'counter-revolutionaries' – the worst of crimes under a Communist regime. The Red Guards retaliated by pledging to smash the authorities; the Army came in against the Rebels and established martial law; and the officials set up their own Red Guard outfit (Nyamdrel) to fight the Rebels. In this deadly version of snakes-and-ladders, the official Red Guards accused their rivals – using time-honoured Communist rhetoric – of being agents of foreign imperialists who wanted to destabilise Tibet. To underline their point, on 10 March 1967, the eighth Anniversary of the Tibetan Uprising, the establishment rushed into print[2] to accuse the Rebels of being no better than Tibetan freedom fighters.

Such deadly abuse, of course, had the effect of endearing the Revolutionary Rebels to young Tibetans, who were only too willing to join in any attack on the hated regime, and who in any case relished the sight of the Chinese tearing each other to pieces instead of them. In April, after over 8,000 more Revolutionary Red Guards arrived in Lhasa from China intending to thwart the officials' attempts to save their jobs (and their lives), young Tibetans joined them in a mass rally to denounce the bureaucrats. As the Revolutionary Rebels proclaimed that they had seized power throughout the Tibet Autonomous Region – 'The country is ours, the masses are ours' – many of the top Party officials prudently left Tibet for calmer pastures elsewhere, leaving their supporters with a war on their hands.

As Red Guards from both camps fanned out all over the country, each trying to recruit the local 'progressives' into their ranks, the fighting spread to smaller towns like Gyantse. The Gyantse Red Guards put on their red armbands and joined in the fray.

'They were all completely out of control,' remembers Emme-la, who was then still at school. 'The battles between them were really violent. We weren't Red Guards but we couldn't help joining in and most of us sided with the Revolutionary Rebels who wanted to get rid of the officials and promised to increase our food rations if they came to power. They even promised us freedom to practise our religion, though I can't think they were being serious.

'I remember that one day the Rebels arrested the local Party officials and took them away to be tried as "counter-revolutionaries". The group had to pass through the main market and I happened to be there carrying a baby on my back to help a neighbour. I didn't know what was going on at first, but when I realised who these people were, I did what everyone else seemed to be doing. Some of the grown-ups had equipped themselves with homemade spears and axes. I picked up the thigh-bone of a calf (in Tibet, when animals died, they were left unburied by the roadside) and, with the baby still on the other arm, I started hitting the officials with the bone as hard as I could. I must say

I got quite a kick out of doing it. I think we were all able to let off a lot of steam at this time.'

These young Tibetans, carried away by their resentment of a regime that had for so long persecuted them, and by the adolescent thrill of cocking a snook at authority, were too naïve to foresee the terrible tragedy in the making: the excesses into which the Cultural Revolution would drag them. The actual fighting was simply an extension of the endless Chinese political power struggle, but the battleground on which the warring groups strove for supremacy, each one eager to outdo the other in ferocity, would be Tibet itself and all it stood for. For Tibet, unrepentantly Buddhist, still aware of its distinctive nationhood and language, still clinging to its 'decadent' culture and customs, symbolised everything that Mao was urging his cohorts to destroy.

'One day,' remembers Emme-la, 'our Sports master at school called us together to talk to us about the Red Guards, and their life-and-death struggle. It was our struggle too, he lectured us, and we were to devote our whole selves to it from now on. It was a struggle of the have-nots against the haves, and the have-nots were bound to win in the end. Our teacher got very excited. In fact, most of our teachers got caught up in the fighting, and eventually there were so few of them left in the school that most of the students started staying at home and the school was closed down.'

But not just yet. The worst horror was yet to come. One afternoon in September 1967, one year after the first Rebel groups had been formed in Lhasa, 'we were told we had to go to the monastery next day and destroy it. My mother was beside herself and begged me not to go. But I had to. What's more, I had to take along a little girl-cousin who lived with us, while my mother went to work. She too was having to work from dawn to dusk, without food or drink or payment, destroying old buildings and putting up new ones.'

Early next day, Emme-la's class were taken by their embattled teachers to the Pelkhor Choede Monastery and told to dismantle it. It was called 'volunteering to destroy the centres of superstition'. 'When we got to the monastery, we were called to a meeting in the courtyard. There we found one of the Red Guard leaders, a Tibetan girl called Tsamchoe, who was haranguing the crowd. She told us how pleased she was that we had come to listen to what she was going to tell us – that we were to begin destroying the monastery. Just like that. We were divided into different work units and everyone was given detailed instructions as to where to go and what to do when we got there.'

Under the red banners that proclaimed their servitude, with the sound of their own trumpets, cymbals and trumpets ringing mockingly in their ears, and waving the red flags of China, the young Tibetans proceeded with their work of desecration. Brick by brick the monastery was torn apart, the stones eventually to be ground down to small pebbles with which to pave the streets. Gold pinnacles on the roof were pulled down and taken away to be melted down. Some of the children were instructed to deface frescoes, behead Buddhas, trample stone or clay images into the ground, or dismantle intricately carved pillars and beams for future use in Chinese building projects. Others were detailed to gather up any artefacts made of gold, silver or bronze, fine brocades or ancient hangings and take them to a Chinese warehouse where they were given some kind of receipt. This part of the demolition process had been meticulously planned in advance, with nothing left to chance. Senior Red Guards supervised the operation, armed with booklets denoting the precise market value of everything. From the warehouses the treasures would be crated and sent to China for eventual sale on the antique and curio stalls of Hong Kong or Tokyo.

Emme-la's class of 10-year-olds were led to a chapel and ordered to smash the commercially valueless offertory bowls used for offering water to the deities. 'We had to pick them up and drop them hard on the ground. When we finished, we were taken to the courtyard of another chapel, where another work team was busy throwing out the religious texts, wood carvings, monastic dance masks and costumes, out of the window of the chapel. We had to gather up all these things and throw them onto a giant bonfire which had been lit at one end of the courtyard. When we'd done that, we were sent to one of the main prayer-halls where we saw huge mounds of sacred books. We had to throw these too on the bonfire. I remember that bonfire all too well. A month later we could still see and smell the smoke from it. I think I can still see it and smell it.'

Those scriptures which were not burned had to be dishonoured, used as latrine paper, as padding for shoes or for wrapping saleable goods in the Chinese shops. The wooden blocks which traditionally bound the texts were broken up for floorboards, washboards, chairs or handles for tools. Papier-mâché statues were thrown into the river or smashed and scattered in the streets for people to walk on. Clay images were ground down and turned into bricks with which to build public latrines. Nothing was spared, no humiliation was too disgraceful. And everyone knew that *thamzing* lay in store for anyone mad or reckless or stupid enough to complain.

When all was done, dynamite was brought in and the monastery was blasted to a shell. Later, the Chinese would be able to claim, with literal truth, that it was the Tibetans themselves who had done these things. It was they who had destroyed their own monasteries. And indeed such things were being done all over Tibet, where those few monasteries which had avoided complete destruction after the Tibetan Uprising were now finished off, their treasures looted, violated, smashed or turned into firewood through cleverly orchestrated mob hysteria.

The Tibetans did all these things, on the instructions of their own Red Guards, while the Chinese watched from the sidelines, well satisfied with their work. For most of the Tibetans it was an act of desecration, and they knew they did violence to themselves by taking part in it. Some went insane. Some killed themselves. 'We felt violated by what we did. We had all been brought up to respect these artefacts, not to destroy them. When we smashed the water bowls and pitched the scriptures onto the bonfire, we tried to tell ourselves it was some kind of game, or we tried to think of something else and pretend it wasn't happening, we weren't really doing these dreadful things. We hated what we were being made to do and felt terribly uneasy. But we simply had no choice. Still, children are always little opportunists – I must confess that when we were carting away the religious texts I hung on to one of the leather cords used for binding them. I knew it'd be useful at home, though of course we were supposed never to steal anything that belonged to a monastery. That night my mother spotted the cord. I hadn't given my parents any details about what we had been doing, but they guessed most of them anyway. My mother was terribly distressed and angry and gave me a good whipping with the cord before hurling it into the stream.'

Shortly afterwards, it was time for the school autumn

break, traditionally the time when every child went to work in the fields to prepare for the harvest. In that autumn of 1967, the Red Guards were in charge, and, under orders to be 'pitiless, wrathful and zealous' in their work, they were in no mood to uphold traditional practices. They had their own priorities. Emme-la remembers them visiting the children's work-camps, 'dressed in smart uniforms with scarves round their necks, calling us to endless meetings and study sessions on the sixteen points in the booklet and on The Thoughts of Chairman Mao'.

In a sort of collective frenzy, the Red Guard factions vied with each other in 'smashing the Four Olds' – 'the poisonous weeds' of the past. (As one woman put it, 'The Four Olds are all things Tibetan, and the Four News are whatever the Chinese say they are.'[3]) To the tune of a massive propaganda campaign vilifying the 'old society', 'they swept into all the village houses,' says Emme-la, 'and cut or slashed people's long plaited hair – sometimes half-shaving them, so that they'd look more like Chinese. They killed all the domestic pets, removed cooking implements, tore off rings, earrings and the conch shell bracelets that all Tibetan women wore. In our village they didn't actually take the jewellery away, but in others they either carried the items off or smashed them to pieces. They broke into our altar-rooms and confiscated all the religious objects they could find and threw them on the still-smouldering monastery bonfires.' Prayer flags were removed from the roofs of all the houses, replaced by the hated red flags of the People's Republic. Prayer wheels and beads had to be collectively thrown into the river.

The whole landscape changed, as familiar chorten pillars and the heaps of inscribed *mani* stones which had always stood in welcome in front of Tibetan towns, the rock-paintings and sacred mantras which adorned the hillsides, the 'wind-horses' which once had carried prayers into the skies on countless tiny bits of paper – all were banned and demolished, replaced by over-blown scarlet daubs from The Thoughts of Chairman Mao. A woman in a neighbouring village who made a mistake while transcribing one of the Thoughts onto a rock face was promptly shot. All references to religion, all religious practice, all burning of incense or lighting of butter-lamps, all prayer, the sacred words *Om Mani Padme Hum*, were henceforth taboo. Even to be seen moving the lips in prayer was from this time forward a crime, and the Public Security Bureau made sure there were plenty of paid informers around to denounce the guilty.[4]

While loudspeakers spewed out an uninterrupted stream of adulation for Chairman Mao, everyone without exception had to learn by heart the Thoughts contained in his Little Red Book. The personality cult of Mao took precedence over everything else. 'We had to hang Mao's portraits (we had to have not one but several) and have extracts from his Thoughts painted on the walls. We were all given a free copy of the Thoughts and of course we had to carry the book around all the time, everywhere we went. We were tested at nightly meetings, and often the Red Guards would stop us at random in the street and make us recite from the Thoughts. Anyone who couldn't do so or who made a mistake was either beaten up or arrested. In time we came to put up with it as being part of the over-all craziness of life.

'Reading Mao's Thoughts morning and evening, day in, day out, was simply something you had to do. We tried to blot it out and it really didn't leave any lasting impression on our minds. Sometimes they made us gather in front of a huge picture or poster of Mao and shout "Long Live Mao, May He Live A Thousand Years." That sort of thing meant nothing – it was just a stupid routine and all we did was mouth the words. In spite of it all, people never really lost faith in their religion or their traditional culture. If anything, the fact that they were totally banned and driven underground made us more attached to them. It was difficult to practise Buddhism even in your own home, because spies were everywhere, but we went on saying prayers in secret, even during the most difficult periods. Monks and lamas weren't allowed to perform any of the traditional rites, but sometimes they would visit us as friends, dressed in ordinary clothes, and quietly say prayers with us. Parents tried to pass on Buddhist teachings to their children and even kept statues and scrolls hidden in the house. The portraits of Chairman Mao on the wall very often had a portrait of His Holiness hidden behind them. People would hide their precious images and texts in the hills, in barns, or even among the animal fodder in the storerooms – those things had no commercial value at all but were infinitely precious to us. Everyone knew the penalties would be terribly severe if they were caught – you would be accused of trying to resurrect the past. That meant you could be dunce-capped and paraded round the streets, or even killed – but that didn't stop anyone.'

A Shigatse man remembers learning Mao's Thoughts by heart at school, and the afternoon self-criticism sessions in which the pupils all had to accuse each other of crimes. 'Mostly it was trivial stuff like not cleaning up properly or being lazy at work. But if someone had said anything at all bad against Mao, he would almost certainly be taken away and executed. I myself had a very narrow escape. Someone reported that one day while I was reading the Thoughts I'd allowed a drop of ink to fall on Mao's face. I swore it was an accident, that I truly loved Mao and had just fallen asleep for a minute. But they made me face *thamzing*, first in my own class-room, then in front of the whole school. After that I had to write out a whole sheaf of depositions about my loyalty to Mao and about how foolish I had been. They posted my "confession" up for a whole week every-where in the school.'

In a frenzy of Sinicisation, traditional Tibetan gest-ures, phrases of greeting and respect were forbidden, and the comfortable Tibetan *chuba* gave way to the charmless Maoist uniform of buttoned-up blue boiler-suit and peaked cap. The Tibetans were ordered to give their children Chinese names, though in the event, only Party members did so. There was to be no more drink-ing of *chang* – drinking was 'anti-Motherland sabotage'. No more festivals and fairs, no more Tibetan proverbs and folk songs, no more Tibetan dancing. In place of the latter came Chinese dance routines with Chinese costumes, and songs stuffed with quotations from The Thoughts of Chairman Mao. Emme-la's eldest sister belonged to one of the new song and dance groups whose songs were dedicated to the praise of socialism and of Mao. 'Like everything else it was just something they did because they had to. All the dances and songs were Chinese. The Tibetan girls didn't understand any of it, it was a routine, it meant nothing to them, they just had to go through the motions.'

What this determined annihilation of 'the dead past' meant, of course, was that it was utterly forbidden to speak of having been either free or happy in old Tibet. The whole of the Tibetan past had to be trashed: anyone caught praising it (or even not roundly condemning it) would be hauled up for *thamzing*.

* * *

When the autumn holidays were over, the children returned to school to find it changed out of all recognition. 'Most of the subjects we had been studying had been abolished. Our main, almost our only, task now, apart from a bit of sport, was the study of Mao Tsetung's Thoughts. The only criterion for being a good student was to be as revolutionary as possible in word and deed. "Chairman Mao is the bright red sun in our hearts," we all sang. It wasn't enough for us to have destroyed the monasteries, our indoctrination into socialism had to be stepped up. Part of the indoctrination was through plays and performances. They put on a play at school called: "Under the Old Regime, the People Were Worse off than Dogs". We had to sit through that and other similar offerings which portrayed in great detail the atrocities supposed to have been carried out in old Tibet.'

The main villains were the Dalai and Panchen Lamas, those Enemies of the People whom the Tibetans insisted on regarding as their real leaders. Denunciations of these two reached hysterical levels during this time, the Dalai Lama being described by Radio Peking as 'a political corpse, bandit and traitor', and by the *Peking Review* as 'an executioner with honey on his lips and murder in his heart'. Fantasies of this kind gained momentum as night after night in compulsory political meetings, the Tibetan people were ordered to speak against their beloved leader. 'Who master-minded the revolt?' went the stock question, to which the stock answer was 'The Dalai Lama'. To the next question, 'What sort of life did he lead?' they were supposed to reply that he was a profiteer and a womaniser who sold his country out to the imperialists. Many of them refused to play the game, some going so far as to say,

'He is our god, our leader.' One woman recalls that for saying something of the sort, she was picked up by a Chinese official and hurled to the ground, where she lost consciousness. Many of those who refused to co-operate were themselves given *thamzing*. A former Tibetan cadre who later fled to India wrote:

> During these meetings everyone had to cry out, 'The gods, lamas, religion and monasteries are the tools of exploitation; the three serf-owners made Tibetans poor; the Chinese Communist Party liberated us and gave us food, clothes, houses and land; the Chinese Communist Party is more kind than our own parents. May the Chinese Communist Party live for ten thousand years. May Mao Tse-tung live for ten thousand years. The crimes of the three serf-owners who ate the flesh and drank the blood of the people are bigger than the mountains and cannot even fit in the skies; from this day forward we will destroy them.'[5]

The absurdity of the allegations did not make them any less horrific. In their hearts, the Tibetans simply could not understand why the Chinese appeared to swallow such obvious nonsense but they dared not speak out. Understand or not, they had to go along with the madness.

Before the Cultural Revolution began, only those suspected of aiding the guerrillas or taking part in the Tibetan Uprising had been arrested. But the Cultural Revolution ushered in a terrifying period of undiluted class hatred. Anybody who had ever held a position of authority, anyone who had received an education – any senior monk, any teacher – was, by virtue of that authority or education alone, arrested and struggled against.

Posters were put up, denouncing them. Many of them simply disappeared.

Everywhere, as paranoia grew, new class enemies were being unearthed. Those who had once willingly collaborated and others who had until now somehow escaped the net were subjected to the most degrading punishments:

> dragged into the streets and paraded in paper dunce hats – beaten and spat upon as they passed, tags listing their crimes pinned to their naked chest – in processions led by Red Guards beating drums, cymbals and gongs. Lashed to heavy religious statues lamas were bent double, while ex-aristocrats and merchants had large, empty vessels, once used for storing grain, roped to their backs.[6]

Sithar Phuntsog, a man in his middle sixties, had been one of the teachers at Emme-la's school. Once he had run (unpaid) one of Gyantse's four Tibetan schools, but when the Chinese closed them all down they sent him to teach in their own school. With the advent of the Cultural Revolution, his fate was sealed – he had once employed others to work for him, and was therefore a 'serf-owner'. Though liked and respected in the village, he was denounced as an enemy of the people, to be struggled against by a People's Court.

His health wrecked by repeated brutal *thamzings*, he was nevertheless forced to leave his teaching post and do manual labour. 'All day long,' recalls Emme-la, 'they made him carry heavy loads of bricks from one place to another, and then mix mud with water to make new bricks. Quite often he was so exhausted he could barely stand, and his fellow-workers used to prop him up on each side. Eventually he grew too weak to continue, so the authorities sent him back to his home village, not far from ours. But they didn't leave him in peace: he had to continue with the brick-making and the brick-laying. We used to see him on our way to school and would feel terribly sorry for him. We were forbidden to help him, but secretly everyone did what they could. When we thought the Chinese weren't looking, we would try to smuggle tea and bits of food to him. Those who worked with him would try to make sure he was given only light duties, fetching water or cooking meals for the others. But the Chinese were determined to go on hounding him. Eventually the poor man was so crippled he was unable to get out of bed to go to work. He died alone, none of us was allowed to go and help him.'

The Venerable Lobsang Tendar was a Tantric practitioner at the Pelkhor Choede monastery. People used to go and see him when they were ill, when they needed prayers or pills or healing. But under the new dispensation, the Ven. Lobsang was accused of preventing his patients from going to the Chinese hospital, of murdering them by poison – some of his patients had unfortunately died in spite of his herbal pills. He was subjected to a whole series of *thamzings*, during which he was referred to as *Dugthong,* 'the poisoner'. He was paraded through the streets, beaten and tormented until he finally died.

At the Nyangchu River outside of Gyantse, whole families, including the wives and children of men who had been condemned as class enemies, 'were made to stand in freezing water for five hours, wearing dunce-caps, heavy stones strapped to their legs'.[7]

'The reactionary people won't die,' a Chinese general urged a group of villagers, 'unless the masses destroy them, just as the dust in the room won't go unless we sweep it out.'[8]

With nothing that remotely resembled law to protect them from such misery, many of the Tibetans, especially the older ones, sank into a state of deep shock. Seeing the destruction of their faith and their whole way of life, many chose to leap from cliffs or drown or hang themselves rather than face the humiliations and tortures of the *thamzing* sessions. Others went mad or just lost the will to live. Pa-drung, Emme-la's father, was one of the latter. He had hated and feared the Chinese from the start, and had not attempted to hide his dislike. In 1968, exactly twelve years after Emme-la's birth, the calamity foretold by the Oracle descended on the family. In despair at the destruction of the monasteries and sacred scriptures, at the loss of everything he believed in and held dear, Pa-drung fell into a melancholia from which nothing could rouse him. He was taken to the People's Hospital where he died, a broken man. 'We gave him a sky burial,' says Emme-la, 'but we were not allowed to recite a single prayer for him. No ceremony was permitted. It was our Tibetan Buddhist custom to have the body cut up and returned to the earth as a sign of our oneness with nature. The final act of the traditional ceremony was to mix the brains to a paste with tsampa grain to nourish our brothers, the vultures. But in 1968 we had no tsampa grain to spare.'

Tashi Tsering, a Tibetan who had despised the old society,[9] and after a spell in the West had gone back home again to help build a new society, was horrified when he returned to Lhasa as a Red Guard.

There was nothing for sale in the streets any more. Gone were the cramped booths heaped full of wares, the voices of salesmen and customers laughing and haggling, and the many tea and beer shops I used to frequent. In their place were a few poorly-stocked government stores ... Food was rationed ... there was almost no meat or butter or potatoes. There had always been a lot of food [in the past], and if you had any money to spend at all, you had quite a bit of freedom and choice.

Tashi Tsering's discovery that, whatever its faults, the old society had had some redeeming features, would eventually earn him a long sentence in a Chinese jail. The regime did not lightly forgive its critics, however supportive they might be.

With many of the Tibetans supporting the rebels and growing accustomed to attacking the Chinese officials with impunity, the next stage might have been foreseen. By the end of 1968 a number of popular revolts had swept the country, led for the most part by the young Tibetan cadres who had been trained in China to carry out social change in Tibet, but who were fed up with the Chinese contempt for all things Tibetan. In 1969 in Nyemo, not far from Gyantse, a 25-year-old Tibetan nun called Thinle Choedon put herself at the head of a group of fifteen Tibetan Revolutionary Rebels. One day, in a trance, she declared that the Tibetan religion and culture were being obliterated by the Chinese invaders, and that it was time for all Tibetans to rise up against them. The people of Nyemo immediately rushed to attack a Chinese military post, killing soldiers and officials and slitting the throats of known spies and informers. A major revolt was under way and awareness of the fact seemed to awaken the Tibetan cadres from their torpor. The young woman rapidly become a legend and, as her fame spread, twenty-nine different districts of Tibet rose in revolt.

Suddenly it was no longer merely an ideological struggle between the left and the right wings of the Chinese Red Guards, with Tibetan hangers-on on either side. A sea change had mysteriously come about, and the struggle had turned into one of Tibetans versus Chinese. Yet it was not so much a nationalist rising as a furious protest at the wanton chaos of the Cultural Revolution which had brought Tibetan culture to its knees. When the Chinese realised what had happened, they reacted with venomous fury. By the time the twenty-nine districts were pacified, they had been reduced to ghost villages, with no one left but old people and women: the nun, Thinle Choedon, and the ringleaders of the revolt everywhere had all been executed (shot in the back of the head), most of the young people were either dead or in prison. But a new sense of solidarity had been born among the Tibetans and would not be forgotten – either by them or the Chinese. When a new revolt in the summer of 1970 spread to sixty of the seventy-one districts within the Tibet Autonomous Region, it claimed the lives of 12,000 Tibetans and more than 1,000 Chinese soldiers.

With the whole of Tibet now in a ferment, the Chinese decided to stop the rot with a massive purge at all levels of Tibetan society. They began with the Tibetan Communist cadres, the class which they had nurtured but which had betrayed their trust. Arresting thousands of cadres, they subjected them either to *thamzing*, imprisonment or summary execution. In the case of the latter, the families of the accused were summoned to attend the execution ceremony. When it was all over, they were made to thank the executioners for their kindness in ridding them of a 'bad' element – and then had to pay for the bullet. After which they were graciously allowed to remove the still-bleeding body and bury it in an open grave.

'In our village,' says Emme-la, 'there were two sisters, one of whom, the younger one, was a government employee, working for the Chinese. They were in the lowest, "clean" category and, in our view, had always been far too friendly with the Chinese. But in 1970, when the Han organised their crackdown on the cadres, they arrested the younger girl on charges of corruption, and searched Lhamo's, (the older sister's) house while they were about it. They found scriptures, statues, thangkas and hidden photos of the Dalai Lama. They pretended to be very shocked and put all this treasure trove on public display. Then they arrested Lhamo's husband, Tenpa, put him through *thamzing*, stuck a dunce's hat on his head, marched him through the streets and took all his privileges away. He was sent to prison for a year and because of the dunce's hat[10] was given all the worst and filthiest jobs.'

'The thing was, the Chinese had never really trusted the Tibetan cadres. Even when they gave them a high rank, they always had to report to a Chinese member of the Communist Party – with the same rank as themselves – who was there to keep an eye on them. Somehow the Chinese had always suspected there was a certain fellow-feeling among Tibetans on both sides of the political divide. But after Nyemo, they knew for certain, because so many Tibetan officials had taken part in the uprising. Then their mistrust turned to furious hostility, and thousands of the cadres were removed or put to death at one fell swoop. After Nyemo, we Tibetans knew that most of the officials were still Tibetans at heart, they were only being used by the Chinese as instruments of control. We sort of grew closer together after that.'

On the other hand, the Chinese had rammed home the message that they, and only they, were the masters of Tibet.

CHAPTER 6

Golden Bridge, Wooden Bridge

The People's Commune is a Golden Bridge to Socialism where there is no oppression or exploitation. It is a socialist paradise.

> Chinese propaganda for the Commune system in
> Tibet

When Emme-la's school reopened in 1968, his 'unclean' class background meant that he was excluded. He was a bright boy, just eleven years old, but as only the politically 'clean' classes were entitled to education beyond the primary level, his school days were over. He had learned to read Tibetan and to write it a little, but that was about all.

There was another crisis now, to add to all the others. Though the left–right Red Guard struggle had officially ended in September 1968 when the People's Liberation Army set up a Revolutionary Committee which took control, fighting would continue for several more years. For the Red Guards it had become a way of life and would not easily be abandoned. But in 1968 the Chinese became convinced that they were surrounded by enemies abroad[1] as well as at home, and that a nuclear holocaust was imminent. (They had recently acquired the hydrogen bomb themselves, and were busy building up their own nuclear strike force – on Tibetan territory.[2])

In the areas close to the border with India, Gyantse among them, massive military preparations got under way. 'As a matter of fact, we were rather wishing there *would* be a war; it might make China get out of Tibet if someone actually attacked it. But we never really knew who the enemy was supposed to be. We thought they probably meant America,' says Emme-la. 'They called America "the paper tiger" and there were posters everywhere saying "Down with US imperialism and all its running dogs".'

The enemy this time, however, was not America but China's former ally, the Soviet Union, which was currently deploying an army of over a million soldiers on its borders with China. There had already been sporadic clashes, and the drift to outright (nuclear) war seemed inevitable. Tibetan society was swept by another upheaval. 'The war fever changed our lives yet again. After a long day's work in the fields, and hours of meetings where we had to recite the Thoughts of Chairman Mao from memory, everyone of all ages, but especially those from fifteen to fifty, had to do military training. No one was exempted, not even old people or young children. My older sister, Dawa Phentok, was one of thousands of Tibetans sent to build a new road near the Sikkimese border. Her job was to carry supplies and ammunition to the soldiers in the front line. Day and night the Tibetans had to carry these supplies on their backs. It was dangerous work and many were killed or maimed while doing it. Fortunately my sister was unharmed. If she had died, the authorities wouldn't have cared, they would just have given the family a certificate of honour to hang over the door!

'For those of us who stayed put there was some training in the use of weapons, but mostly it was civil defence stuff. We had to build deep trenches and tunnels, bunkers and fall-out shelters – some of the bunkers under the old Gyantse fort are still there today. And there were the air-raid practices, when we all had to leave our homes and go into the bunkers. They were never-ending. And worst of all we were very hungry. Our food rations were cut, and any surpluses simply went to feed the army.'

The immediate threat of war subsided in 1969 after the Chinese Premier, Zhou En-lai, met the Soviet Prime Minister Kosygin and negotiations began. It had been a close-run thing and had brought home to China the fact that she had no friends in the world other than Albania ('We kept hearing about Albania, we were sure it must be a big, important country to have China for a friend') and North Vietnam which was engaged in a war to the death with the USA. Zhou now persuaded Mao that it would be politic to mend its fences with the USA, with whom China had been technically at war ever since the Korean War of 1953.[3]

The war preparations exacerbated food shortages which were already at a disastrous level in Tibet. During the Red Guard battles, one of the largest grain storage depots in central Tibet had been cut off from Lhasa with devastating results. Tibet's already precarious system of food distribution came apart at the seams and famine became a reality once again. It seemed to the Tibetans that everything, even nature itself, had turned against them. Emme-la recalls with horror a series of natural disasters, all of which resulted in widespread crop failures. 'There was a sudden dramatic change in our climate, heavier snowfalls than we'd ever known, and a long-lasting drought. The barley-grains withered inside the husks. And we were invaded by a pest which had never before been known in our area – a microscopic insect which destroyed the grain. We Tibetans believed that this combination of climatic change and deadly insect was a punishment for our destruction of the monasteries. The earth had lost its essence. What little barley we managed to harvest tasted sweet and putrid.'

The Chinese introduced a new system of pest-control, a variation on an earlier policy by which Tibetan schoolchildren, in flagrant disregard of their Buddhist reverence for all sentient life, were made to kill a daily or weekly quota of dogs, mice, insects etc. 'This time,' says Emme-la, 'everyone had to take part, not just the children. We all had to kill rats, mice, dogs, birds and any grain-destroying insects. You couldn't argue or ask questions. We had to hand in the tails of any rats and mice, the feet of any birds, the skin of any dogs we had killed. Some people saved themselves the trouble of going out to search, by breeding their quota of pests at home. Those who did well were rewarded by a tin badge with Mao's portrait on it.'

In the past, those bad old days they had so roundly to condemn, whenever famine threatened, the government would come to the rescue with emergency stores of grain. 'But the Chinese refused to help us. Even when the crops failed and people were dying, we had to say what wonderful harvests we were having, thanks, of course, to the genius of Chairman Mao.'

The prime cause of the present famine, however, was the introduction of the long-dreaded commune system.

To the disgust of Mao's revolutionaries, central Tibet, alone among the minority races within the People's Republic, had so far been spared the commune system. A few experimental communes had been set up in some areas in 1962, but they had been abandoned. The Tibetans loathed the very idea of communes, suspecting with reason that they represented a gigantic slave-system in which the last shreds of their freedom would be taken away. They were well aware that after the commune system had been forced on eastern Tibet in 1954, annual production had indeed increased every year but the harvests had been systematically siphoned off to feed the Chinese. Ever since, famine had been endemic in the east.

When Tibet became an Autonomous Region in 1965, the process of communisation was stepped up, but in most places the softly softly approach was still in force. Three years later when Emme-la left school and began work on his parents' farm, his village of Chagri Gyab was still uncommunised. 'We still had our own animal fodder, our own hay and our own vegetables. We were watched carefully by the Chinese, of course, but we were still able to keep back some of the produce for our own use.'

But the Red Guards were about to change all that, since all of them, whichever faction they belonged to, considered it their missionary task to boost agricultural production by dragging Tibet by the scruff of its neck into the commune system. The kid gloves were abandoned.

However, as Communist piety held that communes

were never imposed on an unwilling population, the people had to 'ask for' them. They must sign documents to the effect that they yearned for communisation; and then the authorities would graciously consider their request. (Since the people had been so demonstrably eager to enter communes, how could they possibly complain later on when things went wrong?)

A handful of model communes were set up by way of encouragement, one hundred or so families, (a thousand people), holding the land and everything on it in common, divided into tightly-controlled production-teams and given all the animals, tools and equipment they could wish for. The former activist Dondhub Choedon[4] was in the first of these, the 'Red Flag' Commune, hailed as the 'Golden Bridge' to the Socialist Paradise. 'Since our commune was the first to be introduced the Chinese gave us 10 pigs, 5 Mongolian sheep, 2 donkeys, 2 horse-carts and nine carts,' she wrote. 'Later when thirty-six more communes were established the Chinese did not give them anything.' Those villages which asked to follow suit were congratulated and told that they were now among those fortunate few who were walking the Golden Bridge way to Paradise. The rest, the canny ones who kept their mouths shut, were dismissed as Wooden Bridgers, too stupid to recognise a good thing when they saw it.

For as long as they had the strength to hold out, the Gyantse peasants were determined Wooden Bridgers. 'We knew that once you were communised, you couldn't own anything at all. Everything had to be pooled: land, animals, farm implements, right down to pots and pans, even needles. All possessions – even the bits and pieces distributed to people during the first "democratic reforms" – were divided up, even the number of matches each family had was counted.

Everything was subject to official quotas, there was no possible way of hiding anything from the authorities. You were supposed to get compensation, but even on paper the compensation offered was a joke. In practice most people ended up with nothing. Then there were the crippling taxes, eight of them in all. When the Han first started the Reforms, we'd been told we would no longer have to pay rent in the form of grain. But what they did was introduce a Love the Nation tax which was supposed to be a voluntary offering out of love for the Chinese Communist Party, and which in fact robbed us of all our choicest grains.'

Farmers had to work for a specified number of hours a day with a virtually impossible quota of work to fulfil. Once a year they were allocated a food-grain ration by the commune, on the basis of the work-points they had earned – but *only after* the eight different taxes, including a war-preparation tax, had been deducted by the state. No rations were ever provided for young children or aged relatives who were unable to work. It was down to the working members of the family to share their rations with dependent relatives.

'It was a great system for the Chinese,' reflects Emme-la bitterly. 'They were the ones who gave the orders and made all the decisions. Everyone over the age of sixteen had to contribute towards the costs of starting the communes, and as no one had any money they had to borrow from the Chinese, which meant of course that taxes had to be raised still further. Communes cost the Chinese nothing, and the benefits were enormous. They could fill their granaries with the grain they took from us, and they no longer needed to supervise individual families on their farms. They exercised total control over the communes and I think they really enjoyed having such power over us. When the seeds were sown and the shoots were about five inches high, the Chinese officials would come to the commune and estimate the probable size of the grain yield at harvest-time. After the harvest, when the day came round for the annual allocation of work-points and food-grains (based on the amount each individual had produced), they would come again and sit there from morning till night, checking and cross-checking, marking down discrepancies of even a few grains. Nothing escaped their attention. And after the harvests you could see their lorries driving away filled with all our precious grains.' As one Tibetan put it, the people were 'like bees collecting honey, with no benefit to themselves'.

During this period, the government shops were completely empty. 'The Chinese were so preoccupied with fighting each other and preparing for World War Three there was no one available to bring food in from China, things like sugar, tea, cigarettes, matches and kerosene. There was nothing but a few potatoes or radishes. We had no cooking oil, and we had to use mud instead of soap. We had always used our tea-leaves for a second time, adding some salt gathered from the marshes. But now tea become so scarce, we used to dry the used leaves and keep on using them again and again until there was not the faintest trace of tea left in them. Most of the families roundabout had run out of matches and candles and we lived in total darkness. If we still had a fire, we'd bank up the embers at night, and in the morning if it had gone out we'd look to see if we could see smoke coming from anyone else's chimney. Then one of us children would rush over there with a broken piece of pottery or a tin spade to cadge a few glowing embers, or, as we put it, to "borrow their fire".

'Kerosene was a real necessity for us. In the past we

used to get it from India and store it in homemade pots. But since the Chinese invasion we'd had to import it from China. I remember a day in 1969 when my mother had collected a few dozen eggs – the Chinese were very fond of eggs – and sent me with them to the PLA barracks to exchange for kerosene and matches. The barracks was about three hours' walk away. When I got there, I went first to the married quarters, and when the Chinese women saw the eggs, they offered me all kinds of goods in exchange, soap, towels, luxuries like that. But I turned them down, because I knew my mother would be cross if I went home without the kerosene. I exchanged the eggs for some matches and the kerosene, but when I got them home, my mother discovered that the kerosene tins were filled with a mixture of oil and water and were completely useless.'

The Tibetans had a phrase for these years when all their skill was needed merely to survive: 'the tide of emptiness' they called it. It is a phrase that still conjures up the image of people wandering the streets with empty shopping bags, hoping to borrow some tsampa from neighbours or to retrieve what had been borrowed from them, on and on and on, without end and with very little hope.

Once the communes were established, the harsh system of work-points and food-grain allocation rapidly reduced the Tibetans to starvation. 'The grain ration used to run out three or four months before the end of the year – everyone had to concentrate on eking out what little food they had for as long as they could. Many died from sheer exhaustion. They had to go on working even when there was no food left, no concessions were made, no extra food was ever available, no excuses were acceptable, they just had to wait for the next twelve-month allocation before they could eat. They would go in search of grasses, wild mushrooms, roots, or anything edible they could find, but they were never allowed to do so in working-hours. The quotas must always be met, no matter what. Even when people were dying.' 'We were starving,' says a young woman from the area. 'We had to dig up with our bare hands whatever herbs and roots we could find, and many of them were poisonous and made our hands and faces swell.' Nothing would induce the Chinese to reduce the grain taxes, or to help the people to survive with contributions from their own well-stocked granaries. Whatever grain reserves there were were strictly for the occupation forces of the PLA. So the Tibetans' grain ration plummeted still further, till it was barely enough for a few months in the year.

No word of criticism was permitted, all negative comments about the commune system had to be instantly denounced. One harvest-time, Lobsang Phuntsog, a farmer from the lowest class in the Lhoka area, complained[5] that since no one had enough to eat anyway, there was no point in working hard, one might just as well set fire to the harvested crops. Later, a small fire broke out among the stacks, and, without any evidence, the Chinese arrested Lobsang Phuntsog, subjected him to *thamzing* and threw him into prison. He was never seen again.

About a million Tibetans are estimated to have starved to death between 1968 and 1973. 'Almost the entire population of Tibet,' wrote John Avedon, 'took, often with fatal results, to living off the land, returning, as they had in the early sixties, to picking undigested grain from the manure of PLA horses, stealing discarded food thrown by the Chinese to their pigs and chickens and digging for worms.'[6]

Gyantse resisted to the bitter end, but one by one its villages formally 'requested' to join the system; the people having come to realise that unpleasant as life might be inside the communes, it would become even worse outside them. Not that this made the prospect any easier to bear. Emme-la's family and neighbours dreaded their turn coming. 'We started hoarding some grain – it was against the law, but we were desperate. When all the villagers were brought together for the compulsory meetings – and hunger was no excuse for absence – you couldn't mistake the ones that belonged to the Golden Bridge. They were so pinched and hungry-looking. All their food was controlled by the Chinese authorities and people were really suffering. Crowds of peasants from the surrounding villages used to come to our village and beg for food. It was terrible. Their bodies were swollen with starvation and covered in sores. When they fell ill, they went to the hospital for medicine, but their bodies were so weak they could not tolerate the medicine. These people used to go a bluish colour and by the time they died they could not so much as lift their heads. Of course, we weren't allowed to say they had died of starvation, starvation didn't exist in the Socialist Paradise, anyone who said it did was denounced as a "rumour-monger and an enemy of socialism" and was given *thamzing*. Another explanation had to be found. The Chinese said that they had been suffering from indigestion or from eating the wrong foods. The wrong foods! What was wrong with them was that they had no food at all. We know that the old Tibetan system was unfair in many ways, but in that old society which they forced us every day to condemn we never had anyone dying of starvation or committing suicide because of fear of being struggled against. Suicide was common now. There was a distant relative of ours, a man called Pema. Because he was hungry he stole some heads of barley and tried to prepare some kind of porridge from the grains. The Red Guards caught him stealing grain from the fields and because he couldn't bear to face a struggle session, he hanged himself.'

In 1971, Emme-la's village, Chagri Gyab, was finally sucked in to the commune system. From then on, they would have nothing to call their own, they would be forbidden to move outside the confines of the village: to go further afield, even just to gather firewood would require a special permit. Their day would begin two hours before sunrise with the playing of 'The East Is Red' over the tannoy system,[7] they would work from five in the morning until it was too dark to see – eight or ten at night according to the season – and they would then attend compulsory lectures on Marxism-Leninism or The Thoughts of Mao Tse-tung until midnight. And if they were ill, permission to stay off work might require as many as twelve official signatures. They had been right about communes: they *were* the ultimate prison.

The changes that were supposed to have made Tibetans masters of their own lives had instead given power over every aspect of their lives to the Chinese. A whole people was being enslaved. In Dondhub Choedon's words, 'The "great change", which the Chinese said would make us "masters in our own house", resulted in the Chinese having power over everything that was in our land.' 'For my mother and sisters,' says Emme-la, 'life got tougher and tougher by the day. They were quite sure the Chinese would allow

103

them to die of starvation, and their only consolation lay in thinking that surely it couldn't be long before the Dalai Lama would come and save them.'

CHAPTER 7
The Death of Mao

When Mao Tse-tung used the masses (the Red Guards and the Revolutionaries) to destroy his opponents in the Party leadership, he allowed the people to witness and to take part in an ugly drama of power-struggle between himself and the so-called "capitalist-roaders". The prolonged struggle and the denunciations of one leader after another enabled the people to stumble on the truth that the emperor had no clothes. When Mao Tse-tung died in 1976, the country was in a state of political disintegration. Obviously if the Party were to continue to govern, it must change course.

Nien Cheng, *Life and Death in Shanghai*

In the year that his family's farm was communised, Emme-la was fifteen and old enough to work full time. His sister, Pasang Dolma, was packed off to another farm within the same commune, while Dawa Phentok,

105

the eldest sibling, having married a farmer from the village of Gang, twelve miles from Gyantse, was out of contact. Emme-la, who would have preferred to be studying at school if only he had been allowed to, found the full-time farm work followed by evenings of political indoctrination hard going.

After the various revolts in Tibet had been crushed and order had been reimposed, a new programme, known as the Four Freedoms, was proclaimed in the summer of 1972: freedom to worship, freedom to buy and sell privately, freedom to lend and borrow with interest and freedom to employ casual labour. The last three Freedoms did not excite the Tibetans much, but the first one did. As Emme-la says, 'When they said there'd be freedom of religion, everyone simply exploded with joy. The Chinese were stunned to find that everyone, even the young people, was delighted to be allowed to worship again. Suddenly there was a massive religious revival and they just couldn't believe it. They really thought they had succeeded in inoculating the young against religion, but if they had, the young people would never have behaved like that.'

The ban on wearing Tibetan dress was lifted and rebuilding work started on a few temples. But the change was short-lived, and by the end of the same year, the Four Freedoms had been replaced by One Struggle and Three Antis, the One Struggle being against counter-revolutionaries, and the Antis more or less wiping out the last three freedoms, now renamed 'bourgeois extravagance, capitalistic profit motive and economic waste'.[1] The Three Antis resulted in thousands of arrests and mass executions.

Most Tibetans had given up trying to make any sense of the various changes that came and went. The central fact of existence for them was that the Chinese had total control of their lives: they had to work till they dropped, they were hungry, and still they had to attend the nightly political meetings. 'When the work in the fields went on till dusk, the political meetings would be held just the same, late at night, finishing about midnight. If the field work finished early, then the meeting would be earlier, and at least we could get to bed a bit earlier. There was no escaping the meetings, and whichever way it was, we were exhausted.'

The ups and downs of change, of course, were related to the state of affairs in China itself. Round about 1974, the evening political education sessions became especially tense, as the latest phase of the old left–right power struggle in the Chinese Communist Party played itself out. This particular bout was the result of a spat between Mao and his old buddy, Lin Biao, the defence chief who in April 1969 had been recognised as heir apparent by the Ninth Party Congress held in Peking. Such recognition was in fact equivalent to a kiss of death since Mao, like other Chinese Emperors before him, was famous for despatching those whom he suspected of having even half an eye on the ultimate power. But in 1969 Lin Biao's star was still rising and he could do no wrong. He and his good friend and brother, Chairman Mao, were often photographed together. Throughout the Cultural Revolution Lin Biao had been hailed in the official press as the embodiment of all the virtues. As Commander-in-Chief of the Army, he had supported Mao's beloved Red Guards, and, in an Introduction to the Thoughts, had praised Mao as 'the greatest living Marxist of our time'.

But when, on the advice of Lin Biao's only serious rival, Prime Minister Zhou En-lai, who had been Prime Minister since the very beginning in 1949, Mao began seeking a rapprochement with the USA and plans were known to be afoot to invite President Nixon to Peking, Lin Biao saw that the writing was on the wall. By 1970 Mao had begun to resent his ambitious heir and plan his downfall. Realising that the glory days were over, Lin went onto the offensive, plotting to assassinate Mao in September 1971 by planting explosives on a train the latter was due to board. When Lin's own daughter betrayed him to the authorities, he fell back on a contingency plan and commandeered a plane in which to escape to the USSR. The plane was forced to land and everyone on board was arrested, but Lin managed to escape the surveillance and took off on his own for Outer Mongolia. Alas, his luck had run out, the plane was shot down and Lin Biao was killed.

The news of his death was kept from the public for some months, those in the know being threatened with severe punishment if they talked. Then suddenly books by and pictures of Lin Biao disappeared from public view. Mao, a sick old man in the grip of a profound paranoia, set out to prove in the time-honoured Communist way that the man who had been his boon companion was in reality a black-hearted traitor who had plotted to kill him. A campaign of denunciation began, in which the earlier fulsome hero-worship was stood on its head. He who had once embodied all the virtues was now the very incarnation of evil. 'Everything Lin Biao did that we had been told was good now turned out to be bad after all,' wrote a Chinese woman.[2] 'All his virtues had been turned into vices.' At the end of every political meeting, the audience had to rise en masse to shout slogans expressing their collective hatred of the fiend. Emme-la recalls the fuss made in Tibet: 'We had to write huge posters denouncing the terrible crimes of Lin Biao, though none of us had the least idea of who he was or what he had done.'

Lin Biao's death meant that the more moderate and popular Zhou En-lai could now control foreign policy and the day-to-day running of the economy. Hence the proclamation of the Four Freedoms. But Zhou, like Mao, was terminally ill (he had cancer of the liver), and no longer had the stamina to see his policies through. He too needed an heir, and quickly. That someone proved to be Deng Xiao-ping, a relative moderate – 'capitalist roader' – who since the early days had been in and out of Mao's favour with the rapidity of a yo-yo and who had been imprisoned on Lin Biao's express orders during the Cultural Revolution. That, of course, was now in his favour, and Deng was brought back to Peking in March 1973, to be made a Deputy Vice-Premier of the People's Republic.

Mao was worried. Though it was generally agreed that the Cultural Revolution had been an unmitigated disaster, in his eyes it remained a triumph. Zhou and Deng were setting out to destroy what he regarded as the greatest achievement of his political career. As Deng showed his preference for production over revolution, and began to put the latter into reverse, Mao was enraged at the speed with which he and his brainchild were being dumped. His paranoia was fed by his wife Jiang Qing, a woman whose passion for power was equal to his own, and who, supported by a group of cronies known as the Gang of Four, intended to succeed her husband as the real ruler of China. Needless to say, Jiang Qing (also known as 'Madame Mao') hated both Zhou and Deng.

Jiang Qing had already schemed her way to total control of the press and all major publications in China, and was personally directing the posthumous denunciation of Lin Biao. Subtly she set out to widen the campaign by combining with it a campaign against –

Confucius! The 'Criticise Lin Biao' campaign became the 'Criticise Lin Biao and Confucius' campaign. Many Chinese must have scratched their heads in puzzlement when article after article condemned the long-dead philosopher who, they were told, had, at the age of fifty, become an official in the Kingdom of Lu, and was for a short while acting Prime Minister. As such, Jiang Qing's newspapers claimed, he had been 'a reactionary and an enemy of progress', a searcher after 'the golden mean' who had opposed the radical approach to politics espoused by some of his colleagues. Ah, *there* was the clue! In this really rather obvious swipe at Zhou and Deng who were themselves searchers after 'the golden mean', Confucius was being marked out as a forerunner of the 'capitalist roaders'. Gradually, Lin Biao's name was dropped from the campaign altogether. He had served his purpose, the dead were safely dead, it was the living who were dangerous.

If this was confusing in mainland China, it was all the more so in far-distant Tibet, where Confucius was an even more unknown quantity than Lin Biao. By now the habit of denunciation had become an unstoppable force: as one campaign slackened in force, another one blew in like a typhoon, as the Maoists tried to keep stoking the revolutionary fire. To this day, Emme-la has no idea what the anti-Confucius campaign meant. It was just another of the many pretexts for making the people shout denunciations and write big-print posters. Down with Lin Biao, down with Confucius. And as it was drummed into them that 'Confucius, Lin Biao and the Dalai Lama are three lamas from the same monastery' it was no wonder that the Tibetans were thoroughly confused. The only thing they could be sure about was that this was yet another attack on their traditional way of life. Down with the Dalai Lama and his reactionary

Confucian ideas. And down with his reactionary clique.
Down too with the Panchen Lama, despite the fact that
for many years the latter had been languishing in a
Chinese jail. 'They were always being denounced, but
it got worse at the time of the attacks on Lin Biao and
Confucius. They were said to share the same ideology
or something. We didn't know what it was all about,
but we had to write these huge posters denouncing all
four of them, and stick them up on walls all over the
Gyantse area.'

Once again the two Lamas had to be vilified by
everyone present at the evening meetings, with the
added twist that the Chinese improvised lampoons to
be performed, denouncing these two 'jackals from the
same lair'. One ex-monk, ordered to translate one of
these into Tibetan, was threatened with terrible punishments when he refused on the grounds that his Chinese
wasn't good enough. He had already suffered greatly
and this was the last straw: 'Something in me snapped,
and for a while I lost my sanity and went mad. My
parents and elder sister all died around this time, of
exhaustion, hunger and despair. I wanted to die too.'[3]

It didn't matter that the accusations waxed ever more
ludicrous. Travelling exhibitions were taken on tour,
displaying a rosary of 108 cranial bones supposedly
from victims 'sacrificed' to the Dalai Lama, together
with an arsenal of weapons with which the Panchen
before his arrest was alleged to have planned an
Uprising.[4]

In private, the Tibetans thought the whole thing was
barking mad. As always happens in repressed societies,
jokes, no matter how puerile, surfaced as a safety-valve.
Emme-la cites one of his neighbours who sent up the
whole business in private. 'One night when he got back
to his one-room dwelling after a *thamzing* where the

Dalai and Panchen Lamas had been "struggled against",
he caught a mouse. Holding it up by the fur of its head,
he addressed an imaginary assembly: "Look, I have
caught the rat who is responsible for gnawing through
the tsampa containers of the proletariat." Turning to the
mouse, he demanded fiercely: "Villain, who sent you
here? Was it the Dalai or the Panchen? Whichever of
them it was, you ought to be skinned alive from top to
tail. But naturally this would not be in keeping with the
merciful nature of the Chinese Communist Party." By
this time the terrified mouse was wriggling and trying
to escape. "Ah, you confess your crimes," said the man.
"Then in that case I've no more to say." Going to the
corner of the room where his wife had already fallen
into a sleep of exhaustion, he shook her awake and
pulled her to her feet, saying, "Come on, mother, wake
up, it's your turn to struggle against this counter-revolutionary rat." '

Just occasionally a victim actually managed to brazen
out a *thamzing* session. At the height of the mania for
communisation, when the Maoists were waging war to
the death against the 'capitalist roaders', a villager called
Pasang Tsering bought an ox cheap because one of its
horns was broken. It went without saying that with this
purchase he had become an out-and-out capitalist in
the eyes of the authorities, so when the villagers were
summoned next day to a *thamzing* meeting, they had
no doubt at all that it was Pasang Tsering they were to
struggle against. 'When they dragged Pasang out to the
platform, he decided to make a fight for it. After all,
what did he have to lose? Before the attack could get
going, he shouted out: "*They* accuse *me* of being a
capitalist, yet the only possession I have in the world is
a wretched ox with one horn. On the other hand, when
you look at the cushy life our commune leaders lead,

I wonder how they've got the nerve to call *me* a capitalist?" Turning to the bemused officials on the platform, he said airily, "Let's forget about all this nonsense, shall we? Let's have a cigarette." He helped himself to one from a packet on the table, while the commune leaders sat in stunned silence. The meeting ended as soon as it began, Pasang Tsering being allowed to go home with the others.'

But the tide was already flowing more strongly in favour of the 'capitalist roaders'. At the Fourth National People's Congress in January 1975, Zhou, in the last stages of cancer, announced the Four Modernisations, aimed at developing agriculture, industry, technology and defence. The whole emphasis was on production, and Deng Xiao-ping was in charge. Quite clearly 'Madame Mao' would not like that at all.

After a year or two of full-time farm work, Emme-la's never very robust health had deteriorated still further and his eyesight was beginning to fail. In 1973 his mother managed to have him apprenticed for a year to a master carpenter so that he might learn a less strenuous trade. This relieved the pressure, though as he had initially been registered as a farmer, he still had to work on the farms during the busy seasons. 'Once you were categorised as a farmer, you were always a farmer, no matter what else you might be doing. If the authorities had decided I was needed for work on the farms, they could have taken me away from my carpentry at any time. There was never any arguing with their decisions.'

As a result of the Four Modernisations, a few prisoners had been released. Among them was Emme-la's family friend, the former trader and Resistance fighter Loden Katsanub. Loden's final prison had been the infamous Drapchi outside Lhasa, where he had done hard labour: bricklaying, breaking and carrying stones and bricks and so on. Over the years, lack of food, absence of even the most basic sanitation, inadequate clothing and bedding, and the constant beatings he had received in a succession of prisons had reduced him to a human wreck. 'In 1975, they sent him home, a physical wreck, and stripped of any political rights or control over his own life. He returned to Gyantse suffering from sweating attacks and bouts of pain all over his body which often caused him to lose consciousness. The pains in his chest were particularly severe, but no medical treatment was available for him. The only thing that brought him any relief was placing loosely woven balls of wool on his chest and massaging him with them.'[5]

By 1975, Deng's emphasis on production over ideology was taking effect and hydroelectric power stations were springing up all over Tibet. The Chinese were building one on the 520-km long Nyangchu River (a tributary of the Tsangpo, or Brahmaputra River), recruiting the labour force from the different communes within the Gyantse system. As his carpentry teacher had already been set to work on the project, Emme-la was sent to assist him, one of six or seven workers from his home village which was within a half-hour's walk of the work-site. They were to build and erect the wooden scaffolding for the power station, prepare all the necessary tools, and construct wheelbarrows for carrying concrete and other building materials from one place to another. As a skilled labourer, he was paid six mao a day, of which three and a half had to be handed over to the commune in tax. In exchange he received six workpoints. (Unskilled workers earned only three mao a day,

On the doorstep of Emme-la's former home
in Gyantse, 1987. Left to right: his niece; his mother; his aunt,
Bhunchung; and her daughter, Kyilue.

In front of Pelkhor Choede monastery and
the great Kumbum Chorten of Gyantse, 1987. Left to right:
Emme-la's nephew; his sister, Dawa Phenthok; and her son.

Gyantse, Emme-la's home town.

Emme-la after leaving Tibet, 1982.

Emme-la with refugee dancers from the
Ngari province of Tibet, 1995.

Emme-la in Dharamsala.

Emme-la with his wife and baby son in Dharamsala, 1997.

Emme-la with a troop of TIPA opera performers.

of which one and a half went to the communes, earning them just four work-points.)

It was hard work. 'Probably the hardest thing of all was putting on the roof. The power station itself was three storeys high, and the roof, unlike the flat Tibetan roofs, had to be sloping. We younger ones were to put the crossbeams in place. These were not secured in any way, and we had to inch our way forward with them very cautiously. If we had lost our grip we would have fallen and been killed instantly and when we looked down from a height of three storeys, we could see that we would fall right onto the jagged pieces of building material down below. We were sick with fear, and I still shudder when I think of it today.'

Because he was engaged on carpentry, Emme-la only had to work during daylight hours, whereas there was no limit on the hours his fellow-workers had to put in. Often the Tibetans were ordered to work overtime, starting work again after supper, anything from two to four hours with no extra pay or food-points. It was not like that for the Chinese labourers who had been brought into Tibet with the incentive of many perks and privileges. 'When they did the evening work, they were given nine mao for two hours' work and food vouchers entitling them to about half a pound of grain, an enormous amount by our standards. The Chinese workers always did very well out of it. I remember one husband and wife team of architects who had designed the power station. When they eventually went back to China, it was with a truck-load of household and other goods. But the Tibetans never had anything at all to show for all their hard work. Not only were we given the hardest and most unpleasant jobs, but the authorities treated us very badly. For instance, there was an old man called Karmae from one of our villages. His job was to cut and shape the stones for building the power station walls. One day an inspection team came round and for some reason they were not satisfied with the work the old man was doing. Either he was being too slow or else the stones were not quite the right shape. The chief of the inspection team dragged him out by his beard and beat him hard on both sides of his face with a water-bottle. After that, we were all scared when the inspection teams came round. When we saw one coming, we used to work twice as fast as normal. We were always afraid it would be our turn next to be beaten.'

In spite of everything, Emme-la regarded himself as lucky: at least he was still alive. 'Two other young men I knew, Pasang and Buchung, were made to dig tunnels. But because everything was completely disorganised and there was no such thing as safety precautions, the tunnel collapsed and my two friends were buried under the rubble. Pasang was rushed to hospital and survived, but Buchung was dead of suffocation when they got to him. The Chinese announced that Buchung had sacrificed his life for the good of his commune and that his family would accordingly receive 300 yuan by way of compensation. (I don't think they ever got it.)'

It was while working at the power station that Emme-la met his first girlfriend. He used to walk to and from work, as the site was within half an hour of home. 'One day, my mother sent me a message, asking me to come home during the lunch break. I managed to get the necessary permission, and on my way home met a group of Tibetan girls going towards the power station. They were girls from a remote village who'd been sent to work there. There's an old Tibetan folk custom: if the girls outnumber the boys in any group, they play a rather childish trick. A number of girls will gang up on the weakest boy in the group and rough him up. Well, this time I was on my own, so I knew I was in for trouble. They pushed me to the ground, and four girls each grabbed one of my limbs, while a fifth sat astride me as though I were a horse or a donkey. Then they swung me from side to side, to make me admit that boys were inferior to girls. What usually happened was that if you grovelled they let you go, but if you didn't they would strip you naked, tie a stone onto your penis and march you around to visit the neighbours. Pretty embarrassing. Anyway, that day, I was one against a whole crowd of girls and I'd no choice but to submit. I did a convincing grovel, saying that girls were so much more wonderful than boys, and they let me off lightly. I was rather smitten by one of the girls, Penpa Dolma, and afterwards I couldn't get her out of my mind. She seemed to feel the same, and at the power station she used to bring her farm implements for me to repair. I always took a lot of trouble with them, wanting to please her. In Tibet, you know, there's not usually much verbal communication between lovers, courtships are carried on through a third person. If a girl fancies a boy, she will knit him a pair of check-patterned socks and send them via a friend. Well, that's what Penpa Dolma did – she knitted me the most beautiful pair of socks I'd ever seen and a mutual friend brought them to me. Through the same friend I sent her a scarf. In this way we acknowledged our feelings for each other. But, given our circumstances, I didn't really have much hope that anything could come of it.'

China was in the throes of yet more convulsions. In late 1975, as Zhou En-lai lay on his deathbed, Mao (or more accurately his wife, Jiang Qing, for Mao was now senile and only months away from death himself) contrived a last vicious twitch on the political strings. Deng was sent packing and was rumoured to be under house arrest, while the Gang of Four poured verbal vitriol on him and the dying Zhou En-lai. Mao retained just enough hold on sanity to refuse to hand over his power to his wife and her Gang of Four. Instead, he chose Hua Guo-feng, a devoted but dull disciple, as acting Prime Minister and his political heir. If it had come to a crunch, Madame Mao could probably have made mincemeat out of Hua. In 1976, therefore, with Mao at death's door, China's future – and therefore that of Tibet – hung in the balance.

Early in 1976, Zhou En-lai's death was closely followed by that of Zhu De, the founder of the People's Liberation Army. China suffered a massive earthquake; and some time in August a comet was seen to blaze in the night skies. The astrologers had forecast that the Chinese Year of the Dragon would be unlucky and they were being proved right. Clinching proof of the year's 'inauspiciousness' came on 9 September when Mao Tse-tung, so long thought of as indestructible, also died.

The moderates moved instantly and by night to stop the ambitious Jiang Qing in her tracks. By October, the Gang of Four was smashed, Jiang Qing and the others being in prison awaiting trial, and though Hua Guo-feng managed to hold on to his position, Deng Xiao-ping was brought back from house-arrest and reinstated. Within two years, Hua would be side-lined, Deng would be Chairman and all the power would be in his hands. The Cultural Revolution would at last be truly over.

'The Chinese officials seemed to know all about Mao's death long before they told us,' Emme-la says, without much surprise. 'They told us one evening during the political meeting, and they got very emotional about it. They talked about the Great Helmsman and wept when they said that 'the Red Sun of Our Hearts, the beloved Chairman Mao' had passed away, adding that now there was a great danger that imperial forces would launch a war against China, so we would have to intensify our preparations for war! Again! On no account were we to show any sign of gaiety – there must be no songs, no music, we were to make sure that our facial expressions registered grief at all times. We were all issued with a black armband and a white paper flower to wear in our buttonholes. Then we had to go in procession to a certain place and show our grief in public. We did this, of course, but deep down we were very happy that Mao had died. We associated his name with our sufferings and felt that with his death one of the major obstacles to our happiness had been removed. But of course we didn't dare say anything of the sort. We all went round with long faces, showing what the Chinese called "the correct attitude".'

To console the Tibetans in their 'grief', their clothing ration was slightly increased, a special gift, it was said, from the new Chairman Hua. They were much more pleased by the fact that sugar, which had almost disappeared from their lives, was suddenly available again.

But not long after Mao's death, a new and sinister development began. In 1962, Mao had sworn that as soon as Tibet was sufficiently stabilised, he would settle 10 million Chinese there. So far it had seemed like an empty threat: there had only been the PLA soldiers, a certain number of political officers and a handful of technicians. Red Guards had come and gone, but even they had made little difference: the physiognomy of Tibet was still recognisably Tibetan.

One day in 1976, Radio Lhasa announced quite casually that a number of Chinese settlers were due to arrive in Tibet. 'We didn't realise what was happening,' says Emme-la. 'It was not long after Mao's death that about twenty young men came to Gyantse from China. We were sent out to welcome them at some distance from the town, and then they all had to be billeted in different houses. We were made responsible for their accommodation and welfare. Each commune unit had to find housing for them and provide them with whatever they needed, domestic utensils, bedding, cutlery and so on. At first it didn't occur to us that there was anything sinister about their arrival, but we did notice one strange thing. Normally, whenever the Communist officials held meetings, the local people were excluded. But these new Chinese arrivals were invited to everything. They had, in fact, been brought in to fill the lowest administrative posts – which had until then been held by Tibetan cadres. Obviously the Chinese were not about to trust the Tibetan cadres ever again. The newcomers had been told to learn everything they could about local conditions, to familiarise themselves with the way the people of Gyantse lived and thought. Until they were properly trained, they were to be as unobtrusive as possible, doing everything the local people did – such as farm work and crafts.

It was the thin end of a very big wedge. From now on, the Chinese settlers would keep coming into the country, swamping the Tibetans in ever-increasing numbers. Within less than ten years, exiled Tibetan sources would estimate that at least one-third of the inhabitants of Greater (ethnographic) Tibet were Chinese. Within twenty years, it would be over one-half and the Dalai Lama would have publicly denounced the process as the Chinese 'Final Solution' for Tibet.[6]

The electricity was formally switched on at the new power station on 10 June 1977. It was, the authorities boasted (just as they had with the communes), a project for the people, built by the people for the sole use of the people. They promised that free electricity would soon be available for everyone. 'In the event,' says Emme-la, 'all of the families who might have got the electricity were ordered to pay for it, and as it was far more expensive than kerosene, hardly any of them could afford to do so.'

CHAPTER 8

Towards the Abyss

Such a wide gulf, basic prejudice and antipathy. I used to think that at the central level in Peking it was not fully understood what was going on, much it did not realize, but Peking knows enough now. It is the central government which in the long term wants Tibet sinified, so that there is a majority of Han and Tibetans become a minority in their own land.

Fredrick R. Hyde-Chambers, *Lama: A Novel of Tibet*

Once the power station was finished, most of the workers were sent back to their own villages to get the harvest in. This was standard policy: 'It was reckoned that on the farms we could build up our strength and be ready for the hard work waiting for us in the construction industry during the winter months. Every year, you would see people getting weaker as the months dragged by, until the harvest season came round again and they could go back to their villages to recover their strength.'

Emme-la was among a handful of skilled wood-workers retained to do additional building work for the agricultural sector: putting up four large workshops and two smaller ones for making and repairing the farming implements, each with its own store-rooms, living quarters and communal kitchens. 'We were given an impossible quota for each day, and it was back-breaking work. Every evening when we went to bed we ached all over and were almost too tired to sleep.'

Many of his fellow-workers had been brought in from Dromo County (also known as Chumbi Valley), near the borders with Sikkim and Western Bhutan. As the wood itself also came from there, and had not been paid for, the Dromo authorities asked Gyantse to send them some skilled carpenters in lieu of payment. By September, when most of Emme-la's brigade were starting work on digging canals to divert the water away from the power station in order to irrigate the surrounding areas, Emme-la was sent instead to Dromo.

It was the first time he had ever been away from home, and it was like finding himself in a foreign country. The beautiful Dromo valley with its flowering plants and conifer trees was actually part of his own province of Tsang, yet it felt alien somehow, not lush but misty, damp and cold. He could not follow the dialect and even the architecture was strange, with sloping roofs and verandahs outside the decaying houses. The journey took him up to and through the former market-town of Phari – at 15,000 ft, the highest inhabited town on the planet – guardian of the icy border passes with India and Bhutan and crowned by the awesome Chomolhari, 'Mountain of the Goddess Lady', third highest peak of the Himalayan range.

Below was what he had been told was a thickly forested area, but looking down, he had seen 'nothing but sawn-off tree-trunks as far as the eye could see, with only the occasional tree left standing'.

Later on, when his ear had grown more attuned to the unfamiliar dialect, he heard from the villagers that the Chinese were cutting down all the trees as far as the Bhutanese border – and not planting replacements. 'The name "Dromo" means "warm" ', they told me, 'but a better name for it today would be "Drangmo", which means "cold".' Stripped of its trees, the whole area now stood bare and unprotected from the winds – its once great forests reduced to ugly stumps. A decade or so ago Dromo had been a kind of earthly paradise, a staging-post and commercial centre used by traders on the way from Gyantse to Sikkim, Bhutan and India. But the signs of prosperity had long since vanished; the main town, Sharsingma (known to the Chinese as Yadong), was a ghost town of decaying houses, served only by one large government store and a shabby commune restaurant.

Ordered to repair the government store, Emme-la and his co-workers rebuilt its main entrance, replaced all the floors and interior walls, retimbered the underside of the roof and made various display tables, shelves and cupboards. The work was lighter than any they had known and though Emme-la was homesick for Gyantse, he was beginning to recover his spirits. There were other compensations: the air was like wine, there were black-birds singing – and he didn't have to get up at the crack of dawn. And even though on weekday evenings they all had to watch dreary propaganda films, at least they had Sundays free. Wandering about on these unaccustomed free days, he discovered that most of the Gyantse contingent were employed in cutting down more trees, as timber for building new Chinese army barracks all over south-western Tibet.

This relatively happy interlude in Dromo was short-lived and within three months, in January 1978, he was on his way back to Gyantse. It was freezing cold as he left Dromo, the valley and hills were covered with snow and ice. Passing once again through Phari (surely one of the coldest places on earth in winter, when the temperature sinks to 26 degrees below zero), he was 'amazed to see nomads wandering round with their animals, when we ourselves could barely breathe in the icy temperature'.

When Emme-la arrived back in Gyantse, he was brought down to earth with a bump. There was no question of being allowed time to recover from the long trek. Without further ado he was sent to rejoin the rest of his brigade who were digging the irrigation canals. It would be worse than anything that had gone before.

The brigade was divided into units, each given a ten-day quota. 'Each unit was made to compete against the others, and those who came bottom of the list each month were often tortured and beaten, especially anybody who'd once been a "serf-owner" or an official in the old government service. So we had to work harder and harder so as not to be in the bottom group.'

The workers slept in tents, regardless of the weather. They got up at dawn. Sometimes they were allowed a light breakfast before starting work, but mostly they had to work for several hours before breaking for food. At first Emme-la was relieved to find that he was doing carpentry work again, making the wheelbarrows and mending the tools. But this time was different. After finishing their quota of woodwork, the carpenters were sent to join the others digging the canals. 'It was punishing work,' says Emme-la. 'The canals were really deep and when we dug the mud we had to throw it up high onto the bank. For those of us who were used to lighter work it was even worse than for the others, we just didn't have the strength. And instead of our usual dinner break at one, they moved it to three in the afternoon. As a result we were hungry as well as dog-tired. After the first day I was so exhausted that when I went home I didn't care whether I lived or died. But there was no respite. Next day was exactly the same. And the next. I felt more dead than alive and didn't know how I could possibly survive.'

The pay was almost non-existent, and the workers were being driven to a state of collapse. One day, a work brigade from a neighbouring commune went by the canal on their way back to base camp, and were so appalled at the pitiful state of the labourers down below that they rushed to help them. 'One of them was Penpa Dolma, the girl I'd been keen on. I was terribly embarrassed that she should see me in such a state – and she was pretty upset too. But gradually we forgot our embarrassment and when it was time for us to go back to base-camp, I let her help me carry my long-handled spade for removing mud. I had no pride left. In any case, I had already accepted there was no future in our relationship. It had never really stood a chance. She came from a "clean" background, whereas my class background was all wrong. If we'd married, I would have been dragging her down and she'd have been made to suffer for it. There was another thing too. If in the years to come she had fallen out with my mother, she would automatically be presumed right in any dispute. Again because of class, my mother would always be the guilty party. So nothing was able to come of our brief romance.'

Class struggle was still a potent and deadly force. Among the workers on the canal was a man classed as a 'former serf-owner'. 'They always made him do the worst, most back-breaking jobs. He had to haul sacks of cement and other building materials from one place to another. One day, his hand slipped and the wheel-barrow went out of control, overturned and smashed. Immediately, the officials in charge of our brigade rushed up and arrested him. Because of his bad class, they dragged him to the main office, in front of which stood a flagpole flying the Chinese flag. They tied him to that flagpole with metal wires and left him there for about six hours, hurling abuse at him and beating him all the time. When they let him go they imposed a huge fine on him – which of course he couldn't pay as he had no money. So they deducted the amount from his pathetically low wages.'

Just before the Tibetan New Year in February 1978, the Chinese authorities summoned everyone together to allocate the work for the year. 'I spotted my cousin, Sonam Wangdu. I hadn't seen him for ages, not only because I'd been in Dromo, but because we were in different work units: I was a carpenter, he an agricul-tural worker who spent his day shovelling earth from one place to another. As soon as the meeting was over, he came over to me and said how well I looked! He thought my skin had improved – I suppose that was because of the moist climate in Dromo. But when I looked at him, I saw that his face and arms were covered with boils and welts. He told me that his whole body was like that, and then burst into floods of tears. Not long before, the authorities had allowed him to visit his doctor in Gyantse, and the boils were so painful that he'd stayed for two days to receive treatment for them. But he had not had official permission to be absent from work, and he got into dreadful trouble when he arrived back. They told him that as his father had fought in the Tibetan Resistance, he was the son of a counter-revolutionary, and it would be better for him if he had never been born. They wouldn't listen to his explanations, they just dragged him off and beat him. As if the boils were not bad enough! What's more, they sent him straight back to work in the fields.'

On 1 March they began work on the next major project – diverting the course of the River Nyangchu into which the power station discharged its water, to make it run into the canal – and were told to have the job finished by the 20th. 'We were moved to a new camp, one hour's walk from the previous one. As always, the Chinese officials and their pet pigs came with us. The Han always kept pigs, pork forms an important part of the Chinese diet, and pigs can thrive on any old garbage. One day they killed a pig, then discovered to their horror that its flesh was polluted by a kind of worm – a white egg-like structure which appeared to the naked eye no bigger than a mustard seed. (They're found in their thousands between the skin and the fat of the pig.) Anyway, the Han declared that the pig must be buried and no one must eat the meat since it was contaminated. In the early evening, a group of us was despatched to bury the carcase far away from the camp. As soon as it was dark, we all returned to the place where we'd buried the pig, dug it up again and took it back to the camp. That night we cooked the carcase and had the most wonderful feast any of us could remember.'

But the work was going badly. When at last the river water was released into the canals, it was obvious to everyone that the Chinese surveyors had made a cock-up of the planning. 'There were a lot of blockages, and it was obvious that the construction was faulty. Quite often parts of the canal burst their banks and surrounding fields were simply flooded out of existence. They had to send groups of workers to check different parts of the canal for leakages or damage. I remember a Tibetan called Nyima Wangdu being sent to do one of these checks, the canal banks collapsed and he fell into the water and was drowned. It was several days before they recovered his body. When they did so, they summoned a mass meeting and the Chinese announced that as Nyima Wangdu had sacrificed his life for the Great Motherland, he would be made a posthumous member of the Communist Party as a reward. His wife worked for the Chinese, and the couple were praised to the skies for their selfless dedication. At least, making Nyima Wangdu a member of the Party meant that his children would get an education.

'It didn't always turn out like that. By the time we got the drainage system working properly at the end of May, another boy had died, trapped under a huge landslide which also crushed a girl from Khartoe, a village near mine. Unlike the couple who'd been working for the Chinese, these two were accused of having put their own safety at risk. It was through their own carelessness that they had died – so their families got no compensation at all!'

There was fierce competition now not only between different units but between the three regions whose fields would benefit from the irrigation. Give or take a few unfortunate accidents, the Gyantse authorities were well pleased. A letter from their regional HQ in Shigatse suggested that if only the Gyantse workforce would pursue the class struggle as thoroughly as they had worked on the canal, they could become a model for the whole of China. 'Naturally our local officials were delighted. But instead of praising our hard work and allowing us a bit of relaxation as a reward, they actually increased our workload, by way of toadying to the Shigatse authorities. We were now forced to work harder than ever and our lives were even more intolerable than before. Those units which came last had their food rations reduced.'

In the autumn, Emme-la was sent back to his commune to help with the harvest. As his eyesight and general health had deteriorated to danger level, he braved the wrath of the local authorities by asking for permission to work nearer home. He was not, of course, surprised when they refused. He knew that because of his bad class background they would always send him as far away from home as possible, except at harvest-time.

That year, 1978, was no different from any other. Once the harvest was in, he was sent off to join a co-operative which was reclaiming virgin land in an area some considerable distance away. 'We had to convert a large number of small plots of land into one huge one and make it cultivable.'

Both male and female workers slept in huge tents, where there was no respect for hygiene or privacy. But, if only because they were unable to work at night, at least the workload was bearable. He ran into Dolkar, a girl from his year in primary school. It was good to have a friend to talk to. She told him with some pride that she had already completed her work-points for the year, which meant that she was entitled to the maximum ration of food-grains. For the rest of the year, she hoped she would be able to relax a bit. In reality, both she and Emme-la knew that the dice were loaded against her. Dolkar's father had joined the Tibetan Resistance in 1959 and had been killed fighting the Chinese. It went without saying that the daughter of such a man was an 'Enemy of the People'.

Dolkar met a tragic end. 'Later on I heard that she had fallen in love with an assistant cook at a Chinese staff-training school, a man who was "unclassed" and therefore "clean". She got pregnant and tried to persuade her boyfriend to marry her, but he refused. He didn't want to be reclassed as a counter-revolutionary: if he'd married her, he'd have lost all his privileges. But she was crazy about him and kept on pestering. One day, he told her about some precious dried yak-dung fuel that he'd hidden in one of the caves which the Chinese had dug all over Tibet in preparation for the Third World War. He told her they could go secretly and collect it together. But what he actually did was take her out to that cave and kill her. The police arrested the man, but, although normally anyone found guilty of murder would have been automatically shot, they merely took him off to prison in Shigatse. He was one of their own after all, and she was the child of a counter-revolutionary, a non-person, dangerous to know. The Chinese didn't care, but when we Tibetans found out what had happened, all of us, whatever class we belonged to, were terribly distressed and angry.'

By the end of December when the land reclamation was finished, Emme-la was allowed a brief visit home. Within two days, he was sent off again, to another project, even further away. This time it meant building dykes on another stretch of the River Nyangchu which supplied water to the power station. And although the work didn't actually begin until January 1979, the labour force had been signed, sealed and delivered well in advance. In the previous May, a mass meeting had been summoned to recruit labourers from the three main districts of the Shigatse region, Shigatse itself, Panam and Gyantse. Dorje Tseten, the highest Tibetan official in the region (now minister for civil affairs in Peking) addressed his captive audience. 'This new dyke-building project [he told us] had been ordered by the Central Government in Peking, and was therefore, very, very important – unlike the other "trivial jobs" we'd been doing so far. He said that we in the labour brigade would have to compete among ourselves as to the quality and quantity of our work. In fact he made every Tibetan official working for the Chinese swear on oath that they would complete this project well within the time allocated, and that the quality would be of such a standard as to set an example for the entire beloved Motherland. The officials had to sign the oath and it was collected on the spot.'

In Emme-la's world, where all change seemed to be for the worse, it was just another step downwards into the abyss.

CHAPTER 9

'Hell must be something like this'

Hell . . . any place of vice or misery; a place of turmoil;
(a state of) supreme misery or discomfort; anything
causing misery, pain or destruction.

Chambers' Dictionary definition

January – the mind-numbing chill of a high-altitude
winter. 'The edges of the river were frozen and as we
arrived we could see huge chunks of ice hurtling down-
stream.' To the din of Chinese loudhailers exhorting
them to ever more superhuman effort, Emme-la and the
others put up their tents in a village near the river's
edge. 'The loudhailers were turned on just before dawn
– they were the camp's alarm system, and as soon as
we heard them we had to tumble out of bed. Most of
the time they deafened us with loud Chinese songs, the
meaning of which was quite lost on us. Then, when
we'd been there for a few days, they started criticising

the quality – or lack of it – of the work we'd done the previous day, or they told us about the work we were going to do that day. If there was nothing else to say, they just talked about the organisation of the camp. Anything and nothing. As long as the daylight lasted, the din never stopped.'

After a meagre breakfast, the workers were marched off to the river. 'On the first day we were told we had to build dykes along the edge of the river. This involved digging up the mud and laying huge boulders along the bottom, followed by another layer of large stones, another of smaller ones and a final layer of rubble. Our overseer cut holes in the ice and we had to stand in the freezing water for hours on end. Most of the time we were working up to our knees (and sometimes beyond) in the water, at other times we had to lug heavy rocks about. At first, I had a bit of maintenance and repair work to do on the wheelbarrows and things, but there was not much of that and then it was down to the river to dig the banks. Digging became my full-time job and without a doubt it was the most terrible time of my life. Our limbs became numb and senseless in the freezing water and we all suffered terrible cuts and bruises from the floating ice. The work was so appalling that we could only survive by making up songs that would express our sufferings in some way. One song went something like this: "The sufferings of Hell on earth are the daily lot of us river workers. Every day we come face to face with the terrible Lord of Death[1] in the person of Phuntsog, the man the Chinese have put in charge of us." ' (Ironically, Phuntsog's own boss was the very same sports teacher from Emme-la's old primary school who had first harangued them on the glories of the Cultural Revolution. He had gone far. Later, as Political Commissar of Gyantse, he would become the most powerful (and feared) Tibetan in the whole area. Like all Tibetans, however, he would still be answerable to a Chinese boss.)

The workers had not only to dig up mud, but to excavate boulders from the hillside and drag them down to the river. 'We had to remove the boulders with dynamite, often having to break them into rocks with a sledgehammer and pick or even a controlled amount of dynamite, haul them to the mule-drawn carts and load them. It was just as ghastly as the river work. Some of the rocks were enormous, and it took a large number of people to lift and carry them. If anyone loosed his hold for even a moment, the rock could fall and injure the rest of the group.

'I found it almost impossible to lift these huge boulders at first, and my stronger workmates used to help me out by giving me the lighter rocks to lift. The work made us sweat excessively and gave us a terrible thirst: no matter how much water we drank, we still were thirsty all the time.

'We were down to skin and bone, and our backs and hands were raw and bleeding from carrying the rocks. We were given protective gloves but they lasted no more than two days, and once they'd fallen apart we just had to put up with the blisters and sores. Our shoes lasted longer, ten days if we were lucky, but when they were worn out, we couldn't afford to buy new ones. At seven Chinese mao, they cost just under half our wages for the month. That was what they paid us, plus a little bit of tsampa and oil.

'Tsampa and black tea – we had to toil on that all day long. When our supplies even of tsampa ran out, the only way we could have got any more would have been to walk the thirty or forty kilometres back to our homes at night. We wouldn't have been able to leave till it was dark because we had to work till then, and we had to be back to start work the next day at dawn! So, even though we were desperately hungry, we hadn't the strength to contemplate doing anything about it.

As one of the younger members of the brigade, Emmela had to light the fuses when they were dynamiting the rocks. 'When someone blew a whistle, we had to get ready. At the second whistle we had to light the match, and at the third one light the fuse. Usually there were about five fuses to light, one after the other. It was essential to make sure they were all lit, otherwise there would be no blast. Most of the time it went all right, but there was one occasion when one of the fuses didn't light so I had to go back and relight it. As soon as I'd lit it, I ran for cover, but before I could reach safety some of the fuses started going off. We all lay flat on the ground as the rocks exploded all around us and cascaded down the hillside. Fortunately none of them hit us – if we'd been hit, we could have been killed or maimed.

'There *were* accidents, of course. We had to bring the boulders from the top of very steep hills, many people fell or were crushed, and the same thing happened to horses and carts. The Chinese attitude was instructive. If a man died, they felt the only thing required of them was to remove their cap briefly as a mark of respect. End of story. But if a healthy horse or donkey died, that was a much more serious matter – and we would be severely punished for letting it happen. We were ordered to take all possible care of the animals, because they were vital to the work we were doing. Human beings were expendable, horses and donkeys weren't.

'Before the Chinese came, there had been a small altar at the top of the hill on which we were working, people used to put up prayer flags and burn incense there. According to local legend, there was a lump of solid gold about the size of a young pony hidden in the rock. They may have been right. One day, after a series of explosions to break a large boulder into smaller pieces, we discovered a piece which looked somewhat darker than the others. We packed it onto the cart and took it down to the river, but when the workers down there tried to put it in place, they couldn't get it to fit. When they tried to smash it into shape, they found a lump of gold the size, not of a pony, but certainly of a man's fist. We never really discovered the explanation: possibly it meant that the area was rich in minerals. On the other hand, maybe many years earlier – during the Cultural Revolution perhaps – local lamas had hidden some gold around there. The Chinese geologists who did a survey of Tibet certainly believed that in remote areas where there were altars or stupas or any religious monuments there was hidden treasure to be found. We shall never know for sure: all we knew was that the Chinese took away the gold we found.

'On another occasion, some of our group saw a dead pig floating down-stream. Some of them immediately jumped into the river and grabbed the carcass. They took it back to the camp, cooked it, ate the meat, and made a soup from the bones. Unfortunately, this time the meat really *was* rotten, and the whole brigade got sick. Because we then couldn't complete our work quota, our bosses rounded up all those who were sick, beat them up, and forced them back to work. Many of them were beaten unconscious, Tenzin Norbu most of all – do you remember, he was the boy who had helped me so much during my first days at primary school? The one who showed me the ropes, took care of me, helped me to settle in. But he was the son of a "counter-revolutionary" and the authorities had always had it in for the poor chap. This time they really went to town on him. When I saw him later that day he was barely conscious: his face was a mass of bruises and his body was black and blue from the punches and kicks he'd received.'

Throughout these dreadful weeks and months, Emmela many times found himself thinking back to his mother's stories about life in Tibet before the Chinese came. 'I used to close my eyes and wish with all my heart that somehow the Chinese would all disappear from Tibet and that we could go back to living the simple life our grandparents used to lead. But then I'd open my eyes again and know that the wish was just a dream. Nothing was going to change. We would probably just go on and on in this way until we died from hunger or exhaustion.'

But in mainland China, change was in the air. After Mao's death and the collapse of the Gang of Four, Deng Xiao-ping and his 'capitalist roaders'[2] had been busy blaming every crime that had been committed anywhere in China over the last decade on the Gang. At her trial, Madame Mao had been stung into pointing an accusing finger at the judge. 'And when we were doing all those things,' she interrupted the long recitation of her crimes, 'where were you? Weren't you all part of it?'[3] Few of those present could have denied the charge, but there had to be scapegoats, and the sins of the past could be conveniently loaded onto the backs of the Gang of Four. Hu Yao-bang, the reforming new head of the Party Secretariat which had replaced the old Politburo, claimed that the Cultural Revolution had been a disaster for China. He would later go on record as saying that the country had 'wasted twenty years' because of Mao's 'radical leftist nonsense',[4] and in 1976, after Mao's death, that view was rapidly gaining currency. A major reappraisal was under way.

Settlers continued to pour into Tibet. Maybe this influx (which would eventually swamp the Tibetans and turn them into a minority underclass in their own land) reflected Chinese frustration in the face of what was happening – or not happening – in Tibet. For after quarter of a century of occupation, the Chinese were still regarded as alien invaders, little progress had been made and the discontent which had burst out again in 1968 had rarely been off the boil since. There was no doubt about it, Tibet had proved a disappointment to the Chinese. The land known as the Western Treasure House because of its vast untapped mineral wealth was not only a drain on Chinese manpower and resources but a wretched Third World country in China's own backyard. There seemed no way out of the impasse. Since the Panchen Lama had let them down so badly in the 1960s, there was no single high-ranking Tibetan who could be described as a national leader, even a puppet one. The Tibetan cadres were either unreliable or hostile or both. In short, the country was ungovernable. Except perhaps by one man – the Dalai Lama, the ruler whom the Tibetans still regarded as their leader and whose reputation the Chinese had done everything in their power to destroy. In spite of everything that had been said against him, might the Dalai Lama perhaps be prevailed upon to return and save the day for China?

In the middle of 1977, as Emme-la and his kind laboured at the power station, it was announced from Peking that China would welcome the return to Tibet of the Dalai Lama and the other refugees. To underline their good will, the Chinese soft-pedalled a little on

Tibet: older citizens in Lhasa were to be allowed to circumambulate the sacred pilgrim routes around the Jokhang temple on the anniversaries of Buddha's birth, enlightenment and death. Chairman Hua even said the time had come for certain Tibetan customs to be restored and revived.

In the following year, after fourteen years of imprisonment in a top-security jail (not to mention the brainwashing and torture that had driven him to contemplate suicide), the Panchen Lama was released. The New China News Agency reported that at a public meeting in Peking, he had humbly and sincerely confessed his past folly: 'For a period of time I discarded the banner of patriotism and committed a crime. Guided by Chairman Mao's revolutionary line, I have corrected my errors.' So that was all right then.

Deng Xiao-ping, having decided that the Dalai Lama's return was the only way to pacify Tibet, was ready to make a few concessions. Admitting that mistakes had been made, he suggested a meeting with His Holiness. The latter, who had long since realised that some sort of compromise with China would eventually be necessary in order to win back Tibet's freedom, was willing to explore the possibilities. As a gesture of good will, Peking allowed Tibetans – for the first time since 1959 – to correspond with their relatives who had fled abroad. Thirty-four elderly prisoners, 'counter-revolutionaries' incarcerated since 1959, were released, reinstated and told that they were free to emigrate if they wanted. All thirty-four publicly thanked their captors for so generously re-educating them and appealed to their 'brethren in exile' to return.[5] The Panchen Lama joined his voice to theirs, assuring the exiles that they would find the new society and its standard of living a great improvement on the old.

At first, the people of Gyantse were ignorant of this developing dialogue. (Indeed, the authorities in Tibet had on the whole ignored Peking's request for soft-pedalling, preferring to stick with the old hardline revolutionary policies and introducing a whole new set of petty crimes, 'the Three Antis', which resulted in a nationwide wave of mass executions.) But there was one very popular change in Gyantse: the restoration in 1978 of the popular old June festival which commemorated the founder of the Pelkhor Choede Monastery. Not quite in its original form, perhaps; in fact, completely shorn of all its essential religious significance. The feast was given a brand new name which meant 'festival of business transactions'; there were to be no prayers, no thangkas, no mandalas, no tormas or ceremonial cakes. Moreover, the revived event was merely slotted into the first convenient date whereas traditionally the Festival had taken place every year on the same day in June. But no matter. The essential thing was that, for the first time since the Cultural Revolution had put an end to all social gatherings of the sort, the Festival was going to take place.

The archery contests and horse races were brought back. 'For us workers from Gyantse it meant that we were given a week's leave from our labours, and we were allowed to go back home under guise of celebrating the festival. We got very excited at the prospect of returning to our families, our anticipation grew and grew until the night before our departure it became almost unbearable. But when we got back to our villages most of us river workers had to plunge straight into farm work. We did not get the chance to enjoy the festival, we had to help on the farms, look after cattle and so on. Only those who lived near the monastery saw anything of what was going on, the horse and yak races, the archery competitions. The People's Militia had organised target practice contests, inter-district song-and-dance competitions. And the Chinese government stalls were selling rare commodities like sugar or matches which we normally never saw. Anyone who had any money to spare rushed to buy as much sugar etc as they could, before supplies ran out again.'

The festivities over, the workers returned – to another base-camp, another stretch of river, another losing struggle against despair.

Moving their campsite yet again, they eventually arrived at a place called Dranbu, where they were divided into different units, and discovered to their horror that the workload was to be increased still further. 'Our daily quotas were impossible to fulfil, and the casualty list was high. Do you remember I told you about Buchung who died after being crushed by rubble when we were building the power station. His companion, Pasang, who'd also been buried under the rubble, survived. But when we were building the dykes, Pasang's luck ran out. He was working with explosives, and one day he was blown up by his own detonator, his body blown to pieces all over the hillside. He wasn't the only one: two other colleagues were blown up during dynamiting. The Chinese simply didn't care, as long as the work got done and we didn't lose any donkeys.'

One day in 1979, the Chinese officials summoned all the workers of the region to an annual general meeting. 'We all had to go to this meeting, where the official in charge of the Gyantse, Shigatse and Panam workforce addressed us. His speech was short and to the point. He said the Gyantse workers had got a lot of work done by getting up early in the morning and going to bed late at night. (As if we'd had any choice!) He said he was very pleased with us. However, he said, from now onwards every single one of us was going to have to work twice as hard as before. To show how much he appreciated us, the official gave out prizes to the different village units within the Gyantse area. The unit which had completed its quotas quicker than anyone else was given a poster representing an aeroplane! Second prize was a picture of a train, the third one of a car. Next a horse and cart. My own unit came last, so the leader of our group was solemnly presented with the picture of – a donkey!'

But his words about doubling the workload were not intended as a joke. 'From then on they really did double it and we were expected to work twice as hard. Many of our team got dislocated shoulders, bruised and lacerated backs, sprained joints, broken legs and arms. Almost all of us had terrible open sores on our backs through carrying huge rocks from one place to another. It really was beyond human endurance.'

But some kind of hope was in sight. In March 1979 the Dalai Lama had suggested sending a few exploratory missions into Tibet, to re-establish contact with the people and assess their living conditions. The delegations, he insisted, must be allowed to go where they chose and speak to whomever they wanted. Peking had agreed. Throughout Tibet, food rationing was eased slightly, a few communes were privatised again, pilgrims were allowed back into Lhasa and many more long-term political prisoners were released. Individual Tibetans were to be allowed to visit as well as correspond with their relatives in India (provided they left their families behind as hostages). And for the first time in twenty years, Tibetan exiles would be able to visit their homeland.

In October 1979 the first of the Dalai Lama's delegations arrived in Tibet.

CHAPTER 10

Visitors

Whenever we asked people what had happened since the revolt, they would just start crying. Then, after composing themselves, they'd reply, 'Our country has nothing now. Everything is finished. But . . . our spirit is strong. As long as His Holiness is not in the hands of the Chinese, we have hope.'

Lobsang Samten, elder brother of the Dalai Lama,
on his return from Tibet in 1981

The authorities in Peking were due for a shock. They appear to have swallowed their own propaganda about Tibet and did not doubt that the delegates from India would be impressed by the progress they had brought to the country. Quite clearly the top officials on the spot had deliberately misled them about the true state of affairs, and Peking was only now about to discover that after over twenty years of attempted mind-bending, the

145

Tibetans still resented and feared their Chinese masters and loved the Dalai Lama.

For the Tibetan people the time when the delegations came from India was one of revelation and catharsis, of fierce joy and the release of long pent-up tears. Though Emme-la and his fellow-sufferers on the dyke-building project were not allowed to go and greet the first delegation, they heard all about the visit from friends and family. 'One day in 1979, everyone was summoned to a meeting. Normally the person in charge of such meetings looked very fierce and bullied everyone in sight, especially those who came into the "class enemy" categories. But on that occasion, he was apparently all smiles and charm, even with the class enemies. He told them they would soon be seeing delegations sent from India by the Dalai Lama, and if they were asked any questions about their lives, they should answer honestly, with pride and dignity and confidence in the legacy of Chairman Mao. At the same time, he warned them not to come too close to the delegation members. Shortly afterwards, they were all sent off to do some quick restoration work at the monastery they'd previously been ordered to destroy.'

In August, the first delegation, which included the Dalai Lama's elder brother Lobsang Samten, arrived in Amdo in the north-eastern area of Tibet. Wherever they went, they were mobbed by tens of thousands of ragged, hungry-looking Tibetans, seeking to touch them, hear their voices, speak to them, make sure they were real, seek pictures of the Dalai Lama. The crowd came pouring over the hills, stretching away as far as the eye could see, scenes, according to one eye-witness, that recalled a Hollywood biblical epic. 'Everywhere people were shouting, throwing scarves, apples and flowers,' recounted Lobsang Samten.[1] 'They broke the windows of all the cars. They climbed on the roofs and pushed inside, stretching out their hands to touch us. The Chinese were screaming, "Don't go out! They'll kill you!" All of the Tibetans were weeping, calling, "How is the Dalai Lama? How is His Holiness?" ' The visitors were stunned by their reception and greatly distressed by the sight of all these hungry and frantic people. In spite of which, their Chinese escort kept up a relentless chorus of propaganda about how much better things were now, just look at all those happy people.

By the time the party had left Amdo and were on their way to central Tibet, the official version put out on Radio Lhasa proclaimed that the Amdowas, unable to conceal their hatred of the old serf-owners, had pelted them with dirt and stones. But notwithstanding such wishful twisting of the facts, the authorities in Amdo felt obliged to warn their Lhasa counterparts of possible trouble coming their way. The Lhasa officials assured their provincial colleagues that they were quite capable of dealing with any difficulties that might arise. As the visitors approached, the people were sent out to spruce up the city, told to put on their best clothes – women were actually given ribbons to put in their hair – and remember to speak only when spoken to.

That first morning in Lhasa, 17,000 Tibetans stormed the Jokhang Cathedral where the visitors had gone to worship. They broke open the gates, trampled on the Chinese security guards and mobbed the delegates in a frenzy of longing and grief.

Despite threats and warnings from on high, even more took to the streets next day, and the authorities were powerless in the face of such numbers. However, as the group left Lhasa and approached the towns of Shigatse, Sakya and Gyantse, the local people were hastily assigned work in the fields to keep them busy for the duration of the visit. The Chinese had learned something from the events in Lhasa. 'They had seen the tears of joy and misery with which the people had greeted the delegation,' says Emme-la, 'and they had decided that from now on the people must be kept out of the way. What shocked them more than anything was that the Patriotic Groups of Tibetan Communists were just as enthusiastic about the visitors as everyone else – instead of showing disgust, they were showering the Dalai Lama's representatives with affection and respect. The Chinese couldn't understand it at all.'

Emme-la was disappointed not to have been allowed back to Gyantse to welcome the delegation, but he was happy that they had come at all. 'We learned later on from our friends in the Gyantse area that everyone had been inspired and encouraged by the visit. They had been really thrilled to see Lobsang Samten, and the latter had got up at the crack of dawn every morning to meet as many Tibetans as possible before they were sent off to work in the fields. I can't tell you what a psychological boost it was to us all. We felt as if we were coming alive for the first time. The whole of life acquired more savour just because His Holiness had sent these people to visit us. Before that there was a horrible sameness to everything, our food, our work, our sleep, everything. We functioned like robots. But the delegations changed all that. When they came, we felt a huge upsurge of morale. People even began singing while they worked.'

Emme-la was in desperate need of such a boost to morale. The ever-increasing workload was threatening to destroy him. His back and shoulders were livid with cuts and bruises, and the starvation diet and freezing conditions had caused a serious infection in his lungs. When eventually he became so weak that he was sent back to Gyantse for a check-up, chest x-rays revealed two small punctures in his lungs, for which medical treatment was prescribed. Permission for the treatment to be carried out was, of course, quite another matter. Emme-la returned to his unit without much hope. First of all he saw the head of his work brigade, who 'said that if Phuntsog, his deputy and my immediate boss, agreed to my returning home for the treatment, then he would raise no objection, but he wouldn't give me permission directly. So then I went to Phuntsog and told him his boss had no objections. "Well," he said, "if the boss has no objection, then I suppose I'll have to agree." '

On this dubious basis, Emme-la gained temporary release from the dyke-building and on 8 March 1980 returned home to his village. 'I was treated at the Gyantse hospital for the holes in my lung, and I stayed for a time with my mother and later with my married older sister. I even managed to stay a few days with other relations. As I hadn't really got official leave of absence, I had to lie low, keeping well clear of the authorities, though in fact conditions were becoming much more relaxed since the delegation's visit. The Chinese seemed to have lost a lot of confidence and were anxious about their own future in Tibet. Even the Tibetans who were working for them were sick with worry. I took full advantage of their confusion. We all did.'

A second delegation was on its way, and the Chinese were running around in circles. Learning that this group was to consist entirely of bright young men (specially chosen to demonstrate that the Tibetans had flourished in exile and that their cause was not just one espoused by elderly reactionaries), they forgot that the delegates were supposed to be honoured guests and hysterically denounced them as 'agents of the Dalai's false government'. In the face of this new unknown danger, fresh instructions had to be given to the populace. Pamphlets were issued, covering all possible correct answers to all possible questions, and a crash course in revised Tibetan history (i.e., Tibet as an integral part of China) was hastily given to the Party cadres. Ordinary Tibetans were instructed to have nothing whatsoever to do with the delegates. 'If they were encountered by accident, the people were not to smile, cry, shake hands, stand up if seated, remove their hats, offer scarves or invite them to their homes.'[2]

In the midst of these increasingly dislocated preparations, Hu Yao-bang, General Secretary of the Chinese Communist Party, arrived in Tibet to celebrate the twenty-ninth anniversary of the (in Tibetan eyes, defunct) 1951 Seventeen-Point Agreement. His visit was intended to underline the start of a new era in Sino-Tibetan relations. Hu was almost as shocked by what he saw as the delegation had been. He expressed horror at the obscene poverty in which the Tibetans were living, and apologised for Chinese excesses, wondering publicly if all the money sent from Peking for improvements in Tibet had been 'thrown into the Yarlung Tsangpo'. He even famously exclaimed: 'But this is plain colonialism.' Someone had some explaining to do. Appalled by the way a handful of unreconstructed Maoists had turned Tibetans into outcasts in their own land, Hu sacked the culprits, replacing them with more moderate, pragmatic men, and bringing in a programme intended to improve the living standards, social conditions and basic freedom of the Tibetans.

One of Hu Yao-bang's officials put in an appearance in Gyantse, at the June festival, and Emme-la heard him in near-disbelief. 'He actually stood there and admitted that due to the mistaken policies of the Gang of Four, we Tibetans had been forced to endure great suffering. He said he'd been sent, along with other officials from the Central Government to check on our welfare. From now onwards, he assured us, poor Tibetans would become rich Tibetans, their level of education must be raised, a new Tibet must be constructed. Then he read out a policy statement called Six Major and Eight Minor Policies for Tibet. These meant that over a three-year period there would be greater leniency in the collection of taxes from Tibetan farmers and nomads. And that would definitely help to lighten the load.' As a token of better times to come, a few shops and chang bars were allowed to open, and market stalls began selling a little (a very little) produce.

And in July came the second delegation. These tough, Western-educated thirty-somethings had also come through eastern Tibet and had been greeted by the same emotional outpourings as their predecessors. Everywhere they went they had been mobbed by Tibetans weeping tears of anguish and frustrated longing.

When they came to Gyantse, this time Emme-la was there. 'The Han did their best to keep the delegates away from us. They warned us not to show any deference to the visitors, reminding us that if we did so we would be punished for it later. They brought in units of the People's Militia[3] to keep us apart, but they were useless – right then no one was afraid either of the Militia or the Han authorities. Many people were choked by tears and sobs, but it was clear they felt that for the first time since the Chinese occupation there was someone who cared about them, they understood that they had not been abandoned. That was true not just for the older people but for the younger ones too, even the children, some of whom had hardly even heard of His Holiness before. They were just as carried away as the older ones.'

The usual set-piece visits had been arranged: to the carpet factory and the primary school. (There were, in fact, two other schools, a middle school and an agricultural school for the younger (teens and twenties) workers of farming and nomad communities. But as these were run down and in no fit state to receive visitors, their students were simply locked in for the duration of the delegates' stay.) 'They also visited a farming commune about two hours' walk from our village. Before they arrived, the authorities did what they always did when important visitors arrived: they made sure that all the families – except for one – were out working in the fields. They locked up all the houses, apart from this one which had been specially done up for the occasion, its occupants carefully primed. When the delegates entered, they found a well-furnished house, freshly decorated, with new radios and thermos flasks and plentifully stocked with food. We learned all about it afterwards from the other families in the commune. Of course, as soon as the visitors had gone, officials came and took the furniture and food away again!'

During such carefully stage-managed occasions, the Militias succeeded in keeping people away from the delegates. But it was different when they visited the monastery, which was currently in use as a storehouse for grain and animal fodder. The Tibetans had been sent to tidy up this area and make it presentable. 'It was there that people managed to get close to them and talk to them. Everyone flocked there, everyone wanted to get as close as possible to the delegates, to touch them or just be in their presence. More and more people kept coming, even those who'd been afraid to turn out for the first delegation, had summoned up the courage to turn out now.'

Tenzin Tethong, the Dalai Lama's Representative in New York, led the second delegation. Emme-la was in the crowd with a group of his friends when they arrived. 'Tenzin Tethong told us that His Holiness had sent them to Tibet to bring us his greetings (and those of the other Tibetan exiles) and to say he never for one moment forgot us. He wanted to know what our lives were like under the Chinese, and said that from India he was working hard for our welfare. This news made us all very happy. He went on to tell us about the Tibetan government-in-exile, which we hadn't really known existed. We were excited to learn that His Holiness was well and to hear about his government in Dharamsala,[4] but we didn't take it all in because we just broke down in tears. The delegates themselves were all weeping.'

Flouting explicit Chinese instructions on this subject, everyone clamoured for photographs of the Dalai Lama. 'The delegates didn't have any with them just then, but promised to hand out pictures and mementoes that evening at the guest house where they were staying. So later on we all turned up there, only to find that the authorities had locked the gates to keep us out. But we refused to budge. We just stayed there until they let the delegates out to see us. When they came, they brought pictures of His Holiness, sacred pills and protective cords blessed by lamas and which we like to wear around our necks. We were so very happy, although the Chinese had told us in advance not to receive any photographs from these "dangerous counter-revolutionaries". They had instructed us that if the question of Tibetan Independence came up, we were to say firmly that Tibet had always been part of China, and leave it at that. Well, that night we broke all the rules, we talked to the delegates, we showed our feelings for them, we accepted the photographs they brought with rapture, and although we dared not shout openly for a free Tibet, our feelings on that subject were pretty obvious. We threw caution to the winds, even though some of our friends who worked for the government had warned us that the Chinese were drawing up a blacklist of those who had disobeyed their instructions.

'The People's Militia had been sent out in force, but most of them were as enthusiastic about the visitors as the rest of us. They received the full impact of the speeches, as they were in the front row. One young chap, Namgyal, came from the lowest – i.e., best – class and was known to be an active progressive. As a member of the local Militia, he was one of the few Tibetans the Chinese felt they could really trust. However, when the photographs of the Dalai Lama were being handed out, he was one of the first to grab one.'

The second delegation, whose educated and articulate young men were not at all the sort of Tibetans the Chinese were used to dealing with, had its visit cut short and was packed off home in disgrace. The trouble started when they visited the ruins of Ganden Monastery outside Lhasa, once one of the jewels in the Tibetan Buddhist crown, partially destroyed after 1959, and dismantled stone by stone during the Cultural Revolution. Where over a hundred buildings had once stood, only jagged ruins remained. It was a heart-rending sight. 'It looks,' said a dazed Tenzin Tethong, 'as though it was destroyed five hundred years ago, not twelve.' Then a crowd of over five thousand people rushed towards them. 'Everyone came running down the hill, crying and calling out,' Tenzin Tethong said later. 'I remember a few young boys and girls, teen-agers, grabbing on to my jacket. They were practically howling in tears and refused to let go. People beside them were saying, "Please, you mustn't cry so much," but then they started crying as well, pointing up the hill and saying, "Look, there is our Ganden. See what they've done to it." '[5] Emotions boiled over, cries of "Independence for Tibet" were heard. Next day, outside Guest House No. 2 in Lhasa the exiles, unable to restrain their pent-up feelings any longer, made impassioned speeches to the crowd, who, likewise throwing discre-tion overboard, burst into cries of 'Long live the Dalai Lama' and raised clenched fists in support of Tibetan independence. To the Chinese this was the last straw, and they expelled the visitors forthwith. 'By your actions,' they said indignantly, 'you have deliberately incited the Tibetan people to break with the Motherland and to sever their ties with their elder brothers, the Han Chinese. This amounts to a grave breach in relations between the Dalai and Peking and will not be tolerated.' The delegates were first locked in their rooms, then bundled unceremoniously out of Lhasa – and out of Tibet.

In Gyantse, Emme-la found that the top-ranking Chinese officials were by now very confused indeed. 'They didn't know what was what or which way the wind was going to blow next. In the present climate, anything could happen.'

The third delegation, a group of senior educationists led by the Dalai Lama's sister Jetsun Pema, had already left India and could not be stopped. 'We were already in Nagchuka when we heard that the second delegation had been expelled,' says Rapten Chazotsang, a member of this third group. 'We considered giving up, but the Chinese were actually begging us to continue (though that didn't prevent them showing us considerable hostility). When we reached Shigatse, we sent a cable to Dharamsala, and after three or four days we received our orders to continue. It was while we were waiting for the reply that we decided to pay an unscheduled visit to Gyantse.'

On 28 July, after the second delegation had been thrown out, and nervous of the possible impact of yet another visitation, the local police chief had summoned the people of Gyantse to a meeting. It was carrot-and-stick time with a vengeance. 'He handed out gifts, grain to some, money to others. He said these were gifts from the Chinese Communist Party and everybody ought to be very grateful always to the Party. He warned us that on no account were we to go up to the monastery and waste the money he'd given us on donations for butter lamps. We were in fact to stay at home when the delegation came: we were not to leave our houses and hang around the streets, we might get knocked over by the traffic! Then he came to the real reason why he'd called the meeting: he had accompanied the second delegation round Gyantse, he said, and had been disgusted to see so many of the town's trusty citizens, the bedrock of China's support, up there doing prostrations to the visitors from India. It had been quite an eye-opener to him, he said ominously, implying that those trusty citizens might not be considered quite so trusty in the future. He pointed to Namgyal, the militiaman who'd been the first to receive a picture of the Dalai Lama. "You," he shouted, "a young Communist and a supposed progressive, a privileged member of the people's Militia, you are an utter disgrace, you set a dreadful example to others by your behaviour." Unless Namgyal gave back the Dalai Lama's picture, he spluttered, he would not only receive no cash or grain presents but would lose all his privileges. "And all you others," he said grimly, "you'd do well to remember that the Communist Party has just made you a handsome gift of money and grain. What use do you think a picture of the Dalai Lama is to you? It's not going to feed or clothe you. Go on, try it, put the Dalai Lama's picture on your heads and ask it to feed and clothe you. What a hope! And what a lot of idiots you are!" '

But if their bosses were running scared, the lower-ranking cadres like Namgyal felt able to take more chances. Namgyal refused to hand over his precious picture, and at that time the police chief could do no more than bluster. Banging his fists on the table a number of times, he shouted that a lot of young Tibetans were becoming too big for their boots because the Chinese authorities had been too soft with them. 'He said that if people like Namgyal didn't watch out, they'd end up in prison, just like the monks and other reactionaries after 1959. China was more powerful now than it had been then, he warned, it would be the work of a moment to crush a handful of undisciplined hooligans. He was really furious. The fact is these officials really didn't know what had hit them, and we were able to get away with behaviour which earlier (and unfortunately also later) would have been considered criminal. Right then they didn't know how to handle us.'

A few days after the visit of the police chief, the new First Secretary of the Chinese Communist Party in Tibet, Yin Fa-tang, came to Gyantse. Hu Yao-bang had taken the old one, Ren Rong, back to China with him, in disgrace. Yin Fa-tang was the new supremo and he had come to get the people of Gyantse on his side. 'He told us that he knew Gyantse well,' says Emme-la. 'He reminded us that he had arrived by road from Lhasa in

October 1951 as one of the highest-ranking officials of the PLA's 52nd Division, and had stayed to become the officer in charge of the Gyantse area. We listened to him in silence. Of course, the older ones among us remembered him all too well, and we younger ones knew him by reputation. It seemed to have slipped his memory (but none of the Tibetans present had forgotten) that it was he who had robbed us of all that emergency aid sent from India after the great flood in 1954. He seemed quite confident that we'd be pleased to see him again, recalling that in those far-off days when he'd been in charge, Tibetans had been happy and well-off! Then because of the evil policies of the Gang of Four and officials like Ren Rong, he said, people in Gyantse had undergone much unnecessary suffering. But now he was back everything would be all right again.

'He really expected us to be taken in by this rubbish. The Chinese have an amazing attitude to their own propaganda: they think that if they repeat their lies often enough, everyone will end up believing them. Probably they themselves do end up believing the lies. But of course we were quite unimpressed.'

The third delegation, led by Jetsun Pema, arrived in Gyantse on 14 August 1980, and despite the threats, bribes and blandishments, huge crowds turned out to greet them. 'It was really quite remarkable that all of us younger people, even the children, who had never received any religious education at all, knew instinctively how to make prostrations. And everyone, young and old, was desperate to have a picture of the Dalai Lama. We were particularly keen to meet Mrs Jetsun Pema because she was His Holiness's sister. There were so many who wanted to shake her hand, she was shaking hands with both hands at once, while some of the people were catching hold of her apron and touching it to their foreheads. Her dress was so decent and simple, and she seemed so kindhearted and full of compassion. She brought peace of mind to everyone she met. I thought she was wonderful. Of course, all the time the Chinese kept up a stream of warnings about not talking to the delegates. In fact I made a list of all the things they had told us not to do, and I handed my notes to Rapten Chazotsang, another of the delegates.'

Rapten, like the other members of the delegation, was heartily sick of the relentless orchestration of their visit. 'Whenever we reached any town or village, the Chinese would first summon the local Tibetan officials,' he recalls. 'And we would have to listen to them going on and on about how in the bad old days they had nothing at all, but now they had land under cultivation, animals, tools and so on. So much nonsense – we only had to look around to see how things really were. We used to get mad at them and get into fierce arguments, while the Chinese just stood around and laughed at us all. Then we realised that this was what they wanted from us, they were enjoying watching Tibetans at each other's throats. So then we decided to hold our tongues and not to play their game any more. After all, we knew that the Tibetan officials had no choice but to say whatever the Chinese had ordered them to say.'

He remembers Gyantse – and even Emme-la. 'In both Shigatse and Gyantse, and in Phari too, the people turned out in droves, but, compared with people elsewhere, they were very frightened,' he says.[6] 'Most of them wouldn't approach us, and when we got near them, they would run away. But a few were brave enough to invite us to their homes and give us a list of their dead, for whom they wanted prayers said. Lots of them gave us messages to take back. And there was this young man who was very persistent, tagging along wherever we went. I remember he gave me a written description of all the difficulties he had had with the Chinese, and asked me to assure the Dalai Lama of his undying loyalty.'

The third delegation, like its predecessors, returned to Dharamsala with a mind-numbing report on their com-patriots' fate, backed up by about eight hours of moving documentary film. All those who saw the filmed material wept. But under pressure from China (and unwilling to jeopardise this first possibility of a rap-prochement), the government-in-exile made a conscious decision not to publicise the findings. But all three reports had been damning. China's thirty-year occupa-tion, they concluded, had been disastrous for Tibet. One fifth of the population had starved to death or been murdered; almost all the monasteries and nunneries in the country had been destroyed, their contents smashed, melted down, trodden underfoot, or sold for foreign currency; one in every ten Tibetans was in prison and 100,000 had disappeared into the *lao gai*, the dreaded reform-through-labour camps, while north-eastern Tibet (Amdo) had become the world's biggest gulag, with the reputed capacity to intern 10 million prisoners. Entire mountains had been denuded of their forests and Tibet's unique wildlife had been virtually wiped out.[7] In a privately published pamphlet which conceded nothing to political expediency, an anguished Jetsun Pema confessed that it was impossible to find words to convey the horror of what she had seen and heard: 'Parents had to witness their children being murdered, and if they failed to smile and clap and thank the Chinese for killing their own children, they too would be condemned.' She had spoken to a mother who had made soup from her own blood to keep her children from starving and such things were not unique. 'It was far worse than any of us had expected. When I saw those emaciated bodies and heard their tales of suffering, there was no way to hold back my tears. Throughout our stay in Tibet, most of us were crying most of the time.'[8]

It would be years before any of the delegates recovered from the trauma of the experience. Lobsang Samten, the Dalai Lama's brother and companion of his youth, never did. On his return to India this once jovial man lost all his enthusiasm for life and sank into a melancholia from which he did not revive. When he died a few years later at the age of forty-nine, the Dalai Lama was in no doubt that it was from a broken heart: 'Lobsang simply couldn't understand how the Chinese could be so indifferent to the sufferings they had caused in Tibet.'[9]

CHAPTER 11

Escape from Tibet

The Chinese are sweet talkers and when there is no choice a man will clutch at straws. So for many years I tried to believe their promises. I did what they ordered – even took part in the destruction of religious objects. It would not have done much good to have done otherwise. To the Chinese, if one is not for them, then they regard you as being against them – an enemy to be put down.

Dondhub Choedon, former Tibetan activist,
who later fled to India

Enough was enough. The fourth delegation – consisting of high-ranking lamas – was already on its way. But it was stopped in its tracks while still in east Tibet. This hasty Chinese attempt to stop the rot, however, was already too late: the galvanising effect of the first three groups on the Tibetans cannot be exaggerated. 'They did us a lot of good. We learned from them that the Dalai Lama was alive and well in India, that he hadn't forgotten us and was doing what he could for us in exile. We found out what we hadn't known before, that he had set up a government in a place called Dharamsala, and that they all wanted to help us too. So although we were still under the Chinese and there wasn't much immediate improvement, our self-confidence had been given a real boost.

'In fact, there *were* some improvements. After over twenty years, some of the long-term prisoners were being released, though I think the Chinese had originally intended to keep them locked up for ever. We were allowed to travel short distances outside our villages – travel outside of a ten-mile radius, however, still required a permit. Our workload was slightly reduced and we were allowed to recite Buddhist mantras again. Tibetan dress was brought back, and we were able to drink our tea out of our old wooden bowls again, instead of using those enamel mugs the Chinese insisted on. It was wonderful!'

Emme-la knew, however, that he was now a marked man, and that, even in the present more relaxed atmosphere, his life was in danger. He had been on the Chinese blacklist ever since the second delegation had arrived. 'Before that list was drawn up, my friends and I were regarded as harmless characters who had no need of special surveillance. But once we were put on that blacklist, everything changed. After that, we were followed everywhere by spies who noted everything we did, where we went, who we met, how often and for how long we talked to them, and so on. It was nerve-racking.'

Friends in the know warned that his arrest was only a matter of time – he had been filmed on video camera welcoming the delegations and receiving a picture of the Dalai Lama. Accordingly, he kept as low a profile as he could, and dutifully turned up to help with his commune's harvest in September. 'I was aware that the authorities were watching my every movement. It was only because they still didn't know which way the wind was blowing that they didn't arrest me straight away or send me back to the river and the dykes. But it would not be long before they pounced.

'Why should I let them send me back to the river where I would almost certainly die? For the first time, I thought about escaping rather than continue to live under Chinese rule. I thought of how they'd refused to give me an education, how they'd deprived us Tibetans of our freedom, particularly our freedom to be good Buddhists, how they'd tortured and killed so many of my friends, imprisoned us in fear and misery and driven my father to a premature death. I was twenty-four, condemned to an inhuman slave-labour which would finish by killing me. What had I done, what had any of us done to deserve such a terrible fate?

'I felt in my heart that we Tibetans ought to rise up and drive the oppressors out of our land in order to reclaim our birthright. But how could we do that unless we were living in a country that was free? Anyway, I knew something now that I hadn't known before, that there was a free Tibetan community flourishing in India. Suddenly I made up my mind – I would do everything in my power to join them.'

It was October, that pleasant time of year before the arctic chill of winter sets in. After the harvest had come the threshing. Beating the grain with wooden sticks to get rid of the husks, Emme-la laid his secret plans. The recent easing of travel restrictions made it possible now to visit a relation some distance away, to undertake a pilgrimage or make a business trip. Travel permits for such activities did not even require a photograph – just the name and, of course, the class, of the person. There were those in the village who knew the secret escape routes over the mountain passes, others who had 'connections' and could get permits for the border areas, others still who could provide false documents.

Pilgrims from Kham and Amdo were once again flocking to the shrines of central Tibet, and many of them came to Gyantse. One of these, a man from Amdo called Lobsang Tsultrim, made no secret of the fact that he wanted to get to India, to seek an audience with the Dalai Lama. Emme-la's friends suggested that he and Lobsang Tsultrim should team up.

So the final preparations began in earnest. Emme-la obtained a permit to travel to a village near the border, 'to buy a sheep for the commune and to get married'. Saying nothing to his mother, on the grounds that the less she knew about his escape the safer she would be, Emme-la invested everything he possessed in a pair of stout walking-boots, about 10 kilos of tsampa, a little butter and an emergency ration of chocolate, and hid them in a barn. A date was fixed, 10 October, and then there was nothing to do but wait.

The threshers usually spent the night guarding the crop from marauders, and drank their early-morning tea in the fields. 'But when I awoke on the 10th, the fields were all covered with ground frost as far as the eye could see. I decided to do without the early tea and make my way home. As I approached my house, I could see my mother milking the cows. She waved to me and asked if anything was the matter. I just waved back and assured her I was fine. I went into the house, drank some tea, put on warm cotton underclothes underneath my chuba, with a Tibetan jacket on top made of warm nambu wool. (Years ago, my mother had woven it for me.) Then I went to the barn and put the emergency rations into a small carrier bag. Nothing more. I waved to my mother as casually as I could and walked off. My emotions were in turmoil. My journey out of Tibet was beginning.

'Lobsang Tsultrim and I had arranged to meet at a crossroads where three roads met, one leading to Lhasa, a second to Shigatse and the third going towards Bhutan. Like me, he carried nothing but a small carrier bag with food in it. We did not greet each other, just began walking very casually along the road towards Phari and Dromo. We had decided to travel by day to avoid arousing suspicions – we didn't have watches, but it must have been about ten in the morning. When a group of Tibetans asked us where we were going, we said we were going to the border to buy some sheep for our commune.'

After walking along this rather exposed dusty road for about three hours, they branched off with relief onto a small footpath which at first ran almost parallel to it, but eventually led up into a narrow chain of ice-mountains which formed part of the high Himalaya. Here on this secluded path there was no further danger of Chinese checkpoints.

Three days of hard walking later, they reached a valley hemmed in by vast mountains. In the summer months, it was frequented by shepherds and by boys and girls herding cows, but by October it was already deserted. 'By now, it was evening and there was no one around to tell us the way. We knew that the border between Tibet and Bhutan lay at the summit of Nyingshi La, one of the mountains that rose from this valley. But which one *was* Nyingshi La and how were we going to find out? We searched for the footpath, but there had been a heavy snowfall and we couldn't find it. We wandered off in every conceivable direction hoping to find the path, but in vain. Hours passed and we began to lose hope, even to feel that we'd have to turn back. Then all of a sudden we spotted an empty tin can and in a flash our despair changed to hope. Someone else had obviously been here before us – that tin can was proof that we were on some sort of track. We began climbing with renewed energy, hoping against hope that we were indeed on the Nyingshi La.

'We climbed for three days, sometimes by day, sometimes by night. We slept in the snow without coverings, but at least our clothes were warm. For food we had tsampa mixed with water and a little butter, and some chocolate to revive our flagging energy. As we went higher, the snow grew deeper and before long we were waist deep in it. Still we trudged on. When suddenly we caught sight of some huge mounds of stones and bamboo poles, we realised that at last we'd reached the top of the pass. A few months earlier, there would have been Chinese guards up here, but the passes were thought to be impenetrable in winter and they had gone. We'd hoped to find them gone, but were taking no chances: I had with me a metal tube packed with explosive, and a detonator hidden in the flap of my Chinese cap. If the guards had been there, I'd have bitten off the end of the tube and hurled it. It would have blown us all up.'

The two stood on the top of the pass and looked around, scarcely daring to believe the evidence of their eyes. 'We could see Bhutan to the south, lush, green, fertile, covered with low cloud; and to the north, behind us, Tibet, stark and forbidding but beautiful beyond description. My own country. I felt a stab of anguish as the moment of final decision approached. So many conflicting emotions. I thought again, for the thousandth time, of the reasons that had driven me to this moment. None of my ancestors had harmed the Chinese in any way, and neither had I done anything to hurt them. So why, why, why had the Chinese taken over my life and made it unbearable for me to live in my own country? They had taken everything from me: my education, my religion, my freedom as a human being, my pride in being Tibetan, everything. On the other hand, this *was* my country and I loved it. I was saying goodbye not only to family and friends and workmates but to a beloved and beautiful land. Maybe I would never see any of them again. The same thoughts were almost certainly running through Lobsang Tsultrim's mind. We looked at each other and made a silent prayer. I prayed that I would see my loved ones again and that one day I would return to a Tibet that was both free and independent. I prayed a long-life prayer for all the people I had known in Tibet, including those who had worked with me in the forced labour gangs.

'Then a sense of exhilaration took over. I was wearing one of those Chinese peaked caps that the People's Liberation Army wear. I tore it from my head, hurled it into the void below and laughed out loud.

'At sunrise we began our descent towards freedom.'

Chapter 12

In the Land of the Thunder Dragon

Bhutan, dwarfed by its great neighbours, India and Tibet, and only one-third the size of Nepal, is none-theless ... slightly larger than Switzerland. Its official name, Druk-yul, means 'Land of the Thunder Dragon', the emblem portrayed on its national flag.

Tibet Handbook, with Bhutan[1]

The die had been cast. There were no more familiar landmarks now.

'As Lobsang and I climbed down into Bhutan, while we were still above the tree line, we were surprised to see a large group of bharal, the wild "blue sheep" (a protected species in Bhutan) which had been a familiar sight in Tibet before the Chinese came. We were amazed to see them roaming free on the hillside along with yaks and other wildlife, because in Tibet the Chinese had shot most of the wildlife as food for themselves – or just for sport. Even the fish in the small lakes had become extinct as a result of their activities. So, our first impression of Bhutan was an encouraging one. We felt that in this country not only were human beings free, but wild creatures too. You can't imagine what a shock that was to someone who'd spent his entire life under the Chinese occupation.

'As we went on down into the valleys, we came into a different world of trees and shrubs. The high alpine juniper and edelweiss gave way to beautiful birch, pine, bamboo and rhododendron forests. Suddenly we identified a footprint on the small footpath we were following. It would disappear for a few yards, then come back again. Tracking it carefully, we came to our first Bhutanese village, Nyingshi, called after the mountain we had just crossed.

'It was about noon when we got there, and all the people were busy getting in the harvest. They had no problem with understanding us and were very friendly. Some of them had often visited Tibet on trading trips before the Chinese occupation and still spoke a little Tibetan. But they had bad news for us. The Bhutanese government had recently ordered them not to give shelter to any refugees escaping from Tibet and they would have to turn us in.

'They saw the horror on our faces and went on to explain that apparently, several years earlier, there had been a big row between the Bhutanese Royal Family and the Tibetan government-in-exile.'

It seems that the third King of Bhutan, Jigme Dorje Wangchuk, had kept an extraordinarily beautiful Tibetan mistress by whom he had a son. He also had a legitimate son by his wife, Ashi Kelsang, and this boy was, naturally, the heir to the throne. The mistress, however, wanted to put her own son on the throne and was scheming to that end. When the King died in 1972, trouble broke out. The Queen, Ashi Kelsang, with the support of one of her uncles, took firm steps to thwart her rival and secure the succession for the rightful heir. Two years later, realising that the game was up, the Tibetan woman fled across the border to India. Inevitably, the shock-waves from this saga spread throughout Bhutan, and – perhaps also inevitably – the worst effects were visited on the Tibetan refugees who had settled there after the Chinese invasion of their country. Since the Tibetan mistress had concerned herself with their welfare, they became the unwitting scapegoats for Ashi Kelsang's wrath.

'After the Tibetan mistress fled, the Bhutanese authorities shut down the Welfare Office which the Tibetan government-in-exile had opened, arresting the officer in charge and several members of his staff. They refused to allow their relatives to visit them, not even telling the families where the officials were being held. (Later, we heard that the Head of the Tibet Office and five or six other Tibetans had died in a Bhutanese jail, in very suspicious circumstances.) About thirty other Tibetans were arrested, and severe restrictions were imposed on all the Tibetan settlers. Worse still, they began to dismantle the settlements, sending every second family to another village, so that the Tibetans would simply be absorbed into the host community and become Bhutanese. They were told to cut all links with the Tibetan Administration in India and in future to follow Bhutanese customs and dress in the Bhutanese style. Their children were discouraged from studying the Tibetan culture and language and banned from going to India for further studies.'[2]

'You can imagine how upset we were when we heard all this. In fact we could scarcely believe it because we'd always thought of the Bhutanese as being closely related to us, not only through our common religion and culture but ethnically as well. It was a real blow to our hopes, and we felt that our new life was getting off to a depressing start. The villagers brought food and drink for us in the field, but as soon as we'd all eaten what was by our standards a feast, they had no option but to hand us over to the authorities. Two of the village children came to escort us to the local army garrison. In the light of what we'd just heard, we felt very apprehensive. Things were looking bad for us.

'We reached the garrison[3] just before dusk, but the soldiers there did not understand Tibetan and had no idea what to do with us. They did a body search, went through our belongings in a casual sort of way, then gave us supper and invited us to spend the night in their barracks.

'By next morning they had found an interpreter and began interrogating us about the situation in Tibet, why and how we had escaped, what we had intended to do next, and so on. We answered all their questions and said that we didn't want to stay in Bhutan, it was India we wanted to get to, because we hoped for an audience with the Dalai Lama.

'They had a wireless station, so I suppose they relayed all this information to a higher authority. After that we just had to wait till they got further instructions. To while away the time, we helped them collect different herbs used in the making of incense. They chop these shrubs up small and send them to different monasteries in Bhutan. We collected about two full loads of shrubs a day, and the officer in charge of us, a very devout Buddhist, suggested that we should pray while we worked, since the herbs were destined for some of the most sacred monasteries in the country. Praying as we worked – what a change from singing patriotic Chinese songs! But we didn't actually know many prayers.

'It was almost a month later, on 8 November, that a telegram arrived from military headquarters, authorising us to proceed. Two Bhutanese soldiers were sent with us as an escort. A small mountain still separated us from the interior of Bhutan, but after that the way ahead was all downhill. At the foot of the mountain was a clear stream caused by the melting snow on the mountain tops.

'As we didn't have much to carry, we made good progress and early that evening arrived at a transit camp where we spent the night. By now the scenery was changing, the forests becoming thicker and thicker till finally they were so dense that we could scarcely see the sky above our heads. But still we walked on, passing a number of villages on our way.

'Towards evening on 10 November, we arrived at a major army camp where we spent the night before again being interrogated in the morning. This time the officer in charge of the interrogation was of much higher rank than the ones at the first camp. He told us that it was present Bhutanese government policy to return all Tibetan escapees to Tibet. In spite of all we'd been told about the situation, this came as a terrible shock. We told him that he could put us in prison or even kill us if he liked, but there was no way we would let anyone send us back to Tibet. The officer said nothing, just walked out and left us. Shortly afterwards our two escorts returned and said it was time to go.

'We left there with our hearts hammering, unsure whether they were going to escort us towards India – or back to the Tibetan border, where we'd have had to make a run for it. We walked the whole of that day without knowing one way or the other. Towards evening, we arrived at a fort. One of our escorts, Tsering, was from a family that had originally come from a small village near my own, and he understood Tibetan quite well. He told us that this fort had once belonged to the Tibetans, but that some years earlier the Bhutanese had managed to capture it from them in a skirmish. It was now used for storing the soldiers' rations, and beyond it lay a motorable dirt road into the interior of Bhutan. That night we watched as the Bhutanese flag was lowered, and prayed that next day we'd be on that dirt road.

'Luck was with us. To our great relief, at noon on the next day we were put on board an army truck and driven into the interior – towards Lungten phu, the largest army garrison in Bhutan. Here at last our escorts formally handed us over to the authorities, and returned to their own base.

'We were actually rather sad to see them go, as we had grown quite close to them. To Tsering in particular. He had taught us some basic Buddhist prayers, because, having been brought up under Communism, we were almost totally ignorant of Buddhist practice. We were grateful for that, and for another thing too. The two Bhutanese soldiers had had one automatic rifle between them, and quite often they would ask us to take a turn in carrying it, sometimes for two or three hours at a stretch. We were amazed. Either they felt they could trust us implicitly or it simply hadn't occurred to them that we might use the rifle against them and make our escape. Whichever it was, we couldn't imagine a Chinese soldier doing anything like that.'

The usual interrogations followed, but this time they were longer and more exhaustive. The questioning stretched on for forty days, during which Emme-la and his companion were kept in isolation and saw no one. But when it was at last over three officials of the Tibetan Youth Congress were allowed to visit them.

'It was wonderful to see some Tibetans, we were able to give them a first-hand account of the situation in Tibet, which they intended to pass on to their main headquarters in Dharamsala. They were the first Tibetans we had met in a free land – perhaps the crisis with the Bhutanese government was easing now – and they did their best to cheer our lives up, bringing us Tibetan tea, butter and tsampa, and even giving us five rupees each. Later on, other Tibetans came, representing the various settlements in Bhutan; some of their camps were not far from Lungten phu. They showed us so much kindness that I shall never cease to be grateful to them.

'We knew that the Indians (who had also interrogated us) had to check us out thoroughly, to make sure we were bona fide refugees. All that would take time, but we didn't really mind. Even though we were not allowed to go outside the compound, there was plenty for us to do. Mostly we looked after the orchards and gardens around the barracks, and when fresh food supplies arrived, we helped carry and unload them at the storage depots. At other times we cleared paths or swept roads. The great thing was we were freer than we'd been for a long time, and we were actually being treated like human beings. We ate the same food as the soldiers and even though we weren't paid for what we did, at least, compared with what we'd been used to, it was very easy work.

'Besides, Bhutan reminded us of Tibet. Life was slower down in the valleys, the climate was different, but, as we had always supposed, the Bhutanese and the Tibetans had a lot of common interests. For a start, they were keen on archery, just like us. Well, that's putting it mildly: all Bhutanese males, whatever their age or class, are positively addicted to it. They were also very religious, not just the ordinary people but the soldiers too, they were always chanting prayers and reciting texts. Every day there was a time set aside for the reading of scripture. When we told them how the Chinese were doing their best to wipe out Buddhism in Tibet, they became really agitated and upset. They obviously feared that one day the Chinese might decide to invade Bhutan and try to destroy Buddhism there too.'

In the event, Emme-la and Lobsang Tsultrim were interned in Bhutan for a year and four months. They got so used to being there that it came as quite a surprise when one day they were told that they were about to leave for India.

Early in the morning of 6 March 1982, the two of them climbed into a truck with thirty other Tibetan refugees who had been interned in Bhutan. The Indian government gave them free transport, while the Tibetan officials in Bhutan provided food for the journey. Late that same night they arrived in Siliguri in West Bengal and were formally handed over to a group of Tibetan officials waiting to welcome them to Indian soil.

Emme-la's first feeling was 'one of enormous joy. For the first time in my life, my future was in the hands of Tibetan officials, not Chinese. Secondly – I could scarcely believe what I was seeing – a Tibetan flag was flying from the flagpole. And thirdly, we were all completely overwhelmed by the joy of knowing that, after all the waiting, we really were free at last.'

The Tibetans, including the officials and two cooks, were accommodated in four long bamboo-thatched bungalows, specially erected for the refugees by the Department of Home Affairs in Dharamsala. There were loos and running water and to the refugees from Tibet it seemed like a veritable paradise. Alas, they fell to earth with a bump next morning when they awoke to the full impact of the steamy Indian climate. Their arrival had coincided with the onset of the hot season, the kind of damp uncomfortable heat of which they had had no previous experience. To say nothing of mosquitoes, a plague unknown to high-altitude Tibet.

The piped Siliguri water was another nasty shock. 'It had a metallic taste, almost rusty, very different from the spring water in Tibet and Bhutan. All of us found it difficult to get used to. But the difficulties did not spoil our happiness in having reached India. I noticed one strange thing. Tibet is a mountainous country and the sun there seems to rise from the tops of the mountains and set behind them. But Siliguri was flat, and we were astonished to see the sun appearing to rise out of the earth and in the evening set back into it. It was really odd.'

After a rigorous debriefing by the Indian authorities, they were given a Registration Certificate. This document, the clothes he stood up in and a collection of traditional Buddhist prayers given to him in Bhutan, were Emme-la's sole worldly possessions. He cared little, for the days that followed were the happiest he had ever known. 'To our great joy, many local Tibetans as well as those from distant settlements came to see us. Most of them had escaped just before 1959 or soon after, and some of them were from our own villages and towns. Not that I knew any of them personally, they had left Tibet after the 1959 Uprising when I was not much more than a baby. But there was this affinity between us because we came from the same place. I was so very glad to see them.

'Soon after our arrival, the Tibetan official in charge began teaching us the Tibetan national anthem which of course none of us younger ones had ever been allowed to learn in Tibet. We worked very hard at it, especially as the 10 March anniversary of the Lhasa Uprising was coming up and we wanted to be word-perfect by then. Also we spent a lot of time writing posters detailing the Chinese atrocities in Tibet and so on. Some we pasted up on walls all over Siliguri, others we carried ourselves in the 10 March procession.

'On the morning of the anniversary, our spokesman, Gaga, made a speech to the assembled Tibetans and their Indian guests, telling them how much we had suffered in Tibet. Afterwards, when we joined in the procession, we were able to shout slogans to our hearts' content, to shout or say whatever we wanted, in fact. I can't tell you how wonderful it felt: for the first time ever we were able to express our real feelings about the Chinese in public in a free society. We didn't have to mouth slogans to order. It was incredible. That first National Uprising Day on Indian soil was one of the happiest days of my life, and I shall never forget it.'

Later that afternoon, at the railway station at Siliguri, Emme-la saw his first train. 'We had heard about trains in Tibet, but this was the first time we had ever seen one. At first sight it was so much more enormous than I could possibly have imagined that I felt terrified. The sheer size of it, the power of the engines. Incredible. The biggest vehicles we'd ever seen were Chinese armoured trucks, yet every compartment of that train was bigger than a truck. It was pretty overwhelming.'

Even when all thirty-two of them were aboard the train, there was no end to the surprises. 'Our amazement grew as everywhere we stopped, we saw vendors selling food, tea, sweets. The sight was just as astonishing as the train itself. In Tibet, first of all, we had no money for such things, and even if we'd had the money, there'd have been no food to buy. Nothing was available in the towns and villages where we lived. We couldn't believe our eyes when we saw people spending money and being able to buy whatever items of food they wanted. The variety of food was quite staggering.'

At the end of the long journey from Siliguri they came to Dekyi Ling, a Tibetan settlement in Dehra Dun on the edge of the Indian plains. It consisted of assorted pre-fabs specially set up for new arrivals from Tibet and for those who had recently been expelled from Bhutan. After a warm welcome (and a meal) from the Tibetan Women's Association and the Tibetan Youth Congress, they were taken to unfurnished rooms in the pre-fabs, where they were to sleep on the floor.

The warmth of their reception that evening didn't prevent a certain embarrassment next day. 'We were very impressed by the Settlement, and the people were kind to us. But everybody there looked so clean, and we knew they must have found us dirty and unhygienic. We felt like country bumpkins who didn't really fit in. It made us very uncomfortable and though it wasn't our fault we were dirty, we couldn't help feeling ashamed. Fortunately we discovered that there were some famous hot springs near by, so we were able to go and have a hot bath and wash our stinking clothes.'

The days passed in a whirl. Tibetan doctors gave them a general medical overhaul; rice and dry rations, pots and pans, blankets, sheets, even a mattress were handed out to each one. The Women's Association took them to visit a carpet-weaving factory and an old people's home run by themselves. 'We were amazed at the quality of the workmanship and the cleanliness in the carpet factory. We hadn't ever seen anything like it. And at the home the old people looked so happy – and so clean. They were well looked after, and had nothing to do all day but chant their prayers and recite their mantras. It was so different from Tibet. There the Chinese made the old people work like everyone else and they never had any time to call their own. I suddenly thought of my mother and felt like weeping. How I longed for her to be able to finish her days in such a happy place.'

Wangdu Dorje, a leading official from the Tibetan government-in-exile in Dharamsala, arrived to tell them about the new life that awaited them. 'He told us what it had been like for the refugees in the beginning, the hardships they'd had to face since their arrival in 1959, the difficulties they'd overcome. Then he explained about the situation in Bhutan and the trouble that had recently befallen the Tibetans who'd settled there. He said the Tibetan Administration was doing its best to help all the refugees. Finally, he made us very happy by saying we would all soon be going to Dharamsala where we would have an audience with His Holiness. We were choked with excitement and could hardly wait.'

For the next three months or so '[we] more or less looked after ourselves. Every morning we got up at six, memorised some Tibetan texts before breakfast, then took it in turns (in groups of four or six) to collect firewood and do the cooking – out in the open. We went to school too – for lessons in Buddhism, in the Tibetan language, and a few other things. It was at Dekyi Ling that I was first introduced to the ABCD alphabet.'

At last the waiting was over. In the early evening of

1 April, the refugees left Dehra Dun by bus for Dharamsala. After three or four days of debriefing by the Government-in-Exile's Office, they attended the Tibetan Youth Congress AGM and exchanged experiences with the young delegates from all over India and Nepal. 'We told them about our lives in Tibet, they told us about the work of the Youth Congress and gave us books of Tibetan history (the real history this time) to study. We found it remarkable that these young people were so passionate about Tibet, though most of them had been born in India and had never set foot there. We were so impressed by their dedication to the cause that a number of us promptly enrolled as members.'

Although the next few years would bring a flood of refugees from Tibet to Dharamsala, in 1982 they were still a rarity. The frontiers had been tightly sealed ever since the beginning of the Cultural Revolution and Emme-la's group was only the second to have broken through since it had ended. 'Another group had turned up from Shigatse just before us, but we were still a novelty. We got a tremendous reception from the Tibetans in Dharamsala. It wasn't like at Dehra Dun, we didn't feel at all inferior. The refugees in Dharamsala seemed to us incredibly efficient, clean, well preserved, sophisticated and clever, yet they were also very friendly towards us, they seemed really pleased that we were there. We were invited everywhere, for Tibetan tea, for snacks, and most of all for questions. They wanted to know everything we could tell them about Tibet, they had been starved of first-hand information for so long. I discovered quite a lot of people who originated from Gyantse, though they had lived in India for years. It was marvellous to see them, even if what we had to tell them made them – and us – weep.

'When we met the refugees in Dharamsala and saw

the work of the government officials, the enthusiasm of the Youth Congress, the Tibetan Women and so on, we were tremendously impressed. All those organisations set up in so short a time. We remembered how the Chinese had kept telling us that the Tibetan exiles were enduring terrible sufferings, they were always hungry and lived in dreadful squalor. They painted a graphic picture of children roaming the countryside begging for food. So when we went with the Youth delegates to see the Tibetan Children's Village higher up the mountain on which Dharamsala is built, my stomach was in knots at the thought of what I would find there. They'd arranged games and set up stalls to collect money for the Village. I came to one particular stall where a bright-looking boy was shouting that he had metal boxes for sale for two rupees. I was very naïve, I thought that if I ran and got to the boy before anyone else I'd get a big metal box to put all my belongings in. I dashed up to him, opened my purse and gave him the precious two rupees. He handed me a tin pencil case! It was my first lesson in not rushing into things. Later on I could laugh about it, but at the time I felt very sore.'

The Children's Village put all his fears to rest, it was 'an unbelievable surprise, a real eye-opener. We were almost bowled over by the standard of education, the hygiene, the cleanliness, the smart uniforms and general behaviour of the children.'

Other ingrained fears surfaced when he was taken to see an opera performed at the Tibetan Institute of Performing Arts (TIPA). These were harder to deal with. 'I have to confess that I was uneasy seeing those ancient Tibetan costumes, and the old society they recalled. All my life I had been forced to condemn the decadent old Tibetan culture and everybody who'd practised it. I couldn't shake off those years of indoctrination just yet, and the culture shock of those costumes and those dances was almost too much to bear.'

Before long, Emme-la noticed a strange and unfamiliar breed of people in the streets of Dharamsala. They were Westerners, he was told, Americans and Europeans. 'They were all very tall, but I couldn't tell the men from the women, since both sexes were wearing trousers. They even walked in the same way, whereas in Tibet, the women walked quite differently. It was easy to see that these people were more adventurous and self-assured than the Tibetans – the Tibetans tended to be more self-effacing. Just then I wasn't sure what to make of these extraordinary creatures.'

Emme-la's dream was about to come true, the long-promised audience with the Dalai Lama was at hand. It was principally for this that the refugees had left their country and braved the terrors of the Himalayan peaks. Now that the moment had almost arrived, Emme-la was gripped by an almost painful excitement.

'The audience was to be on the morning of 9 April. The day before we were all in a frantic flurry of preparation. We got our white scarves to offer to His Holiness, we had baths, we scrubbed our faces almost raw, and tried to prepare ourselves mentally. An official from the Department of Home Affairs took us into a storeroom and allowed us to help ourselves to some clothes. I picked a shirt, some vests and underwear, a pair of yellow trousers and a black jacket, though I knew in my heart that next day I would not wear any of these, but the old Tibetan jacket I had worn during my escape from Tibet.

'None of us slept a wink that night. I lay there waiting for dawn to break, and the waiting seemed to go on for ever. At dawn, we got up and washed again – and again

– before having breakfast. The minutes ticked by slowly. Would the moment ever come? Then Mr Sonam Topgyal from the Department of Home Affairs came to collect us and we went up the hill towards the Dalai Lama's residence at Thekchen Choeling. Body searches, more waiting, more interminable delays. What would His Holiness look like? What would he say? My mind was a blank, I had no idea, even though I had had a picture of him back in Tibet. I kept remembering how my mother had told me that when I was a baby she had taken me to see him as he passed through Gyantse on his way back from a visit to India. 1956 had been my first public audience. Over a quarter of a century – and a lifetime – later, would the second one ever happen?

At last we were admitted to the Presence. Slowly we filed past. When we came face to face with him, none of us could utter a word, though each of us had rehearsed what we wanted to say over and over again. We looked at his face for a brief moment, but after that we kept our eyes lowered. All we could see were his shoes, his robes, his knees, we didn't dare lift our eyes any higher. Most of us were shaking and in tears, we were quite unable to control such overpowering emotions.

'Then His Holiness spoke. He said we had all been living through difficult times, perhaps the most difficult Tibet had ever known. But we should try not to worry, the dawn had already broken, we were waiting only for the sun to rise. We all wept with happiness to hear him say that. He came to each of us in turn and placed his hands on our heads. He told me not to cry, but I couldn't stop. His officials must have briefed him about each one of us, because he knew I had left my mother behind in Tibet and assured me that one day I was sure to see her again.'

When it was over, the tears continued to flow, but the

refugees were proud and happy in the fulfilment of their once-in-a-lifetime dream. That night Emme-la poured his heart out in a poem of love and longing. Writing verses was part of Tibetan popular culture. In a land where only Party stalwarts read newspapers, the people used to compose ribald verses or songs on topical subjects. They were anonymous so that when they eventually became public property they could get nobody into trouble. But Emme-la's verse was written for himself alone:

In the hot land of India
There's a cool refuge called Dharamsala.
When first I saw the snow-capped peaks of Triund
I thought in pain of my beloved country.
When first I saw the Bhagsu stream
I tasted in memory the sweet waters of my
    Nyangchu.
And when at last I met the Dalai Lama
I thought of the mother who gave me birth.
Then as I offered him my silent tears
Love and affection rained down upon me.
That compassion, which was a gift from you,
I shall cherish until the day I die.

When, a few days later, the new refugees went on pilgrimage to Riwalsa, a small mountain lake and sacred Buddhist shrine near Dharamsala, their attention was riveted by one small detail. An insignificant thing, perhaps, but symptomatic of the new life which was just beginning for them. 'We saw well-fed fish, hundreds of them. No one was catching them, people were taking turns to feed them. When it was my turn, I thought of the fish in my Nyangchu River at home. Before the Chinese came, almost no Tibetans ate fish.

There was even a government law which protected the natural environment and all wildlife. One of its clauses stated that, apart from the jackal and the rat, no wild animal was ever to be killed. And that included fish. But when the Chinese came, they killed all the wildlife in sight. While we were working on the Nyangchu river, the Chinese officials went after the fish in every spare moment they had. They caught them by rod and line, or with fishing nets or by dynamiting the river in order to stun them. The thought came to me that even the fish born in India were lucky, they must have accumulated better karma in their past lives than those born in present day Tibet.'

CHAPTER 13
Dharamsala

The culture of a people is the sum total of their product accumulated over many generations. Our culture is the foundation on which we stand. Without it we would lose our bearings.

Emme-la, 1997

After the excitement of the audience and the pilgrimage, Emme-la returned to Dehra Dun to await his fate. In June, he heard from the Security Office that he was to go and work at the Tibetan Institute of Performing Arts, the very place which had afflicted his spirit with such misgivings a few months earlier.

Misgivings or no, it was good to be back in Dharamsala, to fill his lungs with the cold, clear mountain air again. After a warm welcome at TIPA, his prejudices began to fade. Jamyang Norbu, the Director, ex-guerrilla fighter, historian, artist, playwright, musician and general polymath, told the new arrivals that as the first group ever to be admitted to TIPA straight from Tibet, he would expect them to set a high standard. And this meant above all studying and working hard. 'We had school lessons, Tibetan language, English, arithmetic, carpet-weaving, tailoring and stitching costumes, pottery, playing musical instruments, performing songs, dances, operas and plays. And physical training was compulsory for all performers. It was hard work, but fascinating and I loved every minute of it.'

But the new life still lacked shape, and in the winter months, with TIPA closed for the holidays and no home to go to, Emme-la was downright lonely. He moped around the Institute, giving Tibetan language lessons to the young children who lived there, but feeling restless and homesick. It was then, in the winter of 1982, that his path crossed that of Anne Jennings Brown, a dynamic Englishwoman who would become a second mother to him and give him at last the sense of direction he needed.

Anne Jennings Brown had led a glamorous and somewhat turbulent life which could scarcely have been more different from Emme-la's experience. On the break-up of her first marriage, this former wealthy London socialite had fled to an old pirate fort on the remote island of Roatan, one of the Bay Islands off the coast of Honduras. With her second husband, an American explorer and treasure-hunter, she had penetrated the jungles of Ecuador and discovered the ruins of the lost Inca city of Coaque. But when that marriage too broke up – Howard Jennings her second husband was later killed in a plane crash – she returned to London to earn a living as an interior decorator. It was while she was doing up a well-known hotel in East Anglia that she met Mike Brown, a company director, who asked her to marry him. Her two previous experiences of marriage having proved somewhat disastrous, and recognising within herself an incurable thirst for adventure in far-off places, Anne doubted that she could ever settle down to routine domesticity. To wrestle with the dilemma, she returned to live alone in her pirate fort on Roatan for a while. Mike did not give up, however. A couple of years later, she finally agreed to marry him, but only on the understanding that she must be left free to take off into the void from time to time, free, as she put it, 'to go in search of other civilizations, other ways of life, far removed from the English way of life which I had always considered stifling'.

Two years later she held her reluctant husband to his promise.

It was after a dinner party, and the women's conversation had droned on and on about things of no importance. Something in me snapped, and on the way home I told Mike I simply had to get away. Now, straightaway, I said firmly. 'What do you want to do?' he asked in a stunned voice. Then, to my surprise I heard myself saying: 'I'm going to help the Tibetans.' It came from nowhere, I'd no idea why I'd said it. I knew nothing about Tibet, apart from reading Heinrich Harrer's *Seven Years in Tibet* when I was at Art College in the Fifties. I hadn't given the Tibetans a thought since, though I suppose I knew vaguely they were being persecuted by China.

Anyway, when I got home I looked up 'Tibet' in the London Telephone Directory. When I discovered that there was a Tibet Society in Kensington High Street, I went straight down there next day and found the Society to consist of one little Tibetan refugee in a lock-up garage, wearing a big sweater and huddled over a one-bar electric heater in the middle of winter. It was freezing cold in there. I remember thinking, 'My God, these people really do need help.' So without further ado, I told him, 'I want to go and help the Tibetans. I've no qualifications, but I'm willing to go anywhere, dig ditches, build shelters or whatever you need. I'm a practical person, so just use me.' I think he was stunned.

'I'm afraid you're never going to settle for the conventional wifely role,' wrote a journalist friend in some amusement. Anne was now indeed firing on all cylinders. Out of a list of possibilities she had elected to go to Dharamsala in the foothills of the Himalayas, home now to many thousands of Tibetan refugees. More specifically, she was going to the Tibetan Institute of Performing Arts (TIPA) which the Dalai Lama had set up in order to preserve in exile an ancient culture which was being wiped out in its homeland. They desperately needed teachers, she had been told. Lacking any experience of teaching, she took a deep breath, bought herself a Tibetan grammar, and booked a plane ticket to New Delhi.

The bus journey to Dharamsala took longer than the flight from London to New Delhi, was much more uncomfortable and, given the state of the Indian roads, the recklessness of the drivers and the clapped-out condition of most of the vehicles, distinctly more dangerous. Dharamsala, part of the North Indian state of Himachal Pradesh, was originally a military cantonment built on a spur of the Dhaula Dhar mountain range which overlooks the beautiful Kangra Valley. This derelict ghost town, miles from anywhere, had been offered to the exiled Dalai Lama in 1960 by the Indian Prime Minister, Jawaharlal Nehru, probably in the hope that if the Tibetan refugees were kept out of sight, they would also stay out of mind. (And that would perhaps reduce the hostility of the Chinese who had been furious when he gave asylum to the fleeing Dalai Lama in 1959.) Perched on a mountainside and surrounded by high snowy mountains, it had the advantage of reminding the Tibetans just a little of home. Lower Dharamsala at the base of the mountain was still a cantonment of the Indian military. Higher up was the new Tibetan enclave of Gangchen Kyishong, where the government-in-exile had built its ramshackle offices; and above that the little town of McLeod Ganj, where at the turn of the century the British had built over one hundred bungalows and which they had intended to adopt as their official summer hill-station – until an earthquake in 1905 made them choose Simla instead. TIPA, at an altitude of 6,000 ft, was higher still, a stiff climb from McLeod Ganj where the Tibetan refugees had now erected hundreds of shacks and set up their market stalls.

Plunged in at the deep end, Anne Brown found herself teaching classes consisting of tiny children, dancers, opera masters, every age from six to sixty-five or even seventy – and was instantly enthralled by them.

What struck me most was their terrible poverty. The people at TIPA were desperately poor, even more so than the other Tibetans in Dharamsala, who seemed to regard dance-drama and the people who took part in it as the lowest form of life. At TIPA everyone suffered from chronic catarrh and malnutrition, they had no sweaters, no pants, no blankets, and the children went barefoot in the snow. They had a single spoon for eating and their sleeping accommodation was pathetic – one thin blanket against the dreadful cold.

Conditions were primitive – no heating, a bucket of freezing cold water for washing, nothing but dry bread to eat; and, for sleeping, 'a mattress that felt more like a table-cloth and on which you were bitten all over by bed-bugs'. Determined to share these living conditions without complaint, Anne Brown found herself battling with the icy cold. 'Indoors and out I wore thermal pants, long-sleeved vests, woollen tights, leg-warmers, slacks, polo-necked under-pullover, woollen blouse, woollen scarf, sweater and anorak. And still I froze! It was only November – I hardly dared think of what it would be like when winter really arrived. And the Tibetans had such thin coverings and no blankets.'

Armed with textbooks, maps and pictures, Anne taught in a mixture of English, sign-language and drawings. She taught her new pupils basic English, and told them about life in other lands, even about life in old Tibet, teaching herself Tibetan history and geography in the evenings, poring over books and maps. ('They often said afterwards how strange it was that the first Tibetan history they had ever learned was from a foreign woman.') She applied her considerable artistic skills to making money for the Institute, cutting out dolls, dragons and everything she could think of from any materials that came to hand, designing T-shirts, even drawing historical maps to sell to the foreign pilgrims, tourists and spaced-out hippies who thronged Dharamsala's dusty streets.

Her attention had been drawn to Emme-la almost from the start:

Someone pointed out this boy who'd recently

escaped from Tibet. He was terribly thin, his face was rather Mongolian, with high cheek-bones and large slanting almond eyes that were dark and sad. I thought he looked like a hunted animal, a panther at bay – he had quick reflex movements of head and limbs and the loping big cat gait of one who is used to walking long distances with ease. He had a sort of closed-in stillness, he kept looking over his shoulder, warily, as if he was afraid someone was following him. I could well believe he'd just come from Tibet – he had that awe-inspiring look of someone from the wild open spaces, someone almost from a different era, a different planet. Unlike the others, who'd been born in India or had lived there for years, he behaved in an old-fashioned way the Tibetans had long since abandoned. He averted his eyes from strangers, stuck his tongue out as a sign of respect, and bowed so low you could only see the top of his head when you spoke to him.

When she began giving extra lessons in her own room in the evenings, Emme-la was one of the first to take advantage of the opportunity. On Sunday 14 November 1983, she wrote in her diary:

After supper of beans and rice – in the dining-room with its wood-burning stove which belches out black smoke all the time – that shy twenty-four year old who's just come from Tibet came to my room, and as he speaks no English, I got out my Tibetan grammar book and we started a stilted conversation, learning about each other . . . His name is Jinpa Ngodup, but everyone calls him Emme-la. He picked up a book of mine called Tibetan Sacred Art, and asked me to tell him how to pronounce those three words, and explain them. How to explain sacred? I put my hands together in prayer and assumed a reverent look. After that, he became one of my keenest pupils, but whenever he picked up that book, he would join his hands and bend over reverently as he pronounced the title.

Many of the students at TIPA were being sponsored by foreign benefactors. Looking around at those who were still without sponsors, Anne decided that of them all, Emme-la and Chung Lang, another boy fresh out of Tibet, were the most needy. 'They are so poorly dressed, and the Secretary agreed they were the two who most need help,' she wrote in her diary. She gave a sum of money to the Secretary and promised to make herself responsible for their upkeep and for 'life's little luxuries', she says wonderingly, 'like food, clothes, soap, toothpaste, writing materials and a tin mug to drink out of'. She had, in short, 'sort-of adopted' Emme-la, to whom she was quite clearly a goddess figure and an answer to all his prayers.

Anne Brown's diary for that winter (she remained in Dharamsala for five months) records her growing affection for Emme-la, the grinding poverty of the refugees, and her own increasing desperation at being unable to solve their interminable problems. In early December she wrote:

Emme-la arrived and insisted on giving me a black woollen Tibetan jacket. I was reluctant to take it, but he was very insistent: his mother had made it for him, and he thought it right that I, his new mother, should have it. However, he does have another jacket, from the bundle of second-hand clothing which came from Holland just before I came. I was very touched. In return I gave him a cashmere scarf I'd brought from

England. When we'd finished exchanging gifts, I showed him the photographs in Sir Charles Bell's book, *The People of Tibet*. He got very excited when he saw the pictures of Lhasa. And when we got to pictures of his home town, Gyantse, he was simply beside himself with joy, and went back to them again and again, with such longing on his face I could have wept.

5 December 1983

Emme-la has a very swollen leg from an enormous boil. I told him yesterday to go to the doctor and have it seen to. He assured me that he'd done so, but I have just discovered he didn't go to the doctor but to a lama at the temple, who blessed a piece of red cord, put it round his neck and assured him it would cure his leg. I was less convinced, so I bathed the boil and dressed it with Savlon on a paper hankie and tied a clean handkerchief round it.

23 January 1984

I have been ill for the last few days and have had to stay in bed. Dear Emme-la brings me a bucket of warm water to wash in every morning and a thermos of sweet Indian tea twice a day. On two occasions he has brought me a slice of hot apple pie from the *Risin' Horizon* in McLeod Ganj. He says he's been given Rs1,000 – about £20 – by TIPA as payment for teaching the young children Tibetan script. (They don't know how to write in Tibetan at all, but Emme-la is very good at it. He writes it beautifully.) Anyway, he wanted to spend some of it on me, hence the apple pie. To-day he brought me a rhododendron flower, dark-red and heralding a very early Spring in the Himalayas.

24 January 1984

Emme-la's room used to be a cement cell with one small window, a bed and a small box containing his possessions. But now he's been given his own room and is thrilled about it. I bought him a few things to make it more habitable and he showed me with great pride his few possessions – the most precious being a picture of His Holiness with a white scarf draped over its frame. There is a tin box in one corner, which he opened and from which he drew out all his treasures one by one. Two woollen rugs woven by his mother in Tibet, a pair of trousers from the Dutch parcel; a shirt which I had given him; a waistcoat which didn't match anything, a child's white sweater and a pair of shorts (clothing from the Dutch parcel was handed out in random bundles) which didn't fit but which maybe would one day, he thought.

From a battered case he then produced a Tibetan flag I had given him, a few old letters from Tibet, three photographs and a pair of socks. On a shelf were a few bits of ragged clothing and two small crumpled books in Tibetan – he hopes one day to have more books, he told me. Lastly he showed me his two diaries – one of them finished, the other half done. I said he must continue to write in them, to write about his life. One day perhaps he will be able to tell the world what it was like in Tibet when he was young. He can speak for all the others who went through the same sort of experience. He is speaking English very haltingly now, and I feel he has great potential.

29 January 1984

Fourth day of snow, high, gusty winds blow down from the mountains and through every crack in my room, water drips down the wall next to my bed. I am never completely warm, no matter how many clothes I pile on.

6 February 1984
I am getting heartily sick of the food here. It doesn't help to find cockroaches in it. To-day I found a live one on my chunk of bread at breakfast and a well-baked one in my soup this evening.

9 February 1984
A leopard has taken two of our dogs. Another one has been severely mauled after fighting off some wild animal, either a leopard or a wolf. Or maybe a bear. The Himalayan bear, I heard to-day, averages 6ft 6 inches in height.

11 February
Losar – the Tibetan New Year. Emme-la brought a ceremonial white scarf and a traditional greeting card with an elephant, a monkey, a hare and a bird symbolizing universal brotherhood, peace and prosperity. Inside this card he had written a message in Tibetan which someone had translated into English for him: 'Dear Mother, Anne Brown-la, I wish you a very happy and prosperous Tibetan New Year for this Water Pig year, with regards, yours faithfully son Jinpa Ngodup.'

Anne's five months in Dharamsala were coming to an end, and her thoughts were turning to ways of making money for TIPA back in England.

I have been paying out for so many basic necessities, arranging sponsorships, organizing medical treatment and so on. God knows what will happen when there is no money available for these poor people. At least three thousand of the refugees are suffering from TB. I begin to wonder how I can ever make people aware of the needs here when I return to the comforts of England.

Just before she left in March 1984, a final entry records: 'Emme-la came to see me this evening with a translator, to tell me something of his life in Tibet under the Chinese. A horrifying story of oppression which I hope he will one day be able to get published.' Later she would recall that at times during his narrative, Emme-la had laughed uproariously, a disconcerting Tibetan trait:

He would be recounting some peculiarly horrible incident and without warning there would be this sudden outburst of merriment which left me stunned by its inappropriateness. He did that quite often, erupting into an almost childish laugh, as, with his head thrown back, he would rock to and fro. It was a strange, harsh laugh, as though there hadn't been enough laughter in his life to teach him to modulate it. I felt shut out by it and never knew how to deal with it – how can one begin to understand such a traumatized mind?

When Anne had gone, Emme-la felt energised by her enthusiasm for all things Tibetan. 'Anne-la did a lot of research into the costumes worn by the dancers at TIPA, she did paintings of the costumes and I think she intended to do a book about them. I found it amazing that a person from the West who seemed to have everything she could possibly want was putting time and energy into research on ancient Tibetan costumes and on a Tibetan culture which had been all but destroyed in Tibet itself. I began to realise that if a foreigner was prepared to do all that, then we Tibetans must do our level best to research our culture and traditions in order to preserve them for posterity.'

Thanks to Anne Brown, Emme-la had found a driving force for his own life and from this point onwards would never look back. From now on he applied himself with enthusiasm to his work at TIPA, learning the historical plays and operas, the traditional songs and dances which would turn him into a valued member of the team.

1985. TIPA was going on tour to the Tibetan settlements in Northern India and Emme-la was part of the thirty-strong song-and-dance troupe. It was his first tour, the first long journey he had ever undertaken freely and without fear. Laden with trunk-loads of costumes they had designed and made for themselves, the troupe were to perform two historical plays and two classical operas, plus a series of songs and dances from all three regions of Tibet. 'They were mainly folk songs and dances which used to be performed on certain auspicious occasions and festivals like Losar. We were also going to do one modern play, based on the life of Yuru Pon, a Khampa Resistance hero who had defended Lithang Monastery for sixty-four days when the Chinese attacked it in 1956,[1] and who was killed by Chinese bullets.'

The journey by bus and train took them eastwards to the state of Arunachal Pradesh, formerly known as Assam. It was a relief to reach the end of the road, and be welcomed by the large Tibetan refugee community in Shillong. Alas for Emme-la's hopes, however. He succumbed almost instantly to an attack of jaundice, and the troupe proceeded to the next settlement without him. Only after treatment from an Indian doctor and two weeks' convalescence in a monastery was he able to rejoin them, just in time to go to Darjeeling.

Here the past came back to haunt him, when he was greeted by an old acquaintance from home, Trogawa Phurbu Namgyal, a member of the land-owning family to which Emme-la's parents had in former days paid rent. Any pleasure Emme-la felt on seeing this man soon turned to horror when he heard what he had to tell. 'He had recently been back to Gyantse on a visit,[2] and told me about an old friend of mine, Tenpa Thinley, a former monk who had married. Like me, Tenpa had decided to escape to Bhutan with his wife, Tsering Wangdu, their children and one or two friends. But they weren't as lucky as me. Just before they reached the frontier with Bhutan, they were arrested by Chinese border guards and brought back in chains to Gyantse, hands tied behind their backs. Trogawa Phurbu Namgyal had seen them paraded publicly in trucks, driven around Gyantse as a deterrent to the local population. After that, they were probably shot. I was shaking with horror, I had known all those people well, they all came from the same village as me, I had grown up with them.'

Next stop was Kalimpong, the town which had for centuries been the focus of trade between India and Tibet and which still boasted a number of houses and estates which had belonged to the important Tibetan trading families. In the nineteenth century it had been the nerve-centre of the Great Game, that power struggle between British India and Tsarist Russia for the mastery of Central Asia. In those days, Kalimpong had swarmed with agents of the Great Powers, shadowy spies seeking information for their political masters.

More significantly for Emme-la, Kalimpong had been the birthplace of TIPA. He was fascinated to learn about its beginnings in August 1959, just a few months after the refugees had fled Tibet in the wake of the Dalai Lama. It had started life on a shoestring, without any idea of making a profit. There was no administrative structure, and not only did the performers earn no salary, they even had to provide their own lunch to take to rehearsals. They survived, because TIPA was first and foremost a tiny fist shaken in the face of China's destruction of Tibet's culture, and their passionate determination saw them through. Their first task was to learn the newly composed Song of the Tibetan National Uprising and a new eulogy of the Dalai Lama, both of which they incorporated into a two-hour performance of traditional songs, dances and short plays. They gave their first public performance in New Delhi at the time of the Afro-Asian Conference later that year (1960), then went on to Mussoorie[3] to present their show to His Holiness.

It was then one year after his flight into exile, and the Dalai Lama was already aware that, with no other country prepared to help them, the Tibetans would have to settle for a long exile. He was therefore determined to help his people start a new life in unfamiliar surroundings, while at the same time trying to save all that was worth saving of their culture. (Many of the old rituals and ceremonial practices he was only too happy to discard.) After he reached Dharamsala, he would draft a new democratic constitution, and with a small seed fund of money set up a medical centre to preserve and dispense the traditional herbal remedies, a library of Tibetan works and archives to store what had been salvaged of the sacred writings and scriptures. That day in Mussoorie, when the song-and-dance troupe came to perform in front of him, he did not hesitate to give them his blessing – and, to their undying gratitude, a little money.

The years passed. July 1988 saw Emme-la taking part in an overseas tour to Switzerland and the UK. The most unforgettable moment of the British tour was at a folk festival in Billingham, when the Tibetan flag flew at full mast among the flags of all the other participating nations. It was a proud occasion, but also, thanks to growing pressure by China on the nations of the world, a very infrequent one.

Emme-la's hard work and patience – with Anne Brown's continuing support – were about to bear fruit. On his return from Europe in the summer of 1988, he was offered the opportunity of a lifetime – to enrol at the Central Institute of Higher Tibetan Studies in Varanasi, also known as Benares or Banaras, a town of great significance to all Buddhists and one of their three most important centres of pilgrimage, for it was in Sarnath near Varanasi that Buddha had begun his teaching. The previous year, the Board of TIPA had decided to set up a research wing and put Emme-la in charge, and, as he obviously would need professional training, had asked the Tibetan Council for Education for help. In November 1988, the Council paid for Emme-la to go to the Tibetan College at Varanasi on a three-year course aimed at enlarging his horizons and skills. He was to study the Buddhist scriptures, improve his Tibetan and Hindi language skills, and do specialist research into the songs, the dances, the instruments of all three regions of Tibet. The three years at Varanasi were undoubtedly the happiest of his life.

In his last year, he was made Director of Dance and Music and met 'scholars from all over the Himalayan

Buddhist world – Bhutan, Sikkim, Ladakh, Spiti, and from all four schools of Buddhism. It was a really cosmopolitan mix of students, and the atmosphere was that of a monastery rather than a school.' Moreover, Varanasi gave Emme-la his first real experience of democracy in practice, for the Director of the Institute was Samdhong Rinpoche, a Tibetan lama renowned for his passionate advocacy of democratic principles. Samdhong Rinpoche's students annually elected representatives to a Student Welfare Council whose function was to listen carefully to all complaints and refer them to the administration.

When the three years were over, the Rinpoche handed Emme-la the coveted certificate, and with it some words of wisdom: 'You are going back to Dharamsala to do very important work for the Tibetan community, he told me. Well, let me give you some advice. Remember, when people praise you, don't let the praise go to your head. And when they attack you, don't let the criticism get you down. Just give of your best whatever you do, whether or not there is anybody watching.'

With Samdhong Rinpoche's advice ringing in his ears, Emme-la headed back to Dharamsala.

CHAPTER 14

Return

Ours is a just cause. We continue to be confident that
truth will ultimately triumph and our land and people
will once more be free. Would the Chinese consider the
Tibetan question so sensitive if our cause was dead?

His Holiness the Fourteenth Dalai Lama[1]

Emme-la, however, had other plans for the immediate
future. On returning to Dharamsala that summer, he
had run into a Tibetan friend who was doing business
in New Delhi. 'This chap seemed to know all about
getting permits for people to visit their relatives in
Tibet,' says Emme-la. 'He planted an idea into my
head. Ever since Tibet was opened up to tourists, even
foreign ones, soon after my escape, my mother and I
had been able to write to each other. In her most recent
letters she had been begging me to go and visit her,
she said that other Tibetans from India were coming

back and she was longing to see me. The thought of seeing her again was irresistible and I couldn't get it out of my head. On my way back to Varanasi for my last term, my friend and I travelled to Delhi together, and, at his urging, I went straight to the Chinese Embassy and introduced myself as a cosmetics salesman eager to try my luck in Tibet. (They used to accept that sort of story without question, but later on they got wise.) I put in an application, filled in innumerable forms, and the official told me to come back in two months.'

He went back to Varanasi for the final term, and three months later, as his course was coming to an end, the permit came through – with immediate effect. So, he returned to Dharamsala just to pick up some things, then went back to New Delhi again, heading straight for the Nepalese Embassy to get an entry visa for Nepal. It was December 1990. Twenty-four hours later he was bumping along the road to Kathmandu on an ancient and rickety bus.

Luck seemed to be with him at first. A friend in Kathmandu gave him a bed for the night and arranged transport for him to the so-called Friendship Bridge which links Nepal with Tibet. There was no problem in getting clearance to cross the bridge. But once on the other side he was in Tibet, and his troubles began. At the border post of Dram (Chinese: Zhangmu), the immigration authorities told him he was just too late – only the previous day the Chinese authorities had issued an order that no visitors were to be admitted until further notice! There was no arguing with that, and the customs officials neither knew nor cared how long the border would stay closed. Emme-la was frantic, but no matter how hard he pleaded with the officials, they were stony-faced. He would simply have to bide his time – and hope that he would get to Tibet before his three-month permit expired.

It was ten years since Emme-la had left his homeland, and the Tibet to which he was hoping to return had undergone many traumas in the intervening years. When he left in 1981, just after the visit of the Dalai Lama's three delegations, there had been some hope of change in the air, some loosening of draconian controls, partly due to a loss of nerve on the part of the Chinese. There was speculation that the Dalai Lama might return, more public worship was being allowed, and shortly afterwards, tourists had been admitted to the once tightly sealed land.

But the dream was always a fragile one, and by 1983 it had more or less died: talks with the Dalai Lama's representatives had stalled;[2] and although the monasteries were being allowed to admit a restricted number of new novices, there were no Buddhist teachers left and little time was allowed for study. (Anyway, the Chinese still had religion in their sights and were still bent on destroying it.) As for the tourists, they had proved to be a mixed blessing from the Chinese point of view. Far from bringing in much-needed hard currency, most of them were impecunious backpackers who travelled on the cheap and poked their noses into matters that were none of their concern. The majority of visitors who had come prepared to admire, were instead horrified by what the Chinese had done to Tibet, and lost no opportunity of saying so – and rushing into print – once they got home.

The year 1983 was when the Tibetans finally lost faith in the promise of better things to come, and independence groups began to surface. To the Chinese, talk of independence was counter-revolutionary (they referred to it as pornography) and a threat to the precious unity of the Motherland. So they tightened the screw yet again, plunging Tibet into a new Dark Ages, not only with a fresh series of widespread arrests and public executions, but by flooding the country with Chinese immigrants, the method they had used to great effect in their other colonies of Manchuria, Mongolia and East Turkestan, to settle the hash of the troublesome natives. Though, as a sop to outraged public opinion abroad, they followed this by disbanding the hated commune system and allowed farmers to have their own livestock again. Nevertheless, with the arrival of the Chinese settlers, food shortages became endemic once again, prices soared and, when the market was flooded with cheap Chinese labour and produce, the majority of Tibetans found themselves unemployed and virtually unemployable. With access to cheap source materials from China, the immigrants were able to take over even the traditional Tibetan crafts such as tailoring, weaving and carpentry. There was little left for the Tibetans to do, and beggars began to multiply in the streets. As Lhasa and the other Tibetan towns were submerged by concrete monstrosities and became indistinguishable from all other faceless Chinese urban developments, Tibetans became the new outcasts, non-persons in their own land. When, in 1985, Tibetan pilgrims went to India for a Kalachakra initiation at Bodh Gaya, the message they brought with them was that the much-vaunted liberalisation had been a sham and was in any case now over. Matters could only get worse.

They did. As the yearning for independence grew throughout Tibet, people everywhere voiced their rejection of the regime more and more desperately. In 1987 and again in 1988, there were spontaneous non-violent protests in Lhasa, and the Chinese sent in the riot squads with rifles, electric stunners and clubs. 'The Chinese are tearing our hearts out,' a woman was heard to say. In March 1989, three months before the demonstration in Peking's Tiananmen Square, and as Communist regimes crumbled in Eastern Europe, there was a spontaneous outburst in Lhasa, an explosion of ethnic rage in which everyone, even young children, joined. The Tibetans were united as never before in their hatred of the regime. The Chinese responded by bringing in the tanks, declaring martial law and unleashing a new reign of terror.[3] Though they officially lifted martial law a year later, they did not relax the terror. The Chinese knew that the Tibetan people had categorically rejected their rule and were determined that never again would they relax their vigilance.

Emme-la had known of this turmoil (after the unrest of 1987, he had joined other young Tibetans in a nonviolent demonstration in Dharamsala), yet he had continued 'to hope that ordinary life in Tibet had improved since my escape. Living standards seemed to be improving everywhere else, so I imagined it was the same with Tibet. As they were now admitting tourists from abroad,[4] surely there'd be improvements, they wouldn't have wanted outsiders to see Tibet the way it was.' His brief sojourn in Dram disabused him. 'While I waited in Dram, I once again saw Tibetans living under Chinese occupation and realised that nothing had changed. Everything was still geared to the Chinese, the Tibetans were underdogs with no stake in the economy at all. The officials were all Chinese, with one or two token Tibetans in inferior positions. Apart from these few, even from a distance I could pick out the ordinary Tibetans – they were so dirty, they looked lost and bewildered, as if they scarcely knew what was going on around them. All the construction work was being done by the Chinese, goods from Dram to Nepal and Nepal to Dram were carried by Nepalese coolies and truck drivers, tourist shops and restaurants were run by Chinese Muslims. The Tibetans had simply been marginalised in their own country. While the Nepalese and the Chinese Muslims could move around as they pleased without any restrictions, the Tibetans couldn't. I saw one elderly Tibetan man walking down the road with a rope in his hand, presumably looking for labouring work or perhaps hoping to be able to carry goods over the border. As he crossed the road, a Chinese soldier appeared from nowhere and scissor-kicked him on the side of his head. The poor old man just stood there looking stupefied.'

Luckily for him, as he cooled his heels in the guesthouse set up for returning Tibetans from India, Emme-la discovered that not only were a couple of the customs officers from his own Gyantse area, but one of them was actually from his mother's home village. That made all the difference, of course, and the official promised to see what he could do. Three days later, Emme-la was given a new permit and allowed to proceed.

By next morning he was on his way home, having been lucky enough to find himself a seat in an Amdo businessman's truck. With scarcely a pause for food and sleep, at daybreak on the following day the pair reached Shigatse where they parted company. 'The truck-driver wouldn't take any money, but he asked me for a picture of His Holiness. I gave him three or four, plus a whole selection of sacred pills from the Namgyal Monastery in Dharamsala. He was delighted.'

At long last he was on familiar territory, among people who spoke his own dialect. Discovering that there were no buses to Gyantse that day, he booked a ticket on the next day's bus and, in order to let the family know that he was on his way, went to the Post Office to telephone a cousin who worked in a Chinese government-run hostel. Then, with time on his hands, he went on pilgrimage to the famous Tashilhunpo Monastery in Shigatse, ancient seat of the Panchen Lamas of Tibet. (Alas, the tenth Panchen Lama had died there on a visit from his home in Peking in January 1989. He was known to have protested to the Chinese against the merciless treatment meted out to the Tibetans after 1987. When they nevertheless allowed him to visit Tibet in the last weeks of his life, he had spoken out very firmly wherever he went, saying that whatever benefits the Chinese had brought to Tibet, they were far out-weighed by the destruction and devastation they had caused. Arriving at Tashilhunpo on the eve of a big religious ceremony, he had retired early to bed, to pre-pare himself for the next day's rituals. During the night, he was taken ill and died. A heart attack, commiserated his Chinese minders. Most Tibetans were and still are convinced he had been done away with.)

Next morning, in a state of high excitement, Emme-la caught the bus to Gyantse. The journey produced mixed emotions. 'I was disappointed at first to find that the other people in the bus were drawing away from me, didn't want to talk to me. But then I realised they would probably get into trouble if seen talking to an exile, someone might inform on them. They had that hunted look, as if they were afraid they were being watched all the time. My second impression was of dust everywhere, we were on a dirt road, unsurfaced, and I was covered in dust from head to foot. And then I saw the river, the Nyangchu, where I had spent so many years of my life under Chinese rule, building dams and dykes. When I saw the dykes, the horrors of the past flooded over me, and I couldn't stop the tears rolling down my cheeks.

'Eventually we reached that crossroads, from where Lobsang Tsultrim and I had begun our escape ten years earlier. I got off the bus there and looked around, almost dizzy with emotion. Surely things would have changed? But one glance towards my native town told me there were no improvements, it had gone downhill even compared with ten years ago. Maybe it was because in the meantime I'd got used to the big cities of India, to surfaced roads with private cars running on them. Gyantse's dirt roads, full of pebbles and gravel and dust, made it look like a desert. The only new feature was the large number of Chinese government shops along the road. The old shopping district, where goods were brought in from India, Nepal and Bhutan, was now full of broken-down carts and looked utterly derelict.'

A number of other passengers had got off at the same stop. Soon Emme-la was surrounded by a group of people who were obviously curious about where he had come from and what he was doing there, but who were still shy of talking to him. It turned out later that this was because his clothes (the ones from the Dutch secondhand parcels) were of better quality than theirs, and they were afraid that if they talked to this prosperous-looking stranger they would be in serious trouble. 'I just stood there, feeling embarrassed, waiting for my cousin to come and find me. Eventually a young girl came running up, shouting Brother, Brother. But then she backed off in confusion, saying, Oh no, you can't be my brother. I asked her name, and she was indeed Phentok, the cousin I'd spoken to over the telephone. So then we hugged each other and wept, while the other Tibetans looked on amazed, some of them crying too.

'I picked up my rucksack and the box I had brought and we walked together towards my house. We passed people working in the fields, and some of them gave a sign of recognition to Phentok, then lowered their heads, minding their own business, not looking at me. Some of them had already guessed who I was, but they still dared not talk to me directly. Not until they could be sure it was safe.

'So at last I came home after ten years of exile. I found my mother, my sister, Pasang Dolma, her two little girls whom I'd never seen, and several distant relations. My sister came and hugged me and cried, as did the others. Not my mother, though. My mother said this was an auspicious occasion and that we should not cry. She was always less emotional than us younger ones.

'My mother was still living in the family home, looking after the animals and attending to the vegetable garden. She had no regular job, but all her various relations made sure she was all right. Pasang Dolma was an assistant in a primary school and still lived in the same village, with her husband, an electrician, and their two children, who, since they're only nine and seven, are still allowed to attend school. My other sister, Dawa Phentok, was living in another village about twelve miles away, with her husband and four sons, aged from about twenty to twelve. Because of their class background, none of the four boys had received an education beyond primary level – all of them just worked in the fields.'

The security police had already learned of Emme-la's arrival through the grapevine. 'Next morning a member of the People's Militia came to the house and ordered me to report to the police station. When I arrived, there were a number of policemen chatting outside in the sun. One of them spotted me and took me inside into his office. He asked me a lot of questions about what I'd been doing in exile. I told him the whole story of my life in those ten years, holding nothing back, even telling him what His Holiness had said about there being no need for tears, the dawn had already broken, we were only waiting for the sun to appear, and that one day I would see my mother again. He listened, then began screaming at me. He said that a few years earlier he'd have had me shot as a counter-revolutionary, but things had changed, and he was forced to welcome me back instead. However, he ordered me never, never, never, not even in private, to mention the words "independence for Tibet". It would bring instant retribution. Also, I must go no further than Shigatse and was forbidden to leave my house before dawn or to be out after dark. Within the limits of those restrictions, I was free to visit the monasteries and to visit my relations and friends.'

Once the news had got around that the exile had returned, he was besieged by relatives, friends and former co-workers, and he was sad not to have gifts for them all. 'However, I did have pictures of His Holiness, some sacred pills from his monastery in Dharamsala, various religious amulets and some blessed grains given me by the Nechung oracle. I distributed these and everyone was more than happy. They were really pleased to hear that the exile community was being run on a democratic system and not under the old one – even those of my former friends who were working for the Chinese were delighted and pleased about this. Of course, the Chinese were always telling them that the Dalai Lama really wants to restore the old feudal system in Tibet, but I was able to assure them that it wasn't so. Talking to these old friends, I got the impression that they were less afraid of the Chinese than they used to be, they were more outward-going, less cowed, less subservient. I felt they were beginning to recover some of their old sense of identity.'

He stayed in Gyantse for about ten days. Then discovering that Kyilu, a girl-cousin from Lhasa, was coming to Gyantse with her husband for the New Year, he decided to visit Lhasa and travel back with them. Despite the strict orders from the security police not to travel any further than Shigatse, he took a chance on it. Hitching a lift to Shigatse, he caught the bus from there to Lhasa, where he reported to the local reception centre for returnees. As he was now, like other foreigners in Tibet, finding it difficult to adjust to the altitude, he rested as much as he could for the next few days.

Climbing to the top of the Potala[5] as a pilgrim a few days later, he looked out over the new Chinese city that Lhasa had become: 'Down below I could see Shol, the tiny section of Lhasa which was still built in the Tibetan style.[6] For the rest, all I could see were corrugated tin roofs and concrete buildings. The Tibetans were not only surrounded by Chinese soldiers but our holy city had been taken over by Chinese developers. Later that day I visited the Jokhang Temple. On the way, I could see policemen and soldiers on the roofs of all the official Chinese buildings, with huge guns pointing in different directions. Those who weren't wielding guns were looking through binoculars. I was quite frightened – it was as if the city was on a war footing. And on the streets I was shocked to see so many Public Security Bureau policemen on motorcycles with guns at the ready. I'd never seen anything like it – they were everywhere.

'But the Tibetans in Lhasa seemed to be used to it all. As this was the traditional season of pilgrimage, the winter months, after the harvest was in, and travel was once more allowed, Lhasa was full of pilgrims from all over Tibet, wearing their colourful regional dress and jewellery. They were prostrating before the temple and openly praying that His Holiness would have a long life and would one day return to Tibet. This, of course, was in defiance of Chinese instructions. Although they didn't actually use the banned (and treasonable) word, independence, the idea was built into their prayer that happiness would return to Tibet. They could have been arrested for that.'

The anxiety that had oppressed him ever since arriving in Lhasa did not diminish. At the great Sera Monastery, only parts of which were still intact, he sensed a lack of spirit and confidence among both monks and pilgrims: 'It was as if the life-force had departed. There was none of the sense of joy and gaiety you usually get from holy places – the essence had gone. It was the same with Drepung, with Nechung, with the Norbulingka. Though there were pilgrims everywhere, just as before, the monasteries and temples looked empty, abandoned, neglected, depressed. There were hardly any Tibetans living in this part of Lhasa. The people were mainly Chinese, the architecture was Chinese, there wasn't a trace of Tibetan-ness anywhere.

'I looked at the stalls, there was every conceivable kind of object on sale, just as in the West, but the stalls were all run by Chinese and stocked with goods from China. I went on to have a look at the vegetable market. There were three hundred or so stalls, only four of them run by Tibetans. These four were selling simple local produce such as radishes, onions, potatoes. The Chinese stalls sold those things too, but they also had a wide variety of vegetables brought in daily from China. The butchers selling meat, the fishmongers selling seafood were all Chinese. I saw tanks full of eels and other sea-creatures. You were meant to choose one and it would be fried in oil before your very eyes, for you to eat. To a

Tibetan this was utter sacrilege, completely alien to everything Buddhism stands for. But it was already common in Chinese-dominated Lhasa. I felt sick.'

On the whole, he was not sorry to leave Lhasa and return with his cousin and her husband to Gyantse. But on arrival at his mother's house, he could see that all was not well. His mother, his sister and all the other relations were obviously on edge. It appeared that a Tibetan who had arrived from India just before Emme-la, and another one who had come a bit later, had both been arrested by the Chinese, one of them while visiting Lhasa. 'Naturally they were bothered about me, and they told me I'd been followed everywhere I went by Chinese spies. Sure enough, I'd hardly arrived in Gyantse before a police official came to the house to see me, to ask where I'd been. I gave them chapter and verse, but they couldn't touch me, as I'd registered at the tourist bureau in Lhasa and been given a permit. Anyway, just to show me that he meant business, the policeman took my passport away.'

As the New Year festival of Losar was fast approaching, the next few days saw the usual annual flurry of soup-making and house-cleaning. On the day itself, they went to the monastery to pay their respects and to friends' houses to celebrate, almost as they had done when Emme-la was a child. But the strain was beginning to tell on them all and Emme-la knew it was high time to go back to India. He was upset by the constant surveillance and realised that his continuing presence could only hurt his family. When he told his mother that he had decided to go back, as usual she showed no emotion, but asked him to wait until the fifteenth day of the New Year when the new prayer flags would be hoisted at the monastery and would be a sign of good omen.

'When it got around that I was leaving, people flocked to say goodbye, bringing gifts for His Holiness, dried yak's meat, dried cheese, things like that. Many families brought gifts for His Holiness on behalf of their deceased relatives.[7] I said I couldn't possibly carry them all, but they wouldn't take no for an answer. So when I came to pack up, most of my luggage consisted of presents for the Dalai Lama.'

As the last (fifteenth) day of the Tibetan New Year approached, the Chinese were becoming jittery. The day was an important one for the Tibetans, and thousands of people were converging on the Pelkhor Choede monastery not only from Gyantse but from many surrounding districts. With the 10 March anniversary of the Lhasa Uprising fast approaching, the Chinese mistrusted all large gatherings of Tibetans and were taking no chances. 'On the night before that final day when the flags were to be hoisted, we were wakened by the noise of motorbikes and other vehicles being driven around. The noise went on all night long. Next morning, as we made our way to the monastery, we saw the reason for it. There were soldiers posted everywhere, and huge numbers of security police as well. I recognised a lot of them, including the officer who'd come to see me when I got back from Lhasa – he was in plain clothes.

'After the ceremony, I went back to my mother's house to say goodbye. (I had found a seat in a truck going to Shigatse.) Most of my relatives were there, some of them in tears, most of them busy giving me advice. All of them gave me white scarves. My mother shed no tears, but as I bade her goodbye, she presented me with a scarf and told me that I must be a good man throughout my life. I left her with a heavy heart and went to the police station to collect my passport. They handed it to me, saying I must leave that very day –

and never come back. I was very upset, and asked for an explanation, but they just shrugged and said that those were their orders. I was to be expelled from Gyantse for good.

'I went to Lhasa via Shigatse and got a re-entry visa for Nepal. By the time I left on 3 March (1991), the Chinese nerves were ragged and they looked as if they might seal off the whole country before the 10th. I knew I must delay no longer.'

When he reached Nyalam, just before the frontier at Dram, the road ahead was blocked by a heavy snowfall. After hanging around for two days and two nights, he decided to make the rest of the journey on foot. It took him nine hours. When he reached Dram, there were no further difficulties, and as he walked across the Friendship Bridge, it was as though a weight had been taken from him. 'I felt an overwhelming happiness, a sense of almost incredible freedom. And a few days later when I arrived back in Dharamsala, it was as though I'd escaped from Tibet for the second time. It felt like coming home.'

Postscript

Emme-la returned to Dharamsala and took up his post as the first-ever Director of Research at TIPA. Since then he has travelled among the various Tibetan settlements all over India searching for old songs, dances and operas to add to TIPA's repertoire and to be documented for the Tibetan archives. It is a worthwhile job and he is happy in it, though occasionally his ambition soars even higher. One day he would like to become Minister for Education in the exile government: 'I dream of offering our pure, untarnished culture to any non-Tibetan who would like to learn something from it. What we have must be used not just for ourselves but for everyone. That is my dream.'

He has made his home now in Dharamsala and is putting down roots. In 1995, following his parents' example of consulting a lama and having divinations made, Emme-la married 20-year-old Pema Choekyi, and in February 1996, their son Tenzin Rigzin was born, to be followed two years later by a daughter, Tenzin Yingsay. Emme-la's mother has never seen her grand-children, and there is little prospect of Emme-la's ever being allowed back into Tibet, though he continues to hope that the miracle will happen. 'Even if it is only in time to die, I'm sure that one day I'll go back home.'

Since 1995, Tibet has almost sunk back into the Dark Ages again. It is commonly supposed in the West (among those few who think about the matter at all) that the liberalisation of the early 1980s, or even the relative relaxation of the early 1990s has continued. Sadly, that is not the case. The Chinese finally realised that they would get nowhere in Tibet if they did not succeed in eradicating Buddhism. They have spent the last few years trying to do just that, whether in the monasteries, in the towns or in the countryside. They are denying now that Buddhism is or ever was an integral part of Tibetan culture – it is, they say, a foreign import, and in any case can only be allowed to exist if it becomes thoroughly integrated into Chinese socialism. Since 1995, a new Strike Hard Campaign is aimed at eliminating the influence of what they call 'the Dalai clique' and at discrediting the Dalai Lama in every possible way. His picture is once again comprehensively banned. Monks and nuns who refuse to take an oath denouncing the Dalai Lama are dismissed from their monasteries; many of them are arrested and tortured, and sometimes the monasteries themselves are closed down. In parallel with this, the Patriotic Education Programme attempts to wipe the slate clean of the last remnants of Tibetan language and culture, to assimilate what is left of Buddhism into a socialist structure. With the Chinese continuing to flood into Tibet and out-numbering the Tibetans almost everywhere, what hope of survival can there be for Tibet?

Emme-la refuses to give up hope. 'There's an old Tibetan saying,' he tells me, 'the Chinese are let down by their suspicions, the Tibetans are let down by hope. Well, it's true, the Chinese suspect their own shadows, and we Tibetans never give up hoping.' Wherever they are in the diaspora, in India, in Nepal, the USA, Australia, Switzerland, France, Germany, the UK and elsewhere, the Tibetans continue to hope. It is to bear witness to that hope in the future that Emme-la and thousands like him are working today. They are determined that when the Tibetans once again become free citizens in their own land, they will still have a heritage of which to be proud.

Is Anyone Listening?

1956

Viewed in its historical perspective, the so-called 'Liberation' of Tibet is the latest and most formidable attempt of the Chinese, prompted by the greed of an over-populated country for the vast area which comprises Tibet and her wealth in natural resources . . . to colonise Tibet in a struggle that has persevered over the centuries. For let there be no mistake about it, the 'Liberation' of Tibet is nothing but a newer form of brutal, ruthless colonialism to be more dreaded than the old, because here the aim is not only the exploitation but the complete absorption of a people – absorption or extermination are the only two alternatives offered to the people of Tibet by the Chinese . . .

It was a blot on the conscience of the world when not a single finger was lifted by any country to prevent the forcible occupation of a free people; it should now be a matter of the deepest shame that not one country raises its voice against the butchery of that people.

(From a letter sent in 1956 to the Indian, Pakistani and US Governments by Thupten Nyingze, a former Abbot of Gyantse Monastery and one-time Governor of Gyantse. It was distributed to US Embassies and Consulates in London, New Delhi, Calcutta, Hong Kong and Taipei – and from there to the State Department, the CIA, the USIA, the Army, Navy and Air Force. The letter – whose contents remain no less true today, forty-three years later – was neither published nor acted upon and the outside world remained in the dark about the fate of Tibet.)[1]

1999

'All is still in the land of the snows, save for the sound of dragging chains.'

'Snow Lion', a poem written by Palden Gyal
for the fortieth anniversary of the
1959 Tibetan Uprising

Notes

Introduction

1 Mary Craig, *Kundun: A Biography of the Dalai Lama and His Family* (HarperCollins, 1997).
2 Joe Simpson, *Storms of Silence* (Vintage Books, 1998).

Chapter 1: Honey on the knife

1 No matter what his social status, it was theoretically possible for a bright boy who entered a monastery to rise to any office within the secular or religious administration.
2 Tibet was ruled jointly by its 200 aristocratic families and the monastic establishment. Each was meant to act as a brake on the other, preventing it from becoming too arrogant and powerful. In practice,

however, the monks always held more power than
the nobles.

3 The Tibetan calendar is lunar and based on a sixty-
year cycle in which animals of the zodiac – mouse,
bull, tiger, hare, dragon, snake, horse, sheep,
monkey, bear, dog and pig are combined with five
elements (each used alternately in its male and
female aspects) to distinguish the year.

4 Perceval Landon, *Lhasa: The Mysterious City* (Delhi,
Kailash Publications, 1905; reprinted 1978).

5 Quoted by Patrick French, *Younghusband: The Last
Great Imperial Adventurer* (HarperCollins, 1994).

6 In the absence of newspapers, street-songs were the
traditional way of voicing popular complaint.

7 The 1904 Lhasa Convention made it clear that
Britain was dealing with an independent country
over which China had no control.

8 It was in this period that Tibet's isolationism began.
Many contemporary travellers believed that it was
the Chinese who encouraged this isolationism, in
order to establish a buffer between China and British
India.

9 One of these was to provide accommodation,
porters and pack animals for government officials
and messengers passing through Gyantse to India
etc.

10 From an interview with Tenzin Atisha in
Dharamsala, for my previous book, *Tears of Blood*
(HarperCollins, 1993).

11 Two Americans, the wireless commentator Lowell
Thomas and his son Lowell Thomas Jr, had made a
fact-finding visit to Tibet in 1949, but were back in
the USA. Heinrich Harrer and Peter Aufschnaiter,
the two Austrians, had taken refuge in Tibet after
escaping from a British prisoner-of-war camp in

India, and were still living there. The three Britons were Hugh Richardson, then in the service of the Indian government as head of their Mission in Lhasa, and two radio operators, Reginald Fox and Robert Ford, employed by the Tibetan government to run their wireless stations.

12 Robert Ford, *Captured in Tibet* (OUP, 1990).

13 The Seventeen-Point Agreement was, however, an international treaty, indicating that the two participating countries were each separate and sovereign.

14 The majority (and dominant) race in China were the Han.

15 Available exclusively in Tibet, its widespread use succeeded in undermining the usual Tibetan currency.

16 His childhood had been a lonely one, his main companions being the 'sweepers', the men who swept the floors of the Potala and Norbulingka Palaces. They did not hestitate to tell him about what was wrong with Tibet, the injustices and corruption that were prevalent. The young boy listened carefully to them and determined that when he came to power he would make radical changes.

17 In *Dragon in the Land of Snows*, historian Tsering Shakya writes that, after 1954, when the roads between China and Tibet were finished, the Chinese were not averse to using the *ulag* system themselves. Their cadres would requisition horses and provisions. 'One Tibetan government official who had to organise corvée labour between Gyantse and Phari said that the frequent arrival of Chinese officials meant that the corvée labourers had no time to rest before they had to go to another assignment.'

18 The 1954 Panch Shila Agreement came about

because Prime Minister Nehru of the newly independent India was convinced that the peace of Asia
depended on friendship between India and China.

19 Palden Gyatso, *Fire Under the Snow* (Harvill Press,
1997).

20 Tsipon or Tsepon was a title given to government
officials.

21 From Sumner Carnahan and Lama Kunga
Rinpoche, *In the Presence of My Enemies* (Clear Light
Publishers, 1995), p. 154.

22 I khel is equivalent to 16 kg.

23 Even before the Chinese came, there was a well-
established community of Tibetan traders and mule-
teers living in Kalimpong, the hub of the flourishing
trade between Tibet, India and the West. This
committee would eventually become the Committee
for Tibetan Social Welfare which, after 1956, would
become the organising centre for the Tibetan
Resistance.

Chapter 2: A deadly mockery

1 Quoted in Warren W. Smith Jr, *Tibetan Nation: A
History of Tibetan Nationalism and Sino-Tibetan
Relations* (Westview Press, 1996).

2 Rinchen Lhamo, *We Tibetans* (New York, Potala,
1985).

3 Such a statue – of an enlightened divinity – was
meant to ensure a happy death when the time came.

4 The animistic religion, Bon, preceded Buddhism
which was first brought to Tibet from India in the
seventh century, and more significantly in the
eleventh century.

5 It was said that evil spirits could not bear the smell
of juniper.

6 In Tibet, where flowers were a rarity, people greeted each other, and greeted significant events, with a long white scarf made of cobwebby silk.

7 Perceval Landon, *Lhasa: The Mysterious City* (Delhi, Kailish Publications, 1905; reprinted 1978).

8 In the Gyantse district as a whole, there were actually 156 monasteries.

9 Official Buddhism is the reformed Gelugpa Order to which the Dalai Lama belongs. The other older sects are: Nyingmapa (the old), Kagyupa and Sakyapa. The Dalai Lama is the titular head of all four, and they all owe allegiance to him.

10 The Buddha of the present era is known as the Sakyamuni Buddha, while the Buddha Maitreya is the Buddha Yet To Come.

11 The yak is male; a female yak is a dri, and there is also a dzo, a cross breed from a yak and domestic cattle.

12 Robert Ford, *Captured in Tibet*.

13 The Tibetans cannot grow tea. They import it in bricks from China, tear a piece off the brick, boil it, pour it into a churn, add yak butter and salt and churn until blended.

14 Landon, *Lhasa*.

15 Tibetan medicine, first introduced in the eighth century, is a mixture of herbal cures and Buddhist practice.

16 Landon, *Lhasa*.

17 Quoted in *Daughter of Tibet*, the autobiography of Rinchen Dolma Taring (John Murray, 1986).

18 Hugh E. Richardson, *Tibet and Its History* (Shambala, 1984). Details of these Chinese atrocities in eastern Tibet were revealed to the world by a report (8 August 1960) issued by the International Commission of Jurists who accused the Chinese of genocide.

19 The story of the Lhasa Uprising of 1959 has been told too often to warrant a retelling here. For a full account, see, for example, John Avedon, *In Exile from the Land of Snows* (Michael Joseph, 1984), or the present author's *Tears of Blood* (HarperCollins, 1993) and *Kundun* (HarperCollins, 1997). Also, Fredrick Hyde-Chambers's superb novel, *Lama* (Souvenir Press, 1984).

Chapter 3: Socialist paradise 1959–66

1 Before 1950, many leftward-leaning aristocrats, ambitious businessmen and some of the less hidebound monks had been attracted by the efficiency and apparent idealism of the Chinese Communists, and genuinely believed that they would help propel Tibet into the modern world. After 1959, most of them became completely disillusioned by the reality.

2 In the three months following the Lhasa Uprising, 18,600 Tibetans were said to have been killed. In October 1960, Radio Lhasa claimed that 87,000 'reactionaries' had been eliminated in central Tibet after the Uprising.

3 *Tibet under Chinese Communist Rule: a Compilation of Refugee Statements 1958–75.*

4 Dondhub Choedon, *Life in the Red Flag People's Commune* (Dharamsala, 1978).

5 Hugh Richardson has an interesting observation on the Chinese understanding of truth. 'Another deeply-seated tendency of the Chinese mind is to believe, without regarding what other people would call facts, that things are as Chinese theory decrees that they ought to be. The reiteration that the Chinese are treating the Tibetans with every consideration and benevolence, and that the Tibetans

want only to be united to China means to the great majority of Chinese that those are the facts.' Quoted from 'Tibetan Précis' in *High Peaks, Pure Earth: Collected Writings on Tibetan History and Culture* (Serindia, 1998).

6   It is estimated that between 1960 and 1962, 340,000 Tibetan peasants and nomads died from famine.

7   Dawa Norbu, *Tibet: The Road Ahead* (Rider, 1997).

Chapter 4: When the wind of destruction blew

1   Not only lamas made pilgrimages. Lay Tibetans frequently did so too. It was a way of life with them. The greatest pilgrimage centre of all was Lhasa, the Holy City.

2   Drapchi is still today the Number One Regional Prison for the Lhasa area.

3   Gyantse and Lhasa are both in central Tibet, known as Ü Tsang, but they are in different provinces, Lhasa being the capital of Ü province, and Gyantse being in Tsang.

4   Drepung was said to be the largest monastery in the world.

5   She remained on the Communist blacklist and died in 1982.

6   The Fourteenth Dalai Lama was anxious to change this and to establish an education system for Tibet.

7   Young Tibetans were sent to China to be trained as future officials of the Communist regime. This did not always turn out as planned. Many of the younger people returned home disillusioned with Chinese promises and many became active underground opponents of the regime.

8   The boy had been discovered in Nationalist China during the Civil War, and when the Communists

took over, they realised what a prize he could be. In Tibetan eyes, he had never been confirmed as Panchen Lama, but their delegates had been forced to acknowledge his position in the Seventeen-Point Agreement of 1951. After that he had been brought back to Tibet and used as a counterbalance to the Dalai Lama.

9 Throughout China and Tibet, people were suffering as a result of Mao's disastrous Great Leap Forward, an ideologically inspired campaign to solve the economy's ills by greater industrialisation. It had resulted in appalling famine.

10 *A Poisoned Arrow: The Secret Report of the 10th Panchen Lama* (Tibet Information Network).

11 Westerners tend to believe – and the Chinese have encouraged them to believe – that the destruction of the monasteries came only with the 1966–76 Cultural Revolution. In fact, between 1959 and 1961, the number of monasteries dropped from 2,500 to 70, and the number of monks and nuns had been reduced by 93 per cent.

12 The 1958 drive to transform China overnight from an agricultural nation to a major industrial power.

Chapter 5: The graveyard

1 Dawa Norbu, *Tibet: The Road Ahead* (Rider, 1997), previously published as *Red Star over Tibet* (Envoy Press, 1987).

2 In their new publication, *The Whirlwind Emergency Battling Newspaper*.

3 Dondhub Choedon, *Life in the Red Flag People's Commune* (Dharamsala, 1978).

4 The Chinese Communist regime operated a tight surveillance over every village, town, city, man,

woman and child in the country. This system, controlled by the Public Security Bureau, spread its tentacles into every aspect of Tibetan life, through neighbourhood committees, communes, Youth Leagues, Women's Associations and so on. No one could trust anyone else, and in the ensuing atmosphere of fear and coercion the work of indoctrination could go ahead. As Dawa Norbu writes, in *Tibet: The Road Ahead*, 'In this way, a civil society, where freedom, individuality and privacy prevailed, disappeared altogether . . . in its place the Party penetrated and pervaded that society as the almighty social god. The Maoist version of totalitarianism violates the very spirit and structure of Tibetan society.'

5 Choedon, *Life in the Red Flag People's Commune*.
6 John Avedon, *In Exile from the Land of Snows* (Michael Joseph, 1984). I myself have met many Tibetan refugees who have described similar treatment meted out to them. See my book, *Tears of Blood* (HarperCollins, 1993).
7 Avedon, *In Exile*, chapter 10, 'The Long Night'.
8 Wangdu Dorje in *Tibet under Chinese Communist Rule*, refugee statements 1958–75.
9 Melvyn Goldstein, William Siebenschuh and Tashi Tsering, *The Struggle for Modern Tibet: The Autobiography of Tashi Tsering* (New York and London, M. E. Sharpe). The author, a poor boy, had left Tibet to seek an education in the West, but had returned after 1959, to help 'reconstruct a new society'.
10 Being designated a 'black hat' meant being in the worst category of criminal offender.

Chapter 6: Golden bridge, wooden bridge

1 The USA was an enemy, the Vietnam War was at its height, India was becoming increasingly hostile, Korea was split into two nations, and relations with the Soviet Union had never been worse. It was probably China's paranoia about being surrounded by enemies that would soon propel her into mending her fences with the USA. Until she did so, the paranoia would continue.

2 China's main nuclear base was said to have been moved from Xinjiang Province (a bit too near the USSR) to Nagchuka, 165 miles to the north of Lhasa.

3 Henry Kissinger visited Peking in July 1971, to pave the way for a fence-mending visit by President Richard Nixon the following year.

4 Dondhub Choedon, *Life in the Red Flag People's Commune* (Dharamsala, 1978).

5 Choedon, *Life in the Red Flag People's Commune*.

6 John Avedon, *In Exile from the Land of Snows* (Michael Joseph, 1984), chapter 10, 'The Long Night'.

7 Tibet was and is forced to keep Peking time, despite being over 1,000 miles from Peking.

Chapter 7: The death of Mao

1 John Avedon, *In Exile from the Land of Snows* (Michael Joseph, 1984), chapter 10, 'The Long Night'.

2 Nien Cheng, *Life and Death in Shanghai* (Grafton Books, 1987).

3 Mary Craig, *Tears of Blood* (HarperCollins, 1993).

4 Avedon, *In Exile*.

5 Loden died in 1981, shortly after meeting members of the Dalai Lama's first delegation.

6 Independent research (1998) puts the number of

Chinese currently in the TAR at 5 to 5.5 million as against 4.5 million Tibetans. In Kham and Amdo, the Chinese outnumber Tibetans many times over.

Chapter 8: Towards the abyss

1   Fredrick R. Hyde-Chambers, *Lama: A Novel of Tibet* (Souvenir Press, 1984).

Chapter 9: 'Hell must be something like this'

1   The Tibetan Buddhist 'Wheel of Life' is an allegory for the ignorance, hatred and desire which bind human beings to an endless cycle of birth and rebirth, until they find the path of spiritual enlightenment which will set them free. The wheel is held by the terrifying and demonic figure of Yama, Lord of Death, who, holding the wheel in his mouth, has the power to bite and destroy it at any given moment.

2   It should be borne in mind, perhaps, that though Deng was a liberaliser in the economic field, he had already announced that he would brook no attack on the Communist system, no challenge to the Communist Party's absolute power.

3   Reported by Nien Cheng, *Life and Death in Shanghai*.

4   W. Christopher, 'A Chinese Lesson: Interest can Overcome Ideology', *International Herald Tribune* (12.10.85), quoted in *Tibet: The Facts* (Dharamsala, Tibetan Young Buddhist Association, 1990).

5   I am indebted for this catalogue of events to John Avedon's *In Exile from the Land of Snows*, chapter 11.

Chapter 10: Visitors

1   John Avedon, *In Exile from the Land of Snows* (Michael Joseph, 1984).
2   Avedon, *In Exile*, chapter 11.
3   The People's Militias had been trained to conduct guerrilla warfare in the event of a new war. But their real task, as everyone knew, was to root out 'class enemies' in Tibetan society, i.e., anybody who resisted Chinese rule.
4   For the first months of exile after their flight from Tibet in 1959, the Dalai Lama and his entourage had been housed in Mussoorie. But in April 1960 they had moved to the 'ghost town' of Dharamsala in the Himalayan foothills.
5   Avedon, *In Exile*, chapter 11.
6   Conversation with Rapten Chazotsang in Salt Lake City, October 1998.
7   Avedon, *Tibet To-day* (Wisdom Publications, 1987).
8   Jetsun Pema, *Three Months in Tibet: A Personal Viewpoint*, pamphlet published by the Tibetan Children's Village, Dharamsala. See also my own *Tears of Blood* (HarperCollins, 1993) and *Kundun* (HarperCollins, 1997).
9   In conversation with the author, June 1994.

Chapter 12: In the land of the Thunder Dragon

1   Gyurme Dorje (ed.), *Tibet Handbook, with Bhutan* (Trade and Travel Publications, 1996).
2   This crisis has long since been resolved, and relations between Bhutan and the Tibetan government-in-exile are once again extremely warm.

3   There were actually two garrisons, one Bhutanese and a much smaller Indian one. Both of them interrogated the two refugees.

Chapter 13: Dharamsala

1   The Chinese had finally bombed Lithang into submission and had exacted terrible reprisals among the village communities which had sheltered the rebels.
2   In the early 1980s, before the riots in Lhasa in 1987, travel to Tibet was a possibility for the refugees in India. It still is, but they have to agree to carry Chinese travel documents while they are there. Many of them are unwilling to do this.
3   The Dalai Lama spent almost a year in Mussoorie after his arrival in exile in 1959. From there he went in 1960 to Dharamsala.

Chapter 14: Return

1   From the Foreword to my book *Kundun: A Biography of the Dalai Lama's Family* (HarperCollins, 1997).
2   The talks were continuing, but the Chinese wished to limit the discussion to whether the Dalai Lama would be resident in Lhasa or in Peking. They were determined it would be Peking. The real issue, the happiness or otherwise of the 6 million Tibetan people, did not come into the discussion, and the Dalai Lama had begun to realise that it never would.
3   For details of this period, see my previous book *Tears of Blood* (HarperCollins, 1993), chapters 17, 18 and 19.
4   The Chinese were now discouraging (and periodically banning) individual tourists and backpackers, and were actively wooing groups of well-heeled Westerners in search of an off-beat holiday package.

Apart from bringing in the hard currency, the theory was that these groups would be less observant, less well informed and less critical.

5   During the Cultural Revolution Prime Minister Zhou En-lai had made a personal plea to the Red Guards to spare the Potala from destruction.

6   Within the last few years, most of this too has been demolished. Lhasa is now almost 100 per cent Chinese.

7   When someone died in old Tibet, relatives distributed food and drink to all passers-by, who were asked to pray for the deceased. Gifts were then made to those who had disposed of the body. The latter had a prescriptive right to the clothes in which the corpse had been decked (his or her Sunday best), and also to a gift of money. The more valuable possessions of the dead person were offered to his or her personal lama (see note below) or to their monastery. Nothing was held back – it was considered unlucky to use any items belonging to the dead.

Note A Tibetan's root-guru or personal lama was assigned to him or her at birth or just after. Every self-respecting Tibetan Buddhist had one and maintained the link throughout his or her life. For a Tibetan, their root-lama was a living manifestation of the Buddha, and therefore was actually held in as much regard as the Buddha himself.

Postscript

1   Warren W. Smith Jr, *Tibetan Nation: A History of Tibetan Nationalism and Sino-Tibetan Relations* (Westview Press, 1996).

Bibliography

Adrian Abbotts, *Naked Spirits: A Journey into Occupied Tibet* (Canongate Books, 1997)

John F. Avedon, *In Exile from the Land of Snows* (Michael Joseph, 1984)

Catriona Bass, *Inside the Treasure House: A Time in Tibet* (Victor Gollancz, 1990)

Sumner Carnahan and Lama Kunga Rinpoche, *In the Presence of My Enemies* (Clear Light Publications, 1995)

Nien Cheng, *Life and Death in Shanghai* (Grafton Books, 1987)

Choedon, Dondhub *Life in the Red Flag People's Commune* (Dharamsala, 1979)

Mary Craig, *Tears of Blood: A Cry for Tibet* (HarperCollins, 1993)

Mary Craig, *Kundun: A Biography of the Dalai Lama and His Family* (HarperCollins, 1997)

Gyurme Dorje, ed., *Tibet Handbook with Bhutan* (Trade and Travel Handbooks)

Robert Ford, *Captured in Tibet* (OUP, 1990)

Patrick French, *Younghusband: The Last Great Imperial Adventurer* (HarperCollins, 1994)

Tsering Dorje Gashi, *New Tibet* (Dharamsala, 1980)

Melvyn Goldstein, William Siebenschuh and Tashi Tsering *The Struggle for Modern Tibet: The Autobiography of Tashi Tsering* (M.E. Sharpe, Armonk, New York, 1996)

Palden Gyatso, *Fire under the Snow: Testimony of a Tibetan Prisoner* (Harvill, 1998)

Fredrick R. Hyde-Chambers, *Lama: A Novel of Tibet* (Souvenir Press, 1984)

Rinchen Lhamo, *We Tibetans* (Potala, New York, 1985)

Dawa Norbu, *Red Star over Tibet* (Envoy Press, 1987)

Dawa Norbu, *Tibet: The Road Ahead* (Rider, 1997)

Panchen Lama *A Poisoned Arrow: The Secret Report of the 10th Panchen Lama* (Tibet Information Network, 1997)

Hugh Richardson, *Tibet and Its History* (Shambhala, 1984)

Hugh Richardson, *High Peaks, Pure Earth: Collected Writings on Tibetan History and Culture* (Serindia, 1998)

Harrison E. Salisbury, *The New Emperors, Mao and Deng* (HarperCollins, 1992)

Tsering Shakya, *The Dragon in the Land of Snows: A History of Modern Tibet since 1947* (Pimlico, 1999)

Warren W. Smith, Jr, *Tibetan Nation: A History of Tibetan Nationalism and Sino-Tibetan Relations* (Westview Press [HarperCollins], 1996)

Tibetan Young Buddhist Association, *Tibet: The Facts* (T.Y.B. Association, India, 1990)

Index